THE DRESSMAKER'S SECRET

THE CHRONICLES OF ALICE & IVY, BOOK 1

A NOVEL BY KELLYN ROTH

Published by Kellyn Roth, Author

Wild Blue Wonder Press

ISBN: 978-1-7341685-0-1

Scripture quotations are taken from the King James Version (KJV).

Cover design by Carpe Librum Book Design

Edited by Andrea Cox

Kelly Lyn Langdon
PO Box 1156
White Salmon, WA, 98672

contact@kellynrothauthor.com

www.kellynrothauthor.com

CONTENTS

DEDICATION

For my mom.
Thank you for cheering me on, helping me with grammar and punctuation, and just being a fantastic influence in my life.
Love you!
~Kell~

CHARACTER LIST

Alice Chattoway (Berck) — A young girl growing up in London.

Miss Claire Chattoway (Berck) — Her mother. A middle-class dressmaker who uses an alias to hide her true identity.

Ivy Chattoway (Berck) — Alice's twin sister.

Nettie Atwater — Claire's former maid who now works as a nanny and governess for Alice and Ivy.

Tom Jameson — Claire's manservant.

Mrs. Bennett — Claire's elderly maid of all work.

Miss Lois Elton — A childhood friend and schoolmate of Claire's. Only living child of John Elton.

Mr. Steven Parker — Miss Elton's cousin. Son of Captain Steven Parker and Miss Patricia Elton. Formerly married to his cousin, Lydia.

Mr. Philip Knight — Miss Elton's cousin. Son of Mr. Edmond Knight, an American, and Miss Amelia Elton. John Elton's sole heir.

Mrs. Hazel Knight — Wife of Mr. Knight. A former resident of Virginia.

Edmond "Ned" Knight — Mr. and Mrs. Knight's infant son.

Kirk Manning — A stable boy at Pearlbelle Park, the Knights' estate.

Katie Manning — His mother

Lizzy Manning — His sister

Charles Chattoway — Claire's brother.

Christina Chattoway-Tinedale — Claire's sister.

Mr. Chattoway — Owner of Starboard Hall. Claire's estranged father.

Mrs. Nora Chattoway — Claire's estranged mother.

Miss Isobel Selle — Headmistress of a boarding school Alice attends.

Lady Mary Cassidy O'Connell — A dear friend of Alice's from boarding school.

Content Warning

Some readers are uncomfortable with certain types of content in the books they read. Though my novels are all closed-door romances with no gratuitous content, contain no swearing, and handle all topics discussed biblically, I have a brief list of content warnings for each of my books below. Some of these may contain minor spoilers. Read at your own risk!

kellynrothauthor.com/content-warnings

"For we are his workmanship, created in Christ Jesus unto good works,
which God hath before ordained that we should walk in them."
~ Ephesians 2:10 ~

PROLOGUE

January 4, 1862
Yorkshire, England

C LAIRE STARED INTO THE flickering flames of her fireplace. The heat warmed her face, almost to the point of discomfort, and she leaned back. "Well, Nettie. I suppose now is as lovely a night as any to run away from home."

Her maid sighed and seemed about to speak, but Claire held up her hand and shook her head.

"No. We must." She played with the edge of the blanket lying on her lap. "If my father enacts a single one of his threats, if he takes the girls away from us ... It's not worth speaking of. We leave tonight."

Nettie's gray eyes drooped as they met her mistress's. The dark circles under the maid's eyes spoke of exhaustion beyond her, of burdens an eighteen-year-old woman shouldn't have to bear. "I don't think you're ready to travel, and, frankly, neither am I."

"We've done it before, and we can do it again." Claire straightened her back and summoned her most intimidating glare. She had to convince Nettie, or she'd never make it. "Besides, you wouldn't ... I know you feel as I do about protecting the babies. I've already failed in so many ways. If anything happened to—"

"I know, but it's not sensible! Where would we go? Two women with no man to support us ... We wouldn't have half a chance."

"But we must try! Surely you can see that." Claire flipped the blanket off her lap and let it drop to the floor. She rose and paced across the room to where two cradles sat side by side. "For them. My father has contemplated murder. He's a madman! At the very least, he'll send them off somewhere. There is no other option for us."

Claire didn't ask if Nettie was willing to travel with her. Since childhood, they had been close friends.

No, Nettie would stay with her, and she would keep Claire from going absolutely insane in the months and years that followed.

There wasn't anyone else. Not anymore.

She bit her lip as she looked down at a small face that Nettie said was like Claire's own in form. The babe might have light hair when it grew in, though Claire secretly hoped she would look like him. At least a bit. It would be a comfort.

"Oh, Ivy." She reached into the cradle and stroked the soft cheek. "What are we all going to do?"

"That's another reason we can't leave." Claire turned to find Nettie behind her, trembling, her arms wrapped around herself. The maid had been unstable since the shaking events of the last few years. Claire hoped she'd calm down soon; it wasn't like Nettie to be upset.

But Claire had been a fool, and it was hurting them all.

"What?"

"Ivy. She's so small, and if her breathing problems continue, travel might ... Claire, I know you couldn't stand to lose her, too. Let's not risk it."

Claire stepped to the side. "At least Alice is all right. Firstborn, least trouble, hmm?"

Nettie's lips quirked up around the edges. "Well, God has His hands on her. She isn't supposed to be here, you know. Neither of them are. But they've both arrived, safe and sound, and that tells you something, I think."

Claire laughed and shook her head in amusement. "I don't know about God, but if we hurry, we can save them both. You know they're about all I have."

Nettie nodded and stepped back, though Claire remained by the cradles, watching her daughters sleep. Yes, they had to leave tonight to get Alice and Ivy safe from all harm.

Claire didn't know how they'd manage, but they must.

Perhaps Nettie's God will help us. It would be nice for Him to do something for me for a change.

CHAPTER ONE

Eight Years Later
London, England

ALICE KNEW HER MOTHER must be home by now, which made sitting still even more agonizing. It had been a long day, and it promised to be a long evening. A little girl ought to be allowed to see her mother somewhere in between morning and night.

She tried to finish the copywork Nettie had set out for her, but she was sure her hand would drop off if she wrote another letter. Besides, Alice was convinced that her penmanship was perfect; therefore, further practice was entirely unnecessary. She twisted her dark hair around her finger and wiggled on her seat, seeking a comfortable position.

Nettie looked up from her novel, and her forehead crinkled, her gray eyes scolding before she spoke. "Alice, I know you can concentrate if you apply yourself. Please stop woolgathering and finish your copywork. I mean it, Miss Grace."

Alice sighed. Nettie used "Miss Grace" or "Gracie" to scold her—because, supposedly, Nettie often had to have an inordinate amount of grace to deal with her naughty charge.

It wasn't that Alice tried to be bad. It was just that there was a lot to get done, and sometimes she had to fight against things getting in the way.

Of course, Nettie sometimes called her "Gracie" when she smiled, too, so really, one could never be sure.

She looked down at her twin, Ivy, who played with the cat on the floor. Alice wished she could switch places with her sister, but Ivy couldn't write much.

Alice placed her pen on the table and rubbed a hand over her eyes, sure she was developing a headache. "Am I done yet? Can—I mean, may I be? I've finished almost the whole page. Please, Nettie! I want to go see Mummy now!"

Nettie glanced at the small watch she kept pinned to her bodice. "Run along, then, Gracie. Please take Ivy with you."

The headache vanished. Alice leapt up, put a hand on Ivy's shoulder, and shook her gently.

Alice felt a flash of envy when Ivy looked up at her. Her sister was a perfect child-beauty: big, dreamy blue eyes and a lovely smile. Alice wished she had pale skin and wavy golden locks instead of perpetually rosy cheeks and dark, straight hair. But, though occasionally she experienced jealousy toward her twin sister, she also felt lovingly protective—except when Ivy was annoying.

"Hello, Alice." Ivy smiled slowly, waking up from her imaginary world.

Alice didn't like to hear other people saying it, but her twin was a bit simple—had been since she was born. But that just meant Ivy needed love. She wasn't less of a person. At least, Mummy said so.

Alice returned Ivy's smile. "It's time to go see Mummy. You want to watch her get ready. Come along."

Dragging her sister, Alice ran to her mother's room. At her vanity sat their mother, brushing her long blonde hair. Her eyes glowed lovingly, and her lips quirked up at the corners in a soft smile as her children entered the room.

"Mummy, are you going to wear that dress?" Alice rushed to her mother's side. "You look so much better in the light-pink one with rosebuds."

Mummy gave way to her light, silvery laugh. Alice thought it was a special sort of laugh that belonged only to Ivy and her.

"That's one thing we three have in common: we all look simply stunning in pink."

"Not me as much." Alice didn't believe she was as lovely as her mother and sister. She didn't mind—at least, not most of the time. "I *did* want to see you in the silk with the tiny rosebuds, though."

"I suppose you're right," Mummy mused. Alice couldn't help but grin. It was wonderful to have a mother who always listened. "But I *am* fond of this dress."

"Leave it on," Alice said reluctantly. After all, her mother had given in to her taste; she had best return the favor. "The cloth is good."

Mummy's eyes laughed, though Alice chose to ignore the implied teasing. "This is an occasion, darling, so if you want the pink ..." She reached past Alice to hug and kiss Ivy.

"No, leave the lavender," Alice said after a moment of thought. "What do you think, Ivy?"

"Pretty," Ivy whispered, fingering the lace at her mother's collar. She offered another hug before sliding out of Mummy's arms, distracted by the rain outside the window.

It was always raining in London, but Ivy liked to watch it. She seemed to find an odd fascination in the dripping water.

Alice picked up a string of pearls that Mummy had left on the vanity and tried it on. She found the necklace too heavy for her taste, however, and set it back down. "When will the guests come?"

"In half an hour," Mummy said, beginning to brush her hair again. "Remember, dears, though you're excited, most people don't ..." She hesitated. "Most people haven't seen you before. You know we don't get out much, so I don't want you downstairs until I call you."

"What do you mean?" Alice said. "We see the Lanskys often in the park, with Nettie, and Mrs. Lansky says I'm a sweet girl. Helena and Rosalind are my dear friends."

The twins rarely left the house, except for regular walks with Nettie. Alice wasn't sure why her mother was so insistent they didn't talk to anyone. She only knew that she was not to do so, and she tried to obey ...

though it was hard. Alice liked to talk to people, and she so badly wanted
to explore the world outside their middle-class London townhouse.

"It's not just the Lanskys." Mummy was quiet for a bit and didn't look
at Alice when she spoke again. "We have a few other guests coming. Old
friends. Ones I haven't seen in a long time, since I was a girl, who might
not ... know about you. At least not all about you. One of them came to
the shop a few days ago and asked to see us, to renew the acquaintance.
Tonight, he is accompanied by his cousin, who was also a friend of mine
before you and Ivy came."

"Oh." Alice wasn't sure what to think of that. She hadn't known her
mother had friends outside of Nettie and Uncle Charlie, Alice's maternal
uncle who visited every few months.

He was the one who paid for their home in London and really owned
Mummy's dress shop, though he did not openly endorse her. Alice and Ivy
weren't supposed to admit they knew Uncle Charlie, either.

"So you two must be on your best behavior. I would like my friends to
meet you, but you must remain quiet and still, and you and Ivy will spend
the rest of the evening in the nursery with Helena and Rosalind."

Alice nodded. "All right. But why did you invite those people if they
won't like us?"

Mummy blinked. Alice thought there might be something wrong with
her smile. "I'm sure they will like you, but they won't understand. Don't
worry; I'll make sure everything goes well. Run along."

Alice and Ivy dashed off obediently, and Miss Claire Berck returned to her
preening. It was important she look her best. Always there was the struggle
to appear, if not be, worthy, and she must try even harder tonight.

She seldom had dinner guests—only the Lanskys, who owned a shop near hers. She lived modestly with a staff of only three—Nettie, of course; an elderly maid-of-all-work; and a manservant. Most importantly, though, she lived secretly, under an assumed name of which few knew the meaning.

Only the Lanskys were aware of Alice and Ivy, and that was because they were the discreet sort. As far as anyone else could tell, the manager of Berck's was a modest spinster who lived by herself in a tall, narrow house wedged between a hundred others like it.

She'd rarely had to explain herself, and her brother's financial backing, little as it was, ensured her safety. But it would be nice to be in contact with the friends she hadn't spoken to in over eight years.

To explain her actions, though that could never be.

At least she was secure now. Charlie had assured her she'd be safe when he'd found her all those years ago. She still remembered going to his arms and sobbing her troubles onto his shoulder.

Of course, he couldn't really rescue her—their father had made sure of that by limiting his funds and keeping him close. Charlie couldn't even visit without losing everything, and Claire would never let him risk that. But his distant acceptance had kept her from despair. With his encouragement, she'd fought for everything she now had.

It wasn't a lot. There was a time when she had been society's latest darling, but now that was gone. She no longer had a sphere she belonged to. The strangeness of the flux state often overwhelmed her.

Nettie came to fix her hair. It was one of the few things she did as a lady's maid now; everything else, Claire had learned to do for herself.

"Tonight will be interesting, won't it?"

"More than you know," Nettie mumbled.

"What's that?"

"Nothing."

"Ah." Claire glanced up then quickly straightened her shoulders and stared forward. Sometimes Nettie said things that made little to no sense—and that was all right.

Claire had her secrets, too.

"Why?" The maid's voice was sharp. Claire might have imagined it, but she thought one of the pins Nettie wielded pierced her scalp. "Why do you think Mr. Parker wanted to see you?"

"He used to care for me." Claire couldn't help but preen a bit at the thought. But that was a long time ago. "I think it's natural for there to be some curiosity about where I've been."

"And why invite the Lanskys, too?"

Claire shrugged. "A bit of a buffer is nice sometimes, I think."

Nettie's hands dropped to her sides. "Mr. Parker would do well to forget he ever knew you. And ... Mr. Knight ..."

"It doesn't matter what he would do well to do." Claire's voice was sharper than she intended, so she softened her tone as she spoke again. "Mr. Steven Parker has found me, though God only knows how. He is coming with his cousin and his cousin's bride to have dinner with us." She met Nettie's eyes in the small, cracked mirror above the dressing table. "Those are the facts. Beyond that, we can only speculate."

"But—"

"No. Please, Nettie." Claire sighed. "It's not worth a discussion."

From the top of the stairs, Alice heard her mother welcoming the guests in a monotone voice. The first to arrive were Mr. and Mrs. Lansky. Nettie hovered nearby to escort Helena and Rosalind up the stairs, where Alice greeted them warmly, and they scurried off to the nursery.

Perhaps fifteen minutes lapsed when Mummy sent for them. Alice, Nettie's hand firm on her shoulder, stood outside the drawing room, heart beating fast.

She wasn't sure exactly why she was so worried about this meeting, only that she was and that her nerves threatened to give way at any moment.

"Nettie, must I?" Alice looked up at her caretaker and stuck out her bottom lip. *I don't want to, Nettie.* She hoped her eyes communicated this silent message.

"Don't be silly, Gracie. It's going to be all right." Yet, Nettie's smile trembled around the edges, and her hand squeezed Alice's shoulder until it pinched.

Alice knew Nettie wasn't going to let her squirm away, so she stepped forward and entered the room.

A hush fell as if the adults had suspended conversation upon her arrival. Alice skittered back a bit, bumping into Ivy. Helena and Rosalind dashed around the twins to their parents, full of wonder over a new doll of Alice's that was furnished with a complete wardrobe Mummy had made.

But Alice wasn't in the mood to discuss her doll's clothing, proud as she was of the carefully sewn pieces. She felt out of place, as three strangers surveyed Ivy and her with narrowed eyes.

The first was a man who stood upon her arrival. He was taller than Mr. Lansky by half a foot and wore a tidily cut suit. Alice could tell he was impeccably dressed. He possessed a neatly trimmed beard, and his hair was so dark it gleamed.

The second was a man who resembled the first one somewhat vaguely, with the same dark hair and eyes, but he was clean-shaven. As her eyes flickered to his face, he rose, looking from her to Miss Berck before settling his eyes back on Alice.

And the third was a woman with hazel eyes and flat brown hair, her dress extravagant and simple all at once—dull colored with a neat cut.

Her eyes were the kindest and her face the softest, so Alice focused in on her. Even as she watched, the woman smiled.

"What darlin' girls! Why, I can't imagine sweeter li'l things! Are they yours, Miss Chattoway? Oh my, how pretty they are. You must be so proud!"

Alice blinked. The woman talked funny, her words all smooth and drawn out. She looked at her mother for guidance.

After the woman spoke, the tension in the room seemed to ease slightly.

"Yes," Mummy said softly. "These two are my daughters, Alice and Ivy Chattoway."

Alice blinked. *Chattoway?* She'd always been called Alice Berck. But if her mother said so, she was a Chattoway. Like Uncle Charlie, she supposed.

"Alice, Ivy, come to me." Mummy held out her hand, and Alice shuffled across the room, leading Ivy.

"The brunette is elder?" said the first gentleman, looking at Mummy rather than Alice. "She's quite a bit taller."

Something hot prickled in Alice's chest. She turned to the gentleman and glared. "My name is Alice, not 'the brunette,' and I'm only older by fifteen minutes, and I'm only three inches taller than Ivy."

"Alice Christina!" Mummy's voice was sharp.

Shame flooded Alice's chest. Had she already done something wrong? Her mother always encouraged her to speak her mind, but perhaps that wasn't all right in front of people. She frowned and crossed her arms. "I'm sorry, but he started it."

There was a moment of shocked silence—even Helena and Rosalind gawked at Alice.

Then the second gentleman laughed a gentle chuckle. "Steven, she's got you there."

The woman smiled. "Yes, Steven, try to be human for once. Alice, how old are you?"

"I'm eight," said Alice, allowing a slow smile to spread across her face. "So is Ivy. We're twins."

"How lovely! I always wanted to be a twin, but all I've got is a mulehead-ed brother who treats me like a baby." The woman's face pinched. "Your dress is simply adorable, you know—come over here and spin for me."

She held out a hand as she spoke, and Alice stepped forward to see her.

"I'm Mrs. Philip Knight, but you can call me Miss Hazel."

Alice glanced at her mother but received no direction, so she nodded. "All right. I suppose you can call me Alice." She nodded with what she hoped was quiet dignity.

"Such a sweet name! I've always loved it." Miss Hazel cocked her head. "And how are you doin' today, Miss Alice?"

"Very well. And you?" Just like a little lady. Alice beamed. *Some* of those lectures of Nettie's had sunk in, no matter how she complained about Alice's inattention.

Before Miss Hazel got a chance to answer, Mummy broke in. "Alice, it's time for you and Ivy to go upstairs with the Miss Lanskys and have your tea. Run along to Nettie."

Disappointed, as she was starting to like Miss Hazel, Alice turned and left the room, dragging Ivy after her. As they ran around the corner, she heard the first gentleman say something like, "Is Nettie still with you?" But she didn't hear her mother's reply.

CHAPTER TWO

A LICE SETTLED IN WITH Helena, Rosalind, and their dolls. Nettie whisked Ivy away to spend the evening reading, so the trio were left to their own devices for the time being.

"Does she have a name?" asked Helena, picking up a beautiful, rosy-cheeked doll from where she sat on a little chair in the corner.

"Yes, Melinda." Alice took her favorite doll from her friend and cradled Melinda close. She never liked the other girls touching her babies without permission. It wasn't done. "Let's put them to bed now."

They did, and Helena said, "Now, our papa would come in and kiss us good night."

Rosalind smiled and patted a blanket down over her doll. "Does your papa come every night after your mama tucks you in and kisses you, Alice? Our papa *always* does."

"I haven't any."

The sisters stared at her, and Alice wondered what she'd said wrong. Her stomach did an odd squirming thing.

"What?" Helena narrowed her eyes.

Unsure now, Alice nodded. "I ... I don't have a father. Mummy says some have them, but I don't. I never have."

"Why, you've *got* to have one!" Rosalind said. "Just about everyone does, I think."

"I don't," Alice insisted.

"Yes, you do. You don't know who he is!" Helena's tone turned from incredulous to taunting in an instant.

"I don't have one at all. There's no need to know him since he doesn't exist." Alice frowned in confusion. "What do you mean 'everyone has one'?"

"Everyone *does* have one." Rosalind folded her arms firmly across her chest, and Alice knew she wasn't teasing. "I know, because I asked my mama once, and she said so. There's no one who doesn't have a father!"

"Why, yes, there is. I don't." Alice persevered, becoming more and more puzzled. "We'll go ask my mother, and she will tell you that I don't."

"I'll ask my mama, and she'll say the same as I do," said Helena. "Everyone's got one!"

"Not me," said a flustered, unsure Alice. Helena and Rosalind didn't—*couldn't*—know what they were talking about.

The door swung open, and Nettie walked in, hands on her hips. "Girls! What *are* you arguing about?"

"Alice has got to have a father, hasn't she?" Helena asked. Though she wasn't an overly reverent child, she respected Nettie's opinion.

Alice understood. Nettie wasn't one to ignore.

Rosalind nodded. "She says she hasn't any."

"I don't!" Alice jumped to her feet. "I really don't! Nettie will tell you."

Nettie hesitated for a moment, then shook her head. "I could hardly say. However, Alice would be likely to know, as he is—or isn't—her father. At any rate, it's time for the Miss Lanskys to return home now."

The sisters scurried out of the room. Alice, thinking hard, dragged behind.

Throughout the rest of the evening, she could think of nothing other than her conversation with Helena and Rosalind. It *did* indeed seem strange that she didn't have a father, but she had always taken it for granted before.

Of course, she knew that her mother was often gossiped about, and that was without knowing that Alice and her sister existed. So it seemed that the situation was unusual.

It was worth hiding, after all. Mummy always said that was because Alice and Ivy were too precious to be shared.

What on earth does anyone need a father for? Alice had lived eight years quite well without one. However, apparently not having one was shameful.

Alice hated to be thought of as shameful. Or to think that her mother was ashamed of her. Why couldn't they live out in the open? Why did it have to be a secret?

Why had the men down in the parlor looked at her like a being from another planet?

In no time at all, Nettie had Alice and Ivy almost ready for bed. A story was administered—one of Ivy's favorites, about the princess who rode a pumpkin to the ball and lost her glass slipper. Next, it was time for prayers.

Kneeling beside her bed, Alice poured all her thoughts out in a rush. "Dear God and Jesus and the Holy Spirit, take care of me. Help me be patient even when it's not easy. Take care of Mummy and Ivy and Uncle Charlie and Nettie. Make Mummy be a real Christian before she dies, so she can come be with us in Heaven. And ... help Rosalind and Helena understand that I'm not bad and Mummy's not bad. Because I don't need a father. In Jesus's name I pray. Amen."

Alice opened her eyes to find Nettie watching her from her seat at the end of the bed, mouth twisted oddly. "Gracie, what did those girls say to you?"

She shrugged. "Not much. But they said everyone has a father—and they didn't like that I don't. I wondered if ... Is that why Mummy won't tell anyone about Ivy and me?"

Nettie rose and walked to the fireplace. She watched the low flames flicker in the grate as she replied. "I'm surprised they haven't brought it up earlier, I suppose. Even in innocence, they must know that something is missing."

Alice glanced at Ivy, whose blue eyes were wide with fright, then returned her gaze to Nettie. "Is ... is something missing?"

Nettie sighed. "I think ... Gracie, as you get older, you're going to have a lot of questions, and I can't answer them. Your mother has asked me not to. But I can tell you that a lot of people would believe, foolishly in their prejudice, that you and Ivy are ... a mistake. That's ridiculous, because God created you both, and He doesn't make mistakes."

"But what about a father? Does God make people without fathers?"

She didn't reply for a long time, and Alice started to feel frightened.

"Nettie?"

"No. No, He doesn't. I can't tell you more. I promised your mother, Gracie, and I won't break that promise." She turned from the fire. Her gray eyes were sad. "You have to be content with that. With not knowing."

Alice blinked. Content with not knowing? That was absurd. What earthly good was living if one couldn't know or find out *everything*?

"But—"

"Shush. No buts. It's your mother's decision. You can discuss it with her." Nettie crossed the room and patted Alice's pillow. "Head here. Let's get you two tucked in. I want to say an extra prayer tonight, then it's time for sleep."

Alice wasn't sure what to do, as she knew she could never sleep without knowing—but Nettie's word was law. She hopped up on the bed and laid down. Ivy did the same.

After tucking them in so tight Alice could barely move, Nettie leaned back. "Eyes closed, hands folded."

There was a moment of silence before she said a word—a moment that stretched on so long that Alice almost opened her eyes to make sure everything was all right.

"Lord God, I pray for Ivy and Gra—and Alice. Life won't be as easy for them as it is for most girls their age, but I know You are protecting and watching over them. I pray for Claire, their mother, as she navigates this situation alone."

"She's not alone; she has us," Ivy interrupted.

Alice kicked her. Everyone knew speaking out of turn during a prayer was wicked.

"Shush now." Nettie's voice was gentle but firm. "As I was saying, help Claire see what she needs to do—whether that is to remain silent or speak up. And guard her heart, as I know she is vulnerable today and will be for some time to come. Help her see You although she is determined not to."

There was another long silence.

"And, lastly, I pray for myself, that I would have the wisdom to tell Alice and Ivy what they need to know while respecting Claire's wishes. I pray that You would help me see what is best for my girls even if ... even if sometimes the easiest route seems to be to tell the whole truth." Nettie stopped again and took a deep breath.

Alice opened her eyes. There were tears on her governess's cheeks. She reached over and slid her hand over Nettie's.

She smiled a bit through the tears. "Thank You, also, for blessing me with such sweet girls in my life. I don't know if I tell them often enough how much they mean to me. I can't share everything with them; sometimes discretion is necessary, but I know they understand that I must remain silent for their own good. Help us all, Lord. Amen."

Nettie opened her eyes and quietly wiped away her tears.

"Why'd you cry, Nettie?" Ivy asked.

"I don't know! Sometimes I get emotional about silly things." She cocked her head. "You have to be patient with me—and with your mother—when we must cry. Sometimes it simply can't be helped. It's because we both love our Gracie-Alice and our Ivy so much—and neither of us feel that life is all it should be for them."

Nettie leaned over to kiss Alice's forehead and squeezed Ivy's hand where it lay against the counterpane. "But God has everything in control, and all will happen on His time, not on ours."

After the longest dinner party of her life, Claire dragged herself up the stairs. At last they had left—after all the barely-under-the-surface drama, the looks cast between various people, the snide comments from Mr. Parker, and the worried eyes of Mr. Knight.

There was also Mrs. Knight, cheerful and charming and so very American. Claire wasn't at all sure what to think of her. Could anyone be that kind?

She paused outside the girls' bedroom. She should go in and make sure all was well, though Nettie had everything in hand. Probably, they had been disturbed by the evening ...

Meeting new people. The confrontation with Parker. Being called Chattoway—when they'd only known Berck as a surname.

Yes, she would make sure they were both asleep, peaceful and safe.

She opened the door. The candle in her hand cast light on Alice, eyes wide open. She immediately shut them and buried her face in the pillow. Claire smiled. That girl.

She tiptoed to the bedside and bent over to kiss Ivy, resting her hand on the dark-blonde locks for a moment. Next she came to Alice.

"Why on earth are you still awake?" she whispered, setting the candle on the bedside table.

A sigh emitted from her little troublemaker, and her eyes popped open. "I couldn't sleep." Alice reached up to put her arms around Claire's neck and kissed her cheek.

Claire sighed and leaned back. "Darling, you've got to sleep! Do you realize the time?" Far too late for a little girl to be up. Where was Nettie? Why hadn't she watched them?

Too much to do, she supposed. With such limited staff, they needed everyone to pitch in on duties they weren't necessarily suited for.

"Oh, it's late." Alice flipped her hand in a dreadfully adult way, apparently thinking it was an unimportant subject. "Mummy, the Lansky girls say everyone has a father. Why don't I?"

Well. Here it was. The moment of truth. Her inquisitive daughter couldn't wait any longer before asking questions—questions Claire could never answer.

There was too much at stake to let an eight-year-old know the truth.

"Not everyone has a father." It wasn't a lie, not exactly. Not if she added further clarification of her idea of fatherhood—and how that place was not currently filled. "Not everyone has a mother, either. There is always a man and a woman who could have been your parents, but parents are only considered such if they care for their child. Your father ... he might have liked you, but you never met."

Alice nodded slowly, her face wrinkled like an old woman's. "But why? Why didn't he ever meet me? If he could have been my father, why wouldn't he?"

"He would have, I think, but it just ..." She sighed. "Darling, sometimes things happen, and we can't stop them. The wrongs can't be made right. I know it's hard for you to understand, but I'm protecting you by not telling you everything."

"But I want to know everything," Alice whispered.

Claire smiled weakly. "I know. I know, darling. And it's going to be hard for you to understand. I love you, though, and Nettie loves you, and I think your Uncle Charlie loves you, though he can't come see us often. It doesn't matter that your father doesn't."

Alice scowled. "I'll talk to him and make him love me. Where is he? I need to meet him."

She would've laughed if it weren't so pitifully impossible. "I can't tell you that."

"Why? He's my father, isn't he?" Alice folded her arms across her chest. "I want to see him."

"But you can't." She forced her tone to be soft and understanding rather than clipped and frustrated. Claire wanted Alice to meet him, too, under the right circumstances. She wished things had turned out differently.

But they hadn't. There was no use in wishing for what couldn't be.

Alice flopped back on the pillow and stared at the ceiling. "Well then. If you won't tell me, I'll find out for myself."

Claire chuckled a bit, as quietly as she could. That was something an eight-year-old could never do on her own. "All right, darling. Find out and tell him to come back to us." She bent forward and kissed her daughter's forehead. "I want you to be happy, but I can't do this for you."

"Why not? You've always done things for me before!"

Yes, that was the perspective of a child. Mummy could do anything. But what did one say to a question like that? Taking a deep breath, she worked her way through the next sentence a word at a time. "He ... doesn't want me anymore. A woman can't throw herself at a man's feet like that. Especially given our circumstances. You'll ... you'll understand when you're older."

Alice huffed. "I don't like that."

"Like what?"

"Being told I'll understand when I'm older." Her daughter was glaring at her now.

Claire didn't like being the villainess, even if sometimes it was necessary in motherhood, so she sighed. "In this case, it's true."

"I think I'd understand. Try."

Again, she repressed the impulse to laugh as she rose. "I love you, Alice. Good night."

"Good night, Mummy," Alice said reluctantly.

Claire took up her candle and crept out of the room, closing the door behind her.

CHAPTER THREE

THE NEXT MORNING, ALICE woke up late. Ivy was already gone, and Alice hurriedly rose and pulled on a simple dress. She took a minute to brush her hair and wash her face; Nettie would throw a fit if she didn't.

She tiptoed to the schoolroom door and glanced in. Nettie was leaning over Ivy, helping her form letters. Alice dashed past the door. She didn't want to begin her lessons; she had some questions to ask first.

She crept down the back stairway and into the kitchen. There, scrubbing the floor on her hands and knees, was Mrs. Bennett, their elderly maid-of-all-work, a plump, dimpled woman with curly, dark hair.

"Mrs. Bennett?" Alice knelt next to the servant. "May I have some breakfast, please?"

Mrs. Bennett smiled and slowly rose, rolling her shoulders as she did so. "Why, it's about time that you were up! Won't you take a seat, Miss Alice?"

Alice sat at the little kitchen table. Though civilities were all very well and good, she was eager to get to the point. "Mrs. Bennett, when did you come to work for us?"

"Oh, six-some-odd years ago," said Mrs. Bennett.

"I was here?"

"Yes, you were a wee little poppet!" Mrs. Bennett smiled affectionately.

Alice did not care to be called a poppet and so decided to distract Mrs. Bennett from thoughts of her poppetness by asking another question.

"Where was I born? Here in London?"

Mrs. Bennett paused halfway through pouring Alice some milk and squinted. "I don't know, Miss Alice. But somewheres other than London, I s'pose." She shrugged.

"Why do you think that?"

She cocked her head as she set the glass in front of Alice. "Because I've heard Miss Berck moved here when you were a wee one—you and Miss Ivy. Everyone says so ... maybe no one knows aught else."

Alice blinked. "Oh. Well. I think we must've come from wherever Uncle Charlie came from. Where was that?"

Mrs. Bennett squinted. "I believe the Chattoways came from Yorkshire. And so did me parents. But they were a grand family, the Chattoways were. I don't know much, but Mr. Chattoway is your uncle, isn't he?"

"Yes."

"Then, aye, you must be a Yorkshire girl." Mrs. Bennett nodded her head companionably as she set a bowl of porridge in front of Alice. "Though, I don't know much. Nettie always says the less I know, the better, and I agree! Not that I would gossip and get such sweet girls as you and Miss Ivy in trouble. Or Miss Berck, for that matter, cold as she seems. She has a right, dear heart in her—strong women often do."

"Oh. If you did gossip, we would get ... in trouble?" Alice wrinkled her nose. What kind of trouble could Mrs. Bennett mean?

"Aye, perhaps. Or at least the gentlefolk would stop hiring Miss Berck, and she'd be out of a job. You'd all starve!" Mrs. Bennett said these dismal words cheerfully, but Alice shuddered.

"Are we ... are we so *bad*, Mrs. Bennett? Ivy and me, I mean." She twirled her spoon about in her breakfast, unwilling to eat until her questioning finished.

"No, there's nothing wrong with you, poppet." Mrs. Bennett smiled. "Now, eat up your porridge before it gets cold. Don't you worry about it! Sometimes people can be finicky if they put their minds to it, but that don't mean you're not a sweet thing. Don't let anyone tell you that you're bad!"

As Mrs. Bennett went back to her scrubbing, Alice took her first bite of breakfast and pondered the servant's words.

But even if Mrs. Bennett says we're not bad, how does she know? After all, if you have to be a secret, there must be something wrong with you. But what's wrong with us?

A thought came to her, and she bit the inside of her mouth for a long minute as she thought about it.

"Can you have a baby and not be married?"

Mrs. Bennett looked surprised but answered calmly. "That sure is switching subjects! Aye, you can, but it's not right. Only naughty people would have babies without being married. Hurry along with that. You're already late enough getting to your lessons."

Alice took another big bite of porridge, but she had more questions. "Mrs. Bennett." She hesitated before plunging in. "Was Mummy married when Ivy and I came?"

The servant turned to face Alice. "Your mother may be many things, but she's not like that. I knew it when I first met her and had me interview. No ... not Miss Berck. I have me standards, same as anyone. I don't know who to, but she was married once. Now, no more questions. Run along!"

With a sigh, Alice dragged her feet out of the kitchen.

Mummy arrived home a little earlier than usual that evening. Alice had to redo an arithmetic lesson, but she hurried downstairs to the drawing room as quickly as she could.

When Alice walked into the room, she found Mummy telling Ivy a story.

"Did the princess stay in the tower forever?" Ivy's eyes were wide.

"Why, she might have, but one day, while she was sitting up in the tower—"

"What was she doing up in the tower?"

Alice grinned. Only her twin would think to ask that question.

Mummy cleared her throat. "Princess Rapunzel was sitting up in her tower eating breakfast when she heard horse hooves in the garden. When Rapunzel looked out the window, she saw a handsome prince on a white horse."

"I want it to be chestnut." Ivy pouted. "White horses get dirty too easily."

Alice nodded in agreement, though, of course, if she had a horse, it would be a brilliant, shiny black, not a dull old chestnut.

"Very well." Mummy nodded. "I had been partial to that coloring. Aren't you going to ask what the horse's name was?"

"What was the horse's name?" Ivy asked.

"I believe it was Fred," Mummy said with an amused smile. Alice had to grin, too. She knew Ivy would never accept that. Unlike Alice, Ivy was good at naming things.

Ivy shook her head emphatically. "That's not a horse name."

"Morning Star?" Alice suggested.

"That's a girl horse's name. I want it to be Starlight."

"The handsome prince rode up to the tower on his chestnut stallion, Starlight. 'Hello! What's your name?' Rapunzel called down to the prince. You see, the evil witch had kept her in the tower so long that she'd never been taught not to speak to strangers."

"She was a naughty princess?" Ivy said, looking awed over the fact that princesses *could* be naughty.

Alice agreed. Princesses were perfect, after all.

"Why, no, she'd just never been taught. And the prince said, 'Fair maiden, my name is Prince ...'" Mummy hesitated.

"Prince Charlemagne," said Ivy, having overheard parts of Alice's history lessons earlier in the day.

"Yes, that was it." Mummy laughed. "He said, 'My name is Prince Charlemagne, and I have come to seek out the fairest maiden to be my wife, and you are the fairest of them all. Everyone knows that you are doomed to forever dwell in that tower; nevertheless, I will rescue you, if I can only find a way.'"

Mummy paused for a moment, her eyes growing troubled. "You should always look for a prince who is willing to rescue you." She kissed them both and continued on with the story. "The princess said, 'I will hang my hair out of this window, and you may climb up.' So she hung her golden locks out the window as she always had for the evil witch, and Prince Charlemagne began to climb them."

"How did he do that?" Ivy inquired.

"Now, Ivy." Mummy had a teasing gleam in her blue eyes that Alice didn't fail to notice. "Everyone knows that, as a boy, Prince Charlemagne climbed trees quite frequently. I don't believe that some fair maiden's hair would be a challenge."

"Oh, I didn't know," said Ivy.

Alice almost laughed aloud.

Ivy's brow wrinkled again. "Did it hurt Rapunzel for him to climb her hair?"

"You know, that is an interesting—" Mummy began, but their manservant, Jameson, entered the room.

"I'm sorry to disturb you, Miss Berck, but Mr. Steven Parker is at the door."

Mummy stiffened, and her eyes narrowed. "Mr. Parker? Did you—has he given a reason for his coming?"

"No, miss. Only—he told me to give this to you." Jameson extended a rectangular piece of stiff paper, which Mummy accepted.

Over Mummy's shoulder, Alice made out the words "We need to discuss certain matters" scrawled onto the back of the calling card in a careless hand.

"Hmm." Mummy's voice was tired as she dropped the card onto her lap. "You may let him in. I'll see him here."

"Yes, miss." Jameson stepped backwards. "Shall I call Nettie down to fetch the young ladies?"

Mummy shook her head. "No. I'll keep the girls here with me. But I would like you to ask Nettie to wait outside the door, where I can ring for her in an instant if necessary."

"Yes, miss." Jameson turned, looking rather confused, and left the room.

As soon as he was gone, Mummy turned to Alice and Ivy. "Darlings, I need you both to be quiet and still unless spoken to, and please do not answer a question unless I give you permission to do so. I'll nod if I believe it's a safe one for you to answer. This is for your own protection. Understand?"

Brow wrinkled, Alice nodded. "Yes, Mummy. But—"

"No buts. Ivy?"

Eyes solemn, Alice's twin nodded. "Yes, Mummy. I won't speak."

In a moment, Jameson entered again. "Mr. Steven Parker," he announced. After him walked Mr. Parker.

Now that she had a moment to really look at him, no longer as frightened as she'd been the first time, Alice realized he looked a bit like a prince in a fairy tale. Mr. Parker was a tall, painfully handsome man who might have resembled the Greek god Apollo save for his dark hair and carefully-groomed beard.

He smiled winningly at both the little girls and nodded to Mummy. "Thank you for seeing me, Claire."

Mummy arched her eyebrows, and Alice knew she wanted to give this Parker fellow a good tongue-lashing. But all she said was, *"Miss Chattoway* will do, sir."

His smile tightened a bit. "Such good friends as us?"

"It's been a long time since we were children." Mummy inclined her head toward a seat opposite her. "Will you sit down?"

"Always the picture of propriety, Miss Chattoway." Mr. Parker carelessly sprawled onto the chair, eyes on Mummy in an uncomfortable way.

Alice scowled. He ought to be more respectful. After all, Mummy was a perfect lady; he should be a perfect gentleman.

"I am glad to see you, Mr. Parker, though it was only yesterday evening when you were here last." Mummy's tone was cutting.

Alice wished all the tension would end. It wasn't any fun.

"It's because of yesterday that I've come." He leaned forward. "Are you sure you want to have this conversation in front of your children?"

Alice wouldn't have believed it if she hadn't seen it, but she was sure Mummy's eyes grew even harder. "Be civil, and I won't have to worry about what you say in front of them."

Mr. Parker cleared his throat. "It's not an easy subject, nor a kind one to little ears. I would rather it just be us—Nettie could be present for propriety's sake, as I'm sure she knows all the details already. But not these girls."

"Yet, I presume, based on your hinting, that it is about them." Mummy inclined her head. "Please. Speak your piece. I'm not able to give all the details at present, perhaps never will be able to, but I will keep the girls with me."

Alice wasn't sure why Mummy wanted them to remain in the room so badly—until she felt Mummy's fingers digging into her shoulder and saw the way she clutched a lock of Ivy's hair.

Comfort. It was for comfort.

Reassured, and knowing her presence was a help, Alice sat quietly at Mummy's side and let the scene play out.

Chapter Four

M R. PARKER CLEARED HIS throat. "I suppose you are not willing to tell me what happened."

"No."

"Tell me how you came to London and are now a businesswoman." He raised his eyebrows. "I presume that's quite a tale."

"Not much of one." Mummy began to relax. Alice supposed because that was an easy question. "I came here almost eight years ago, found I had a talent as a seamstress and, later, a designer. Sometime after, my brother found me and helped finance the dress shop I own now. The styles I designed took off somewhat, as they say, and I've always had an eye for it."

"But that doesn't get to the root of why you must now earn your bread." Mr. Parker forced a chuckle through the stiff smile on his lips. "You were the belle of the season, Claire—"

"Miss Chattoway."

"I can't see how you managed to get to … to where you are now. Somewhere between June 1861 and now, I lost you. You … you know I looked after you disappeared, didn't you?" He was unsure now, a different expression on his face. Like a little lost boy. Alice almost felt sorry for him.

"I'd heard. From Charles."

"Yes." Mr. Parker shifted in his seat. "I worried. I couldn't think what had happened. Now I know why and who—"

"Mr. Parker, please."

He paused and glanced at Alice and Ivy. "Do they not know?"

"No, and I think it's best that way. It will only cause more pain."

He swallowed. "Ah. At any rate, I don't understand why circumstances did not continue as they did from that night on—the certain night in June 1861." Again, he cocked his head. "I wish I knew what had gone wrong. I can't believe he would—"

"Mr. Parker."

"Ah." He sighed. "This is why I wanted to discuss the matter privately."

"It is exactly why I *didn't*." Mummy helped Ivy to her feet, then rose. "I don't think you really have much to say. You ask me for answers I cannot give, and you wish to find solutions for problems that are unsolvable."

"I don't believe they are. I ... Dash it all, Claire! You'll never admit it, but this must be hell for you."

"Watch your tongue! And it's Miss Chattoway."

"Legally?"

She stilled. "Yes. Legally."

"So you are not—"

"I am *not*."

"But were you?"

She drew herself up, and her eyes flashed. "Do you believe it of me?"

Mr. Parker shook his head, eyes solemn. "Miss Chattoway, I don't believe anything of you anymore. I don't know what to think! I fail to understand what could have happened—surely there were no grounds for annulment, but if you say that, in this matter, you were without blame, I will take your word."

Mummy stood still for a moment, her fingers tangled in Ivy's blonde locks and her eyes distant. "I was without blame. I promise you that."

Mr. Parker sighed. "Then that is what I believe."

Alice wasn't sure exactly what they were talking about, but Mummy had forbidden her to speak—so she'd have to ask later. She was certain it was about her father. If only they could talk about it in ways that made sense, ways that gave specifics. That would be ideal.

"Would you leave this life if you could? Would you marry me if I offered it?"

That was unexpected. Based on the expression on Mummy's face, she was as shocked as Alice.

Frightened, Alice cowered into Mummy's skirts. She hardly knew this man—and now he was proposing marriage to Mummy?

"Don't think you need to sacrifice yourself," Mummy said after a long silence. "We're doing well, and I'm sure I'm beyond preserving my honor."

He shifted in his chair. "I'm not the heir of Pearlbelle Park anymore, as the gossip papers probably informed you. I know that was always my best quality." He attempted a smile. "After my fall from grace in Uncle John's eyes, I was promptly disinherited. My cousin, Mr. Knight, is the owner now that Uncle John has passed on."

Mummy cocked her head. "Where are you going with this, Steven?"

Alice wondered where the formal *Mr. Parker* had gone. Mummy almost never dropped formality.

He smiled wryly. "Despite all that, I have a tidy sum to my name, and we could move somewhere where everyone wouldn't know the past. Besides, if I were married, my daughter could come live with me. You know things about little girls." He gestured at Alice and Ivy. "You could care for her as I never had time for. I think it would be the right thing to do."

"Ah." Mummy raised her eyebrows. "So you and Lydia *did* have a child."

"Yes. I thought our marriage would turn the tide in favor of my inheriting, but, unfortunately, it only angered Uncle John further." He cleared his throat. "He blamed me for her death to the day of his. And he wouldn't look at his granddaughter."

"So where is she? She must be three or four years old now—if I'm remembering when Lydia's death took place."

"Yes, she's four and is in Liverpool with my father. He has a nurse who helps him take care of her, and he loves children." Mr. Parker shrugged. "My lifestyle wouldn't benefit her, and I hear she's doing well."

"So you don't go see her?"

He winced. "How can I? It feels as if she took everything from me. A child shouldn't have to live with a father who views her as such. But ... if you were to help me ..." He looked up at Mummy, and again Alice had the impression that he was lost.

"Why did your wife die?" Alice asked.

"Alice!" Mummy snapped.

But Mr. Parker was smiling. "I am quickly learning, Claire, that Miss Alice is a force to be reckoned with. Don't shush her. You'll break her spirit. My wife died when our baby arrived, Miss Alice."

"What's your baby's name?"

"Posy."

"Posy is a funny name."

"Her full name is Patricia Mariah Rose Elton Parker, but that's a bit of a bother to say, I think."

Alice nodded slowly. "Yes, it is a bother to say."

"*Alice*," Mummy said again in that same exhausted tone of voice.

"It's quite all right. I agree!" Mr. Parker knelt before Alice. "I'd have named her Posy Parker and had done with it. But everyone in the family wanted to add something. Patricia for my mother, Mariah for Lydia's, Rose for a grandmother somewhere back. Even Elton for both of us, I suppose." He cocked his head. "Lydia and I were cousins, you see; my mother and her father were siblings."

"Oh." That made sense, she supposed. "I just have Alice Christina. I don't know why."

"Christina is for your mother's sister. And Alice for—"

Mummy caught Mr. Parker's eyes and shook her head, so he stopped.

Alice sighed. No one was ever going to tell her anything, were they?

"I'll take my leave now." Mr. Parker stood. "Claire, please send me a message when you arrive at a decision. I don't believe that, at this juncture, happiness is something to speak of, but you could make a difference in my life—and I would make one in yours."

"I'll consider what you've said."

Mr. Parker stepped toward the door. "I can't be *him*, but in the situation you're in, a man is what you need—someone who can sweep it all away."

"As I said, I will consider it. Thank you for coming this evening."

Mr. Parker nodded to her. "Thank you for letting me in."

"Nettie?" Claire lowered herself onto the edge of her bed and regarded her confidante. She trusted Nettie's opinion, but then, her maid had always been unfavorably inclined toward Mr. Parker.

Nettie dropped down in front of the fire and looked at Claire with a slight smile. "Yes?"

"Well, Nettie ..." *Why is it so hard tonight?* "Well, Nettie." Yet there wasn't a good way to phrase her thoughts.

"Yes, Claire, I'm listening."

That soft confirmation was all Claire needed. She blurted out, "Should I accept Mr. Parker's proposal?"

"You're considering it?" Nettie's eyes widened. From the moment Claire had told her of his suggestion, she'd proclaimed it ridiculous. She'd declared Mr. Parker the least dependable man in the world, a shameless flirt, and never a friend to women.

Where Nettie obtained this information, Claire didn't know. But she still hesitated to override her maid. Nettie wasn't one to rely on intuition or uneasy feelings. She used cold, hard facts in her decisions—or at least she always had before.

"Perhaps." At least she was willing to entertain the thought. After all, a respectable marriage, a regular home, and the ability to be a true mother to Alice and Ivy—and more little ones down the road—would be a great blessing.

Something she wanted more than anything else this life had to offer.

Nettie pressed her lips in a thin line. "I have stated my opinion, and now I shan't interfere with your decision."

"But why have you formed such a decided opinion against a man you have never even spoken to?" Claire pressed. She must know. She couldn't make an informed decision otherwise.

"I'm not sure." Nettie's tone was as careful as a housemaid dusting a priceless vase. "It's merely an impression, but a strong one, based on his actions and attitude whenever I've seen him or heard of him. Think, Claire. Since you were a child, he was determined to marry you. Yet, even while you were in the same house with him—those weeks at Pearlbelle Park—I saw him flirting with others. His cousin Lydia, even while she was only a child. And the maids ... the maids told tales in the serving hall."

"What did they say?"

"That he begged kisses and embraces from them. Sometimes more. He never threatened their jobs, but they feared it." Nettie shrugged. "I cannot trust a man who would do that."

Claire winced. No wonder Nettie couldn't trust him; it struck too close to home. But at any rate, it was to be expected. "Ah well. He was only a boy."

"That's no excuse, Claire."

She sighed. "I know. But surely it wasn't bad. Is that all? Boyhood follies? I'm sure even Charlie has flirted with the maids, and he was honorable in everything else."

Nettie shook her head. "Your brother never looked or said or did anything to make me uncomfortable, Claire. If he has spoken to me, it has been kindly. Parker is different. As I said, he doesn't respect women. Think how he went from you to Lydia! We both know he married her because she was with child. Stop denying it. You just have to look at the dates to see the truth."

Claire suspected that, though she hadn't wanted to voice it. But she knew Steven had loved Lydia, too; his eyes said so when he spoke of her death and their child, even if he was afraid to admit it. "I fear that is the case, but, again, he was young, and he did the honorable thing."

Nettie snorted. "And was disinherited for his troubles."

"I know his uncle wanted him to marry rich and bring a new bloodline into the family. Instead, he married his sickly cousin and sired a daughter." No one wanted daughters. Claire gripped the edge of her nightgown in her fist.

"I believe John Elton might have been tired of so many girls." Nettie's tone almost cracked with its dryness. "He never did have a brother—only Mr. Parker's and Mr. Knight's respective mothers. Then he only had Lois and Lydia, so for a male heir, there was Knight or Parker—neither of them perfect options."

Claire couldn't help but chuckle. "Mr. Parker or a young man who had grown up in America? Oh, I can't believe he was thrilled with his potential heirs."

"Yes, but at least things are settled now. I hope the new Mrs. Knight's child is a boy."

Claire glanced up to see Nettie watching her closely. "Yes," she said. "I believe she may be expecting, as you have surmised. They have traveled to Pearlbelle Park now, probably so she can have the child there. Though, why Mr. Elton would condone his heir marrying an American is beyond me."

Nettie cocked her head. "He did condone it?"

"Yes. Before his death this winter, he named Mr. Knight heir to Pearlbelle Park—and he was married then."

Nettie nodded. "I see. Well, the late Mr. Knight—Mr. Philip Knight's father—was an American, too. Perhaps Mr. Elton didn't mind them as much as you seem to."

"Hmm." Claire reached behind her to pull back the covers. "I just find them shiftless. But let's keep to our original subject: Mr. Parker. I think we're stepping around the biggest issue—if I don't marry him, what future can I offer the girls? And, further, how can they expect to go on without a father all their lives?"

Nettie ran a hand over her eyes and shook her head. "They could get on well without a father—and God will provide regardless. Besides, Claire, you must admit not everything was Mr. Chattoway's fault."

"It wasn't entirely my father, no," Claire said after a few moments of silence. "I'm headstrong—but Ivy isn't, and Alice is at least trainable. Thankfully, they don't take after me as far as personality goes." She sounded more sarcastic than she'd intended, but it was true.

"Ivy inherited her father's mild temperament," Nettie murmured.

A lump rose in Claire's throat that she couldn't swallow. "Perhaps. I would like that. Nettie, sometimes I miss him terribly—do you know that? I get so lonely. I wish he were here, yet I don't." The tears welled, and she dashed a few away with her hand. Still, they came. "How immature it is to think about him at all."

"Oh, I hardly think so. There, don't start crying! You're only sad because it's so late. We had both better go to sleep now." Nettie began to rise from her place, but Claire motioned her back down.

"If it isn't too much trouble, I'd rather talk a bit longer. I believe it helps me think. At least, it always has before."

But she didn't know what to say, how to express the feelings brewing inside. For a few moments, there were no more words between them, then Nettie broke the silence.

"Claire, would you like to talk about him for a time? I would understand, as I always have. You used to go on so."

She swallowed. "I used to love him so." He'd been the center of her universe for a brief period of time—before that, the dearest friend she had every summer.

But now, that friendship was in the past. Oh, life was so horridly unfair.

Nettie sighed. "Claire, you're in love with him, aren't you?"

Her head snapped up. She couldn't admit that and keep her pride intact. "No, most certainly not. I have more sense than to go on loving someone who doesn't care whether I live or die. Besides, it was all a juvenile infatuation. I'll go to sleep now. Good night, Nettie. Sweet dreams." Claire hastily cast aside her dressing gown and snuggled under the covers.

Best to stop talking before she fell apart completely.

Nettie crossed the room and took her friend's hand. "Don't think too much tonight, Claire. Go to sleep right away. I know you are hurt, but

I want to remind you: if you are lost, the only One Who can find you, redeem you, is our Lord, Jesus Christ."

Claire's throat tightened with promises she couldn't accept. If she were a different sort—and if God Himself were a different sort—it would be possible.

But she wasn't, and He wasn't.

"I don't deserve what you say is offered, Nettie," Claire said. "Please don't bring it up again."

But Nettie wouldn't be put off tonight. "I've told you time and time again, but you won't hear it. Jesus can heal you; He can wash you clean! If you could only believe."

Claire gritted her teeth and turned her face away. "Good night, Nettie."

"Good night, Claire."

CHAPTER FIVE

T HE NEXT EVENING, CLAIRE entered Alice and Ivy's bedroom as Nettie closed a book, and the girls begged for just one more story.

Nettie glanced at the small watch pinned to her bodice. "I suppose there's time."

"Of course there is." Claire cleared her throat. "I'll tell the last story. Would that suit?"

"Yes!" Ivy clapped her hands together. "Please, Mummy, tell us a story."

Alice nodded enthusiastically.

"Very well. Nettie, would you leave us?" As her maid left the room, Claire took a seat on a chair near the fire and pulled Ivy down onto her lap. "There."

Alice curled up with her chin resting on her mother's knee and passed the storybook to her.

"No, not these stories. Tonight I'm going to tell you a true story. Would you like that?"

Alice's brow wrinkled, but she nodded. "All right."

Staring into the fire, Claire whispered, "I thought I'd tell you something about your father."

Ivy showed no reaction, but Alice jumped. Those black eyes, flashing and full of curiosity, met Claire's sharply.

"Mummy." Her elder daughter's voice was hushed. "Oh, *Mummy*."

Claire swallowed. "I know you'd like to know more, Alice. I think it's important that you understand ... some of what happened."

Tears trembled on Alice's lashes. "Why isn't he here?"

"He can't be." That much was true, at least now. "I'm terribly sorry, darlings, but he *can't* be."

Ivy smiled and wrapped an arm around Claire's neck. "I don't want him anyway. I love you and Alice most—and Nettie—and Kitty."

That was her little girl. She didn't really like people beyond her own circle.

Alice scowled. "Why is he a secret, though? I don't understand!"

"If people knew about you and Ivy—"

"I know *that*, even though I think it's silly. But what about our father?"

Claire sighed. How should she explain it to her girls? No easy way presented itself, but they needed to know some of the answers or they would be helpless.

"He isn't able to be a part of our life anymore. I'm so sorry, but that's how it is. However, I'm willing to answer questions about ... about him. The man himself. And I believe it might help to tell you a bit about how we ... how we met."

"Can we ask questions?" Alice pressed.

Claire wasn't sure if she wanted to laugh or cry. *That's my Alice. Keep that inquisitive mind. It'll take you far.* "You may."

Alice paused, and Claire could almost see the gears of the child's brain turning like a clock preparing to strike the hour. "Did he love us?" she asked at last.

Claire sucked in a breath. "He never knew you. I ... I regret that he didn't get to know you, both of you, because he loved children. He wanted to be a father—and he would have been proud to be yours."

Alice nodded. "Good. Being our father would be a good job, I think. What did he look and act like?"

Claire half-closed her eyes. *Vague is good. Things that apply to a thousand men. Don't think of him as the exception but the rule.*

"He was tall, a few inches over six feet. His eyes were kind and his smile bright. As a gentleman, he always lent a helping hand where needed, and he was a friend to everyone. He was soft-hearted, sometimes even emotional, but he possessed a gentle strength."

If only he had come back ...

"Where is he now?"

Claire pressed her lips together. "If I tell you, you'll try to go to him, no matter how impossible that is." She cocked her head. "You'd only be hurt."

Alice blanched. "He'd hurt me?"

"No! No, darling. Not purposefully. He's not a frightening man—quite the opposite. But you would be hurt by the circumstances. Trust me."

More hesitation, but Alice slowly nodded. Claire breathed a sigh of relief.

"You said you'd tell us a story, though." Ivy tugged gently on Claire's sleeve. "Mummy, this is *not* a story. This is like *schooling*."

Claire chuckled softly and kissed Ivy's cheek. "I know, dearest. And I am going to tell you a fairy tale—it's about a princess who was foolish."

Alice sighed. "Mummy, is this going to be one of those lesson things again? I'd rather just be told."

Ivy cut her eyes to Alice. "I like Mummy's stories." Her arm tightened around Claire's neck. "Even the lesson ones."

"Shush, girls. No quarreling. Yes, Alice, it has a bit of a lesson ... but not much of one. It's no fable. I don't think Alice was trying to insult me, Ivy dear." Claire smiled and squeezed Alice's shoulder. "Let's see. Where shall I begin?"

"Once upon ..." Ivy said.

"Right. Once upon a time, there was a princess who lived in a wild moor in the north. It was beautiful there, but she hadn't many friends. She had a younger sister, who was very unlike her, and they never got along. And she had a big brother, who was a rough boy she didn't like playing with anymore—now that she was a lady, I mean. And she had a maid, who was her dearest friend, but ... it wasn't the same."

"Nettie is a maid," Ivy observed.

"Yes, Nettie is the same as having the very dearest friend!" Alice said, folding her arms.

I'd forgotten how much they talk during bedtime stories. It's been too long. "You're both right. She did have a very good friend in her maid, but she was still bored. There wasn't much to do, and her parents—especially her father—were difficult to get along with. So it was time for an adventure, as it often is in fairy tales."

"I don't think I'd like an adventure," Ivy said. "Please don't make me have one, Mummy. I'd rather stay with you."

Claire laughed. "Perhaps you'll want one someday, love."

Ivy shook her head emphatically. "*Never*. Alice will have adventures, then she shall tell me about them. I'll like that! It'll be like a story, only real."

"You can come with me," Alice offered. "I wouldn't mind sometimes."

"No ... I don't think so." Ivy glanced across the room. "Unless Kitty could come."

"Oh, she can't come. She's too noisy."

Claire was curious to know more about Alice's proposed adventures—of which she had heard nothing before now—but the minutes ticked away. Soon it would be late, and she wanted to finish this story first.

"Well, much like Alice, this princess was an adventure-embracer." Claire tangled her fingers nervously in Ivy's hair. How could she say this? Even in fairy-tale format, it was difficult. "So off she went to the south, to an estate. And while she was there, quite by accident, she met someone. A prince, of course."

Alice cocked her head. "Was it love at first sight?"

"Oh, I don't believe in love at first sight!" Ivy exclaimed. "I would only fall in love with someone who I knew. I don't like strangers. Mummy, why don't you change the story so they can be best of friends before the adventures?"

"I can satisfy you both, darlings." She bit her lip, trying to remember the excitement of first love before broken hearts and empty longing. "They had been friends for years, Ivy, as children, but now that they were almost adults, things changed between them over the following weeks."

"Oh, all right." Alice shrugged. "Love at first sight just speeds things up a bit, and you can get to the good parts."

Claire tried to conceal a grin. "And what, pray tell, are the good parts?"

"The happily ever after, of course."

"But all the happily ever after entails is just that—'and they lived happily ever after.' And then the story is over." It wasn't over, nor did happily ever after exist for most, but Claire wouldn't shatter an eight-year-old's dreams.

Alice shook her head. "It's not *really* the end, though. They have to live and grow old and have babies. I like to think about it. It's almost like Heaven in fairy tales—happily ever after, I meant."

"Ah, I see." That was an interesting way of seeing it, but she supposed it was true. Happily ever after assumed that the prince and princess never experienced any pain or suffering. That the world ceased to turn on its axis and cause the inevitable tragedies of its turning. "How did you come to think of that?"

Alice shrugged. "I don't know."

Ah, well. Childhood genius couldn't be unraveled, or it wouldn't be so shocking. "Where was I?"

"The prince and princess had met—again—and fallen in love," Ivy said without missing a beat.

"Right. They wanted to marry, as people in love usually do. But the problem was that the prince had not a dime to his name, and the princess's father didn't approve. At all. In fact, he often voiced his disdain for that particular prince—and encouraged the princess to marry another."

Ivy gasped. "Who she didn't love?"

"Yes. The princess wasn't interested, though. She only wanted her one true love—and she was determined to have him. So they eloped ... ran off into the night like thieves and married in France, where it's easier to do these things."

Claire pressed her lips tightly together as emotions overwhelmed her, causing her throat to tighten and tears to well. She couldn't finish this story. Not when two eight-year-olds, not at all disillusioned with the bright and hopeful world they lived in, depended on her.

"And then ... then they lived happily ever after? In France?" Ivy suggested.

"Y-yes. That's exactly what happened."

Alice frowned. "Well, you don't seem happy about it, Mummy!"

"I am! I'm so glad that the prince and the princess found happily ever
after." Claire eased Ivy off her lap and stood, forcing a bright smile to chase
every shadow off her face. "Time for bed, darlings. Hop under the covers
..."

There was time for reality when they were a little older, perhaps.

Mummy was sitting at her vanity putting her hair in a simple bun when
Alice and Ivy ran in to claim kisses early the next morning. They almost
never got to see her before work, but Alice had insisted.

Things had been so topsy-turvy lately that Alice appreciated a hug first
thing in the morning.

This morning there was something different on Mummy's vanity—a
little box with ornate carvings on the outside.

"What's that, Mummy?"

Mummy blinked. "Oh, that's my jewelry box."

"I've never seen it." Alice reached for it, then drew back, hesitating. It
was one of those no-touch treasures. "Can I look?"

Mummy opened the box to reveal a few trinkets, from necklaces to rings
to bracelets. "I rarely wear them anymore, but I can't bear to sell them.
Aren't they pretty?"

Alice carefully picked up an ornate diamond necklace. "Oh, Mummy!
How lovely. Will I ever have anything so precious?"

"Perhaps." Mummy mustered a tight smile. "But at any rate, someday when you are older, you will have some of mine."

"And me?" Ivy asked.

"Yes, and my Ivy." Mummy slid her arm around Ivy and pulled her in for another hug. "Now, I'm on my way out. Would you like to pick a ring for me?" Though she rarely wore necklaces or diamonds or anything like them, Mummy usually wore a simple ring on her right hand.

After sifting through the small collection of jewels, Alice gasped and pounced on a simple ring with a blue stone. "I love this one. Do wear it, Mummy!" She held the trinket out to her mother.

Mummy fairly ripped the ring away from her daughter. "Not that one." She threw it back in the jewelry box as if it burned her hand.

Alice jerked back and stared at her mother for a minute before peering into the box. "Is it a ... I mean, what's wrong with it, Mummy?"

"Nothing. It's my birthstone, actually. Topaz." Mummy stood and walked to her wardrobe only to open the doors and remove nothing.

Ivy picked up the small gold band and turned it over in her hand. "Don't you like topazes? I think they're pretty."

"It just reminds me of something." Mummy sighed and turned to face them. "I'm sorry if I was harsh, Alice. I didn't even remember that I'd saved that ring. I only got the box down because I was looking for a different one. Why ... why don't you take it? I'll get you a chain, and you can wear it around your neck. I have no use for it."

She crossed the room and reached into her jewelry box. "Here. Ivy can have this one. It's a man's ring, but it's not heavy. And the stone is a garnet, which is your birthstone."

Ivy clapped her hands together. "Thank you, Mummy."

Alice nodded, not nearly as excited as Ivy but still appreciative of the gift. "I'd like that."

"Here, I think I have two chains ..."

After the rings were hanging around Alice's and Ivy's necks, Mummy kissed both their foreheads. "I have to go now. It's going to be a busy day, darlings, but I'll see you in the evening."

CHAPTER SIX

CLAIRE'S DRESS SHOP STOOD only a few blocks over, so the fact that she didn't own a carriage wasn't a problem. If she left before it was light, she'd have Jameson, their manservant, walk her to work—and if it was close to dark and she had yet to return, he would sometimes come and walk back with her.

But, in general, she encouraged him to stay with Nettie and the girls. Her own safety was a secondary concern, and it didn't seem right to leave a household of women without protection. She'd be fine. Her dress shop was in a reputable area, and the walk home wasn't a particularly treacherous one.

That was definitely a blessing, if she believed in those. Which she didn't. But it indicated good luck.

This morning, Claire had told Jameson not to fetch her, being sure she'd leave early. Although she hadn't, when she arrived back at her house, she was glad she'd insisted he remain there.

Outside stood a majestic carriage with a matching pair of bays jingling their harnesses. She half-closed her eyes and took a deep breath, trying to keep the anxiety at bay. She would not panic. It was nothing.

Never mind that no one ever came to visit her. Never mind that the girls and Nettie were alone—though, at least Jameson was home. Never mind that Alice had been asking all sorts of questions and that she had more information than ever before about her father.

Heaven help her. There were so many things to mind that, in that moment, Claire whispered the first prayer she had in years. "Dear Lord, let everything be all right."

Surely she was overreacting. She often did as a result of all the things that had happened when she was a young girl that made it difficult for her to trust, to embrace new situations.

To forgive.

Forgiveness was so terribly hard. She thought she was functional at least, but that didn't mean she had moved on or healed.

She picked up her pace as she hurried down the pavement, but she didn't run. She wouldn't give the mysterious carriage the satisfaction of worrying her that much. She was still a lady. She would always and forever be a lady, even if it was hard to see sometimes.

The carriage was empty, though a driver sat at the top and glared down at her as if he didn't trust her for a minute. She probably looked a bit anxious, a bit wild, and she didn't blame him.

Deep breaths. Calm down. It's going to be all right, Claire.

She opened the door for herself and stepped in. Jameson was standing in the hall, looking at a loss. She stepped forward.

"Whose carriage is that?" Her voice was even and slow, surprisingly so. She'd expected it to tremble, to give away her fears, but no, it was everything a lady's voice should be.

Regulated. In control. Unworried.

"Mr. Steven Parker. He's back." Jameson shrugged. "I told him you weren't home, but he insisted he would wait. He was determined, and I didn't want to use force, miss ... should I have?"

"No, Jameson. That's all right." Claire forced herself not to do what she wanted to do, which was rub her forehead and sigh. At least it was just Steven again. It could have been anyone. But it hadn't been. "I'll see him. Is he in the drawing room?"

"Yes, miss. He's been there for about half an hour—but he said he would wait three hours if he must. He tells me he has nowhere to go and must speak to you."

Claire did sigh then. Try to pry all her secrets out from their hiding places, he meant. He wouldn't let her be until he knew everything. She'd been friends with Steven Parker since they were small children, and he was the soul of persistence.

Whether talking her into an impromptu picnic, taking a ride in a rickety boat on a pond at Pearlbelle Park, or even convincing her to forgive him while she sat wet and miserable on the bank, he always won. He was too charming, too clever, and too disarming.

Yet she didn't like Steven Parker. Not really. Well, she did, but another part of her disliked him greatly. He was beyond annoying sometimes. More often than not, actually.

And he would get her to tell him everything if she wasn't very, very careful.

When she entered the drawing room, he was leaning against the mantel looking calm and collected, but he started as she entered the room.

That was new. Steven Parker was almost never nervous. She couldn't remember a time where he hadn't been controlled and gentlemanly.

He was a heartbreaker. Claire wasn't really a great admirer of beards, but his was neat and looked right on him. He had dark eyes, sharp eyes, almost like Alice's.

Yes, Mr. Parker was a handsome man. He probably had half a dozen women chasing him even now that he no longer had a grand fortune like Mr. Knight.

He'd only been married for about a year before his wife died, but she didn't doubt that he'd made use of the "poor widower with a daughter" line since.

Claire took in a deep breath. "Hello, Mr. Parker. How are you this evening?"

He smiled easily and stepped toward her. She stepped back. He would not get close to her, comfort her, or do anything of the sort. Claire needed to keep all contact minimal. It was best that way. She couldn't bear the thought of his finding out what had happened. She just couldn't.

"I'm doing well." He stopped where he was, but that inexplicable smile remained in place. He definitely wanted her to like him. Definitely wanted to find something out.

Dangerous. He was dangerous. A treacherous addition to her life.

Oh, how had he found her in the first place?

"Why ... why are you here?" Might as well begin with what she wanted to know, with what she must know. She believed in honesty, and it often disarmed people. Women who were honest and upfront shocked men, and they couldn't resist being truthful in return.

He didn't seem shocked, though. He was used to her. Always had been.

But she shook off her worries and focused on his answer.

"I came to see you," Mr. Parker said. "I thought we hadn't finished our conversation last time, even though you wanted it to be finished. You're probably mad at me for coming, but you must see that I had to. It was necessary. If I didn't come, you might have ... I don't know what might happen to you, Claire. Frankly, you seem to be on a treacherous precipice."

"I've been on a dangerous precipice for years, Steven." There. She'd return her first name with his this time. It wasn't proper, it wasn't the tone she wanted to set, but it was truthful. It was how she thought of him most of the time—except when she forced herself to do otherwise.

Being childhood friends seemed to do that, after all. She believed that childhood friends could only be childhood friends when they were children, and that after that, they had best adjust to the idea of being adults, but ... still.

She would call him by his first name tonight. And she would expect honesty in return.

Would he betray her? It was always possible. Who knew? After all, men changed. Perhaps he had done so enough that betrayal was in his heart.

But no. He didn't seem like the type.

His expression was genuinely worried now. "I've noticed." He cleared his throat. "Let's talk, Claire. I'm curious to know how you managed to get to the point where you ... have fallen to this level. Yes, I'll call it a fall. After all, you can't expect it to be called anything less than that. I don't understand what happened! How you ... how you didn't work things out. You've always been so good at working things out, Claire."

Yes, she had. Sometimes to her detriment. She was a problem-solver and always had been. But she was in a situation beyond problem-solving, and she didn't live her life for herself anymore. There were other concerns—two primary concerns, which had changed her life in many ways.

"I'll never be the same, Steven. I'm stuck in a world where everything is changed, without a possibility to make it better. But, truthfully, I don't mind. I am proud of the life I have built ... the dress shop, a safe place for my children ..."

Steven's eyes darkened, looking like two black warnings in that handsome face. "What makes you think it's safe, Claire? It's clearly not—quite the reverse of that. You're raising two children in a dangerous, insane way. Why, at any moment, you stand to lose everything. What if you lose your clientele? Surely, if you don't have a way to support your children, things would go horribly wrong ..." His voice trailed off. "Besides, have you thought about their future?"

Claire swallowed. Had she thought about it? Constantly. It was the ever-present worry behind her life, causing her to push herself as far as she could to be a wonderful mother even when it seemed impossible to do so. What would happen if they arrived at a time when Alice and Ivy could no longer be cared for?

"Yes. Of course, I have thought about the future. I've thought about a lot of things. Now, at present, there's no way out, but, if I could save up enough money, and if I were to somehow find a way to move somewhere ... Well, Steven, at least I could present myself as a respectable middle-class widow. I don't know how it would work out exactly, but there must be a way to give Alice and Ivy the future they deserve—even as I am."

After all, hundreds upon hundreds of women had fallen. Where did they go? She wasn't sure. But they all couldn't just die or disappear. Many of them had to find a way to survive—and for many of them, that had to include a way for their children to survive.

So it could be done. It must be done. She only had to find the way.

Steven sighed. "It seems risky. I strongly feel that something must be done immediately, while they are still young, to make things secure for them. Anything could happen. Which is why ... tonight I've come to you with a suggestion."

Claire raised her eyebrows. "And what would that be?"

"I want to repeat my proposal of marriage."

This man would be the death of her.

"I'm not sure what to think of that expression." He was far too suave for a man who had just asked a woman to marry him. "Claire. Really. Say something."

"You didn't give me enough time. I would need at least a few more days. I ... I don't know what to say."

"As proven by your silence." He laughed. "That could also mean you have something to say but are afraid it would be rude, I suppose."

She offered a bit of a smile, hoping it would lighten the mood. "I suppose. This is all so sudden. What ... how did you come to think of it anyway?"

"Well, wouldn't that solve everything?" He cocked his head. "You'd have a husband, the girls would have a father, my child would have a mother." Steven stepped forward, hand extended, as if he actually expected her to take it. "We could go away somewhere. That way we wouldn't ... wouldn't risk any further scandal. Just to Bath or even Scotland. Or to the Continent, if you'd like."

"But ... you ..." How did one phrase this delicately? "Surely, in your current state, you're not looking to add a family to your list of responsibilities."

He flushed. "I could support you. I have some experience with business, and I have a small sum of my own. I can be frugal, and I know you have a bit put away."

Heat brewed under her cheeks. "How do you know?"

He blinked as if that were an unusual question. "I wanted to see how you were doing, so I inquired at your bank."

Claire swallowed. "They let you have that information?"

He raised his eyebrows. "For the right price."

Fury rose in her chest. He had no right. She wasn't his, never had been, and he couldn't come in and take control. He wouldn't. "I wish you hadn't done that."

"I know you probably consider it a breach of trust, but I had to know that there was no immediate danger. I'm not about to let you starve, Claire."

"But I won't starve." At least, not unless her secret got out. Which he was aiding simply by his presence, by his familiarity, by his concern.

"I know that." He used the same tone when he soothed horses.

He and his horses.

"But I had to be sure. I should've trusted you, perhaps, to know what you're about, but you can be so dashed proud, Claire. Sometimes it's hard to tell if you're in control or just unwilling to ask for help."

Fair enough. But that still didn't give him any right to interfere as he had.

He sighed and shook his head. "Let's not get distracted, though. You know you should marry me. What other recourse have you for the girls?"

Claire swallowed. She'd been thinking about that all day. "I actually have a solution."

Plainly frustrated with her, he ran his hands through his hair, looking just like the messy little boy she'd always known. "And what would that be?"

She walked to the window and looked out on the London street below. What would her neighbors think if he stayed too long? The gossip would spread fast.

"I'd have to give them up ..." she whispered. "Let them go, so they can have a life."

Steven was silent behind her, and at last she turned to face him.

"What would you—?" he stuttered out.

"If they were to become the wards of ... of a benefactor." She stepped toward him. "It could happen. Nettie could be their governess as always, and, sometimes, she could report back to me. And I could disappear—I'm good at it. I could go to France. I know the country well."

His chest rose and fell with a deep breath. "I didn't expect to hear you say that."

Claire bit her lip. "Before today, I didn't expect to say it. My brother, Charles, could take them eventually. They could be the children of ... of distant relatives or ... or old friends. It might work."

"More likely, it wouldn't," Steven retorted. "Claire, you're insane. You know that isn't something you can do—I saw the way you looked at them. And your brother is reliant on your father. Who, other than Charles, could take them in? You know I can't."

"Nor would I ask you to." She wrapped her arms around herself. "But perhaps the remains of the Elton family would be able to do it. The Knights certainly have the money—and Mr. Knight and I grew up together."

His smile tightened. "I doubt it would happen."

"It's a thought anyway. I had friends when I was a young lady—surely some of them would have pity."

"I wouldn't count on it." Steven sighed. "The best course of action is for us to marry. I feel an obligation, really, and—"

"Forget your obligations! I'm not interested." The words left her lips before she had time to think. Earlier, she'd been unsure, still considering her options.

But now she knew. She didn't want to marry Steven Parker. The life she would have with him would be a difficult one. It wouldn't be an improvement for her children to have parents constantly fighting than to have no father at all.

Steven Parker wasn't a sure thing. She could imagine him doing so many reckless, crazy, impossible things—and, if he fell, she wasn't going to fall with him.

She wasn't going to fall with or for anyone ever again.

"Oh." He seemed shocked, then a slow smile appeared on his lips. "I'll salvage my pride and not plead. Shall I let myself out?"

Claire shook her head with a wry chuckle. "Sorry. I've been rude."

"No, that's all right. A lady has her rights—one of those rights is to say *no*." He cocked his head. "It took me a while to learn that, but it's true. I appreciate your forthrightness. It's better than to be dangling. I'm not a boy madly in love, so it's not a long drop." He leaned against the mantel again, looking quite debonair. "So, are you really going to try to give your children away?"

"That's not how I would have put it, but ... perhaps." Claire acknowledged the truth in her heart. "I'm not sure I can bear it, but isn't part of love to put them first? Maybe I could arrange it so I could see them sometimes."

Steven shrugged. "Well, I'll leave you, Claire. I'll let you know if I come up with a wondrous solution to your problem, but I doubt I shall. Hopefully your resourcefulness will last. Not every debutante would be able to do what you've done." He grinned. "Have a nice evening."

"You as well," she said distantly.

He left, and Claire sat down to think.

CHAPTER SEVEN

T HE FOLLOWING MORNING BEFORE the sun had even risen, Alice ran to Nettie's room, which was attached to theirs. After hastily donning a wrapper over her nightgown, Nettie followed her through the door.

"I don't know why she got sick again," Alice said disapprovingly, jumping onto the bed next to her twin.

"Shush, Gracie! Don't jiggle her." Nettie hurried across the room and placed a hand on Ivy's flushed, sweaty forehead. "Oh, dear girl, you're burning up. Alice, run for your mother. She's probably still in bed."

Confident Nettie would tend to Ivy, Alice ran to her mother's bedroom and burst through the door. She raced across the room and bounced onto her mother's bed.

"Mummy, Mummy! Ivy's sick *again*."

It was somewhat of a habit with Ivy to be sick. Alice was used to waking up to find her twin feverish, listless, and grumpy. She didn't think much of it, but Nettie and Mummy always did.

The amount of fuss Ivy got was ridiculous, and it made Alice just a tinge resentful. Though, sometimes it was fun to play nurse.

Mummy hurried out of bed and ran to the girls' bedroom. Alice watched from the door.

Nettie stood from the bedside to make room for Mummy. "It seems bad,

Claire."

"It always does." Mummy pressed her hand to Ivy's forehead. "Ivy? How do you feel?"

"Mummy?" Ivy's voice was weak.

"That's right, darling. I'm here. What hurts?"

"My head ... and I feel cold." Ivy clung to Mummy's arm. "So c-cold. Will you make me better?"

"I'm going to try, darling." Mummy smoothed Ivy's damp hair from her forehead. "There, now. Close your eyes. I'm here, and I'm going to take care of you." She glanced up at Nettie. "Why don't you get dressed and wake Mrs. Bennett? Ivy might like some broth."

Ivy shook her head. "I'm not hungry."

"You could be in a bit—and you have to eat to get well. It will give you strength." Mummy glanced toward the door. "Alice, run along. Ivy needs her rest, and we can't have you underfoot."

Alice went downstairs and found her way to the kitchen.

In no time, Mrs. Bennett was up and about, fussing and tutting. The cook was sympathetic, as always, though she did refer to Ivy as "that poor little poppet."

Alice thought, for once, that she was a poor little poppet, too, being ignored by both Mummy and Nettie. But as the day continued, Alice realized it wasn't just like any other time Ivy had been sick. The anxiety in the house was pressing and unforgettable, like a heavy, scratchy blanket on a hot day.

How was this different from any other time Ivy had been sick?

Then she caught her mother and Nettie speaking outside Ivy's room.

"I don't like it, Nettie. She's so weak! What if ... what if we lose her?" Mummy's voice trembled like a glass teetering on the edge of a table. Alice had never heard her mother use that tone before, and she shuddered at the sound of it.

Nettie wrapped her arms around herself and sighed. "Claire, I think we ought to call the doctor. This is worse than her other illnesses. She seems to be having trouble breathing! And perhaps a doctor—"

Mummy shook her head. "We can't risk it! Too many people know about the girls already. If anyone else finds out … It's not even worth thinking about. It's too much of a risk."

"But, if Ivy's dead, she won't need to be protected!" Nettie's voice was a quick snap, and Mummy cringed.

"W-we don't know that she will die."

Nettie nodded. "I'm sorry, that was harsh. I'm just worried; it's hard to be calm."

"No, you're right." Mummy's hands trembled, and Alice could see tears pooling in her eyes. Heart racing, she rushed forward and buried her face in her skirts.

"Mummy, is Ivy …?"

"Hush." Mummy folded Alice in a hug. "Let's send for a doctor. Everything else is secondary to Ivy's health."

As Nettie ran down the hall, Mummy gently turned Alice's chin up so she looked at her. "Dearest, you were wrong to listen to our conversation."

Feeling ill herself, Alice trembled in Mummy's arms. "B-but, Mummy, is Ivy going to d-die?"

"Oh, darling, I … I hope not!"

Hope not? Alice needed a lot more assurance than *hope not*. "But Mummy—"

"No, Alice. Don't worry about it." Mummy turned and went into Alice and Ivy's bedroom, leaving Alice standing in the hall alone.

She wasn't allowed to follow.

Alice resumed her seat between the floorboards and the long carpet that ran down the middle of the hall and hugged herself.

After a time, she rose and paced the floor, hands folded behind her back like Uncle Charlie, head down and frowning in frustration. But this soon grew boring, and she went to her mother's room and sat there patiently.

About an hour later, she made her way down to the kitchen. Mrs. Bennett was cooking some wicked, steaming concoction on the stove, but she at least acknowledged Alice, nodding to her when she entered the room.

"What's that?"

Mrs. Bennett cocked her head. "Poultice the doctor's going to try on Miss Ivy's chest to get her breathing again."

Alice blinked. "She's not breathing?" Didn't people who weren't breathing die? Or rather, weren't they already dead? And, if Ivy were dead, there'd be no getting her back. Alice understood that much—had since Kitty lost one of her babies last year.

"No, dearie, but she might not be soon if the doctor don't get her lungs cleared out." Mrs. Bennett tapped the spoon on the edge of the pot and picked it up with a rag-covered hand. "Now, you stay down here while I take this up, all right?"

Alice nodded and slumped onto a chair at the table. *Maybe Ivy's going to die,* she thought as Mrs. Bennett walked up the kitchen stairway. *God, don't let Ivy die. I love her, after all, and it just wouldn't do.*

Claire watched over her younger child, desperation tearing at her heart until she feared she was the one dying, a slow and painful death of fear and heartbreak. Questions teased her mind constantly, bringing new helplessness, new pain.

I've already borne too much; why me and mine again? Can't we have some cessation? Why couldn't I be the one dying? Must it be Ivy, my darling Ivy? Shouldn't she get a chance at life ... and shouldn't I be allowed to keep her after all this trial?

Nettie spoke the same dry, empty phrases she always did, about God and love and plans for each of their lives. But how could that be true?

As a young girl starving for affection, she had reached out once, begged God to change her parents' hearts, to make them give her love. The next morning, she had found the same violent father and timid mother she'd known all her life.

There was no getting around it—her life was of no interest to God. Or, rather, He saw a need to punish her continually for sins not her own.

"I just don't understand it, Nettie." Claire whispered the words as she paced the floor of Ivy's bedroom in the flickering candlelight. "I could understand if it were me ... After what I've done, I understand that God wants to hurt me. But my child?" She ran her hand over her face, trying to scrub some of the pain away. "My precious girl, my Ivy. My link to the man I loved, my hope of happiness."

Nettie was silent for a long time before she whispered, "There's Alice, Claire."

"I know that, but ... Ivy is the child I should have with me in my old age. Alice won't love me then as Ivy will; she'll have her own life. And I want her to. I want her to soar, but Ivy ... Ivy is my nestling."

Claire glanced to the chair beside the fire and saw a small trembling around Nettie's lips, weak though it was, as she spoke. "I think you're right, but Ivy may surprise us."

"If she lives," Claire snapped bitterly. "If she lives to surprise us! To have a life! This is so unfair. I know she's weak, but I thought we were over the worst of it. And now I have a useless doctor telling me to prepare myself, as if he were talking about a trip to the countryside. Losing my child, Nettie!" The emotions she'd been keeping in check with anger focused behind her eyes finally burst forth, causing tears to leak out. "If I lose her, I don't think I want to go on."

"But Alice—"

"I know! I know. I have a duty to her, and I could never regret that." She dropped onto the chair opposite Nettie and hastily wiped her tears away. "I only fear I won't be able to follow through."

Nettie bit her lip. "I don't know what to say, Claire. Without God, there isn't much hope for me to offer, but I will continue to pray for her and for you."

Claire sighed and shifted so she wasn't facing Nettie but the fire. She couldn't deny that this situation was beyond her, that she didn't know what to do herself ... Yet, something must be done.

She couldn't watch Ivy fade away before her eyes; however, she was helpless to stop it from happening.

Slowly, she returned her eyes to her maid's face. "Nettie, if I were to pray and ask God to save my child, would He do so?"

Nettie blinked. "Well—"

"If He were real, He would have to."

"That's not how it works. He both gives and takes, and it is up to His wisdom to determine which and why. It has nothing to do with anything we do or don't do. I—"

"Then why pray?" It was nonsensical to pray just because praying was what one was taught to do, and Claire knew Nettie was anything but nonsensical. She trusted her maid for good sense, even if she did believe in a God Who had only ever hurt them.

Nettie stood and stepped toward Claire—stopped and folded her arms as if she didn't know what to do with them. "Prayer isn't about getting answers. I know you'll never believe me, but God cares about you, and He always listens. Yes, what will happen will happen, but some of the happenings have to do with us, as we're the ones who put them in motion. The choice is yours: will you beg for Ivy's life or won't you?"

Claire swallowed. "But you just said it might not make a difference." She wasn't going to open her heart only to be disappointed. Purposeless faith in God held no interest to her. She only wanted Him if He was going to save Ivy.

And it would seem that there was no easy way to guarantee it.

"Prayer makes an incredible difference for me, believe it or not. I don't feel right when I don't pray, and I've seen things happen in response to my prayers—"

"Which you just said were going to happen anyway." The amount of nonsense one had to believe to follow God was overwhelming.

"And *I* just gave my response. The fact is, Claire, that we're only human and not in control of life and death, but God is. And He loves us, so we must trust Him to take care of us." Nettie returned to her seat. "Now, I could tell you—"

"Oh, shush, Nettie! I don't want to hear it. Not now." Claire rose and walked toward the door, then paused. Her chest tightened with guilt. Nettie didn't deserve her harsh words; she was everything a good friend ought to be. "That was rude, and I'm sorry, but this subject frustrates me."

Nettie cocked her head. "I don't mind your rudeness. Not if it means we're going to keep talking about these things. I want you to keep thinking about God until you can't help but realize He's there and He wants you."

Claire placed a hand on the doorframe. "I believe that you think it's best for me, and that your persistence is a labor of love. So thank you ... even if I don't think it's doing any good. God can't love me."

"And can He not love me, too?" Nettie rose again and walked over to the bedside. "Despite it all, you've been blessed, really. The things I endured in my past have led women to take their own lives or live a horror-filled existence, but God was stronger than that. I must believe He loves me, as without Him, I was broken and lost, but when I found Him, I was able to embrace life again." She half-smiled. "It could be the same for you. The idea isn't that He'll wipe it all away—not yet at least—but that He'll give you the ability to bear your sufferings and even rejoice in them."

Claire barely restrained an eye roll. "If you were able to go back and change that night, you know you would."

Nettie's smile faded. "It's a useless thought as I never could—but, honestly, with the foreknowledge of what it would bring me, I would make no changes."

More insanity. It had been a long day, and Nettie was raving. Of course, *of course* they would both make drastic changes in their lives if it were in their power to do so!

Then, softly into her mind the names Alice and Ivy were whispered, and she suddenly felt very cold, and her hand trembled on the doorknob. "You're right. There are some things that I could never change."

Nettie's face lightened. "I thought you would say that. Because, after all, what would our lives be without them?"

Claire chuckled. "I'd be rich and respected, you'd probably have found a husband by now, and we'd both be living happily ever after."

Nettie shook her head wryly. "So optimistic of you."

"Realistic." Claire sighed. "I need to get Alice settled for the night, but I'll come back. Please come get me if there's even a slight change." She glanced toward the still figure in the bed. "At least she's breathing easier, but the doctor was hardly positive."

"I'm sure she'll be much better after a good night's rest." Yet, Nettie's smile trembled about the edges. "I can tuck Alice in."

Claire considered it for a minute, but Alice probably needed to see her after their words in the hall. "I'll tuck her in, but you can check on her after we're settled. I have a few things I need to say to her ... I was distressed this afternoon and probably frightened her."

"Oh dear." Nettie twitched in place, obviously wanting to run straight to Alice and soothe her fears with meaningless nothings about a God who loved them, but she remained where she was nonetheless. "I'll have to come in and pray with her after you're finished."

"Of course." Claire might be opposed to religion for herself, but it seemed to comfort Alice and Nettie ... even Ivy, come to think of it. They all prayed and read the Bible and whatnot—and Claire supposed there was a certain reassurance to be had in "God will protect me" and other platitudes.

When Claire walked into her room, she found the bed which Alice was to occupy empty. Alarmed, she glanced about before she saw Alice huddled in the corner.

"Darling, it's chilly with the fire dying down." She crossed the room and held out her hand to her daughter. "You might catch cold sitting on the floor."

Alice stood and held out her arms. "Is Ivy getting better, Mummy?"

There were tears on Alice's eyelashes, and Claire hastened to draw her close. "Oh, Alice, I believe so. At least a bit. But the doctor ... At least she's breathing better. Nettie says that God is in control." She didn't know what else to say. In truth, it was easier to fall back on some all-powerful Being rather than simply saying, "This life is arbitrary and cruel, and I don't know."

Alice nodded fervently, plainly having heard such verbatim before. "Yes, Mummy! He'll take good care of Ivy, unless He needs her. Do you think He needs Ivy in Heaven, Mummy?"

"I ... I don't know." She couldn't imagine what Ivy would be needed for there, unless it was to be the sweetest angel the pearly gates ever welcomed. Though she supposed that old wives' tale about children turning into angels wasn't factual—assuming any of it was.

She *could* see a use for such a sweet girl anywhere. And that was what scared her. Ivy could possibly be taken away as too good for this world ... and certainly too good for Claire.

She shuddered.

Alice suddenly burst into tears. "I wish He needed me instead!" She sobbed, throwing herself into Claire's embrace.

She held Alice tightly until she began to pull away, then drew out a handkerchief to wipe Alice's face and her own. It was good that they both had a quick cry before bed—especially Alice. The poor child tended to bottle up her emotions, especially if she was anxious about something.

Alice attempted a smile. "God will take care of Ivy, but I just ... I just don't want Him to take her *away*. I love her."

Claire squeezed her daughter's arm. "Shush, now. No more worrying. I'm sure ... I'm sure He won't. I'm going to stay up with her tonight and make sure He doesn't." It was beyond her power, but an eight-year-old child wouldn't know that, right?

Alice frowned. "You can't make God do anything, Mummy, but thank you for trying to make me feel better."

She stared incredulously at her daughter before choking out a reply. "Y-you're right, Alice, but we must only be strong enough for today. So let's not borrow trouble. What will be will be."

"That's what Nettie says. Everything's going to be all right, because God writes the pages of our book." Alice tried to look cheerful, but Claire could tell she was fading fast. "I suppose it'll all work out."

"I hope it will." Claire stood and went to the basin. "Come now. Let's wash your face, and then it's time for bed. Nettie will come in as soon as I leave to check on you, but I'll say good night now."

"All right," said Alice, "but I shan't sleep. Not when Ivy is sick. I will stay up all night and pray." She was blustering in that unique Alice way that usually made Claire feel like laughing. It was as if one of the more self-important Dickens characters hopped off the pages and into her child's body and began insisting everything should go according to their plans.

But it was useless to argue when Alice was in this mood. "Of course you shall. I would expect nothing less of a dutiful sister." Claire wrung out the rag in her hand and turned to mop it over Alice's face. "There. Into the bed you go."

Her chin jerked up. "I think I'll stay in my chair, thank you."

"Don't you think praying in bed is much better?"

Alice hesitated. "Why?"

"Because it is. Everyone knows that."

After a stare down that lasted for who knows how long, Alice nodded slowly. "All right. But I won't go to sleep. I'm going to stay up all night."

"Right. Like any good sister." Claire turned to the bed. "Hop up. I'll get you tucked in."

A suspicious look appeared on her face. "I don't need tucked in."

"You need to be cozy to pray properly."

This was when Alice started to catch on. "I do not! You think I'll fall asleep, but—"

"Prove me wrong. Into the bed."

Reluctantly, Alice plopped down on her pillow and scowled up at Claire. "I won't—"

"Sleep. I know." Claire bent and kissed Alice's forehead. "I love you."

Alice answered this with another glare. She was apparently determined to do something noble, and Claire hoped she would pray—if prayers helped at all—but she would fall asleep.

It was the effort that counted, wasn't it? Who knew except God, if He had rules about these sorts of things.

"I'll see you in the morning, darling."

Chapter Eight

The crisis was arriving, the doctor said. They would clear Ivy's lungs and banish the fever tonight—or not at all.

Claire's arms shook as she adjusted the poultice on her daughter's chest. She almost dropped the cloth bundle, and the doctor glared at her.

"Why don't you sit down, Miss Berck? There's nothing much you can do." He was young, and often his tone leaked with sarcasm, probably believing her to be everything she wasn't—and, at the same time, everything she was.

So she did take a seat, near the bed, watching the trembling rise of Ivy's chest.

"What are her chances?" she asked.

"They're decent, but I'm no miracle worker," the doctor replied brusquely. It was clear his proper bedside manner was not gifted to working women like her who possessed illegitimate children. At least, that appeared to be his perspective of them.

She couldn't blame him. A decade ago she had assumed the worst of others whenever something was not as it should be. Better to believe the worst than look for a proper explanation.

Claire didn't fight it. She just sat there. Let him believe what he would. She would neither confirm nor deny—she would not protest to the point of guilt nor tell him he was right—that she was a woman without a husband raising her daughters alone.

If he chose to spread gossip, which she didn't doubt he would, her business would cease to exist overnight. But he seemed to have a few ideas to keep Ivy breathing, and that was enough for Claire. If Ivy lived, there was nothing else to be wished for.

Nettie seemed to be praying again—or that was the only reason Claire could think that she would be kneeling beside the bed with her hands clasped and her eyes closed.

Insanity. It might not make a difference. A dismal outlook on life—yet, her maid, and even Alice and Ivy, believed He was a kind and loving God.

There it was again—the desire to pray, to ask, even if the answer was negative. To find some peace in the situation regardless of the outcome.

Dear Lord. She didn't say the words aloud, but she let them echo about her heart. *Lord God, let my child live. Please don't take her. I live for her.* She swallowed. *I suppose Nettie would say I need to live for You, but ... I can't. You've taken so much from me. So please ... please don't take Ivy. Nettie has told me more than once that we can't bargain with You, and I know because I've tried, and it never works. But I can beg, and so I'm begging. Show me. If You can, let me keep her. And if You must take her, then give me the strength to bear it. Give me the courage.*

She waited for a rush of peace or a thunderbolt or words of guidance spelled out in air before her, but nothing came. Instead, the room remained quiet other than Ivy's raspy breathing and Nettie's murmured prayers.

Still, her soul was calmer, and within her, there was something new—acceptance. The knowledge that what would be would be, and perhaps, just perhaps, a tremor of hope that told her that no matter the outcome, it would be all right. Painful, difficult, and frightening, yes, but a road she must and would travel, one way or another. It would seem that faith, hope, and love made it easier.

That's what Nettie said.

Claire wondered, with a little smile, if she was becoming spiritual but decided that, rather, she was becoming a little bit mad. She rose from her seat to sit on the edge of Ivy's bed and hold her hand. She would be there, near her daughter. Ivy would feel her presence as she ... as she faced this crisis.

She didn't want to think of death and of the strength and determination it would take to face that. So many children died, and Ivy was so weak.

The doctor was here now. He knew how to make small children better. And, even though he was a dour, irritating, judgmental man, between the poultice and the medicine he'd given her, they had half a chance at reviving Ivy.

The night wound on, long and laborious. After half an hour, Ivy was launched into a coughing fit that brought up a great deal of distasteful liquid, and that seemed to improve her breathing. Her fever worsened after the coughing, but they kept her cool despite her insistence in brief moments of consciousness that she was freezing.

When the fever broke and she seemed to rest, the doctor looked more annoyed than Claire was willing to bear. He removed his thermometer from Ivy's mouth, checked it, and shrugged. "Strange how resilient children like her are while little lords and ladies die every day." He wiped the instrument off and placed it in his bag. "She'll do all right."

Claire shouldn't have asked, but she couldn't resist. "'Children like her'?"

He raised his eyebrows. "Misbegotten, unfathered, baseborn. I'll stop there. You don't deny it, do you, Miss Berck? She clearly resembles you—you're 'Mummy,' and goodness knows who 'Papa' is."

Claire raised her chin, refusing to let the fury sparking in her chest reach her words. "I don't deny that she is my child." She kept her words quiet. "I thank you for your help in saving her, though not for your compassion in the act. Now, have you done all you can? Will she recover?"

"Probably." He huffed. "But not through any merit of blood. Resilient, like all mutts."

Out of the corner of her eyes, Claire saw Nettie twitch as if, like Claire, she wanted to rip the man's face off. But that wasn't possible. Anger and violence would only make it worse. "Then leave. Nettie, pay the man for his efforts and show him out."

He rolled his eyes and picked up his bag. "Wait 'til my wife hears about this nonsense ..." he mumbled to himself as he walked out the door.

Once again, Claire sat on the edge of Ivy's bed and watched her child sleep. *Lord, thank You for allowing us to keep her. Now, please don't let that dreadful man steal our livelihood and my reputation ...*

Alice dashed into her bedroom early one afternoon a few weeks later, Mummy following her. Though Ivy was still bedridden, she had been gaining ground rapidly, and there was no reason to believe she couldn't be on her feet within days.

"Hello, Alice." Ivy shifted so she sat up and held out her arms. "You were gone all morning, and I missed you, but I had my doll and Kitty, until she ran away."

Alice walked to her sister's bedside. "How are you feeling?"

Ivy smiled. "Oh, much better. Mummy says I can go for a walk in the park soon. She says I need fresh air. Isn't that so, Mummy?"

"It is so. Fresh air and sunshine would be the quickest cure. And we'll get it for you, even if we have to drive out of London for it." Mummy sat on the edge of the bed and placed her hand on Ivy's forehead for a moment.

"Do I feel all right?" Ivy asked.

"Just perfect." Their mother smiled and leaned back. "Mrs. Bennett will bring up trays in just a bit, and we'll have our luncheon together. How does that sound?"

Ivy wriggled with delight. Alice guessed she was starting to feel a bit shut in after all that lying about. "Lovely! Will Nettie be here, too?"

"Of course." Mummy squeezed Ivy's hand. "Now remember, we must do our best to eat everything on our plate so we can grow strong again."

Ivy nodded solemnly. "Yes, Mummy."

Nettie entered the room. "Claire, there's a letter for you."

Mummy glanced up, and her brow furrowed. "I'm busy at the moment. Can it wait?"

"I thought you'd want to see it now—it's from Pearlbelle Park."

Alice saw a sudden rush of pink in her mother's cheeks before they paled. Mummy held out her hand for the letter and, once Nettie handed it to her, hastily opened it.

Nettie cocked her head. "I thought it might be from Miss Elton. You were close in school."

Mummy glanced up and laughed. "She amused me, and I awed her—foolish, bold girl that I was. But that was when we were children, and we haven't spoken since." She shrugged and flipped over the sheet of paper. "You're right. It is from her."

"Interesting. Mr. Parker must've given her the address." Nettie folded her arms over her chest. "That man can't mind his own business. Surely he has other things to do—children to abandon, houses to burn ..."

"My opinion of him isn't that narrow, but, yes, he does tend to interfere." Mummy shook her head and returned her eyes to the letter.

After a moment, she looked up from the page, eyes glistening with tears. "She heard of Ivy's illness—and her slow recovery. She invited us to Pearlbelle Park, with Mr. Knight's permission, so Ivy can ... can rest."

"Pearlbelle Park?" Alice jumped up. "Is that in the country? Mummy, are we really going to the country?"

Nettie smiled so broadly it seemed her face would crack. "Claire, it's an answer to prayer."

Mummy threw back her head and laughed, really laughed. "Surprisingly, it is. We're to come out with Mr. Parker in a few weeks, if we're able." Her face darkened. "I ... I can't. I have to stay here in London, but you will take the girls?"

Nettie hesitated. "Me, alone?"

"Yes, well, you'll have Mr. Parker with you, much as you dislike him, and it's not a long journey." Mummy slid the letter back in the envelope. "He's not a bad man, and he'll take care of you. I trust him that much. Please, Nettie—Ivy needs the country air, and, if I can get them out of the city now ..." She paused and cocked her head.

Alice couldn't resist interrupting now. "Please, Nettie! I've never been to the countryside, and I would love to!"

"Well, I suppose. It's not far from London," Nettie conceded. "Still, Mr. Parker can be difficult."

"Yes, but bear it for the girls' sake." Mummy stood in her "this matter is decided" way. "I'll go see what's keeping Mrs. Bennett, then I'll have to jot down a message letting Lois know we'll be coming."

After Mummy left, Alice turned to Nettie. "Who is Lois?"

"That's Miss Elton to you, Miss Grace." Nettie playfully tugged on a lock of Alice's hair. "She's a friend of your mother's. I suppose she never married, and so she lives at Pearlbelle with her cousins who own the estate now that her father has passed away. Poor dear must be terribly alone."

"What's Pearlbelle Park?" Ivy asked.

Alice rolled her eyes, because everyone knew that something with a name like Pearlbelle Park must be a big, fancy estate, like one she'd read about in books, but Nettie didn't seem to think it a stupid question.

"It's the home of the Eltons—the Knights now, I suppose. It's a lovely, big property with acres and acres of gardens and fields and tenants ... You'll like it. Ivy, there's a library we'll explore, and you'll love the fountains in the garden. And, Alice, you'll meet the horses at the stables."

Alice had to keep herself from clapping her hands like a child. She was far too old for that. "Oh, Nettie! Will I learn to ride?" She'd only petted horses she met on the street but certainly never been on one.

"Perhaps. We'll see." Nettie smiled. "I hope you will get to. And, even if you don't, we can visit them."

"Did Mummy ever ride the horses there? When she visited, I mean," Alice asked.

"She did, but you know your mummy isn't quite the horsewoman you're sure to be." Nettie winked. "Oh, here's Mrs. Bennett. Let's have our luncheon!"

For half of the journey by train and throughout the five-mile carriage ride to the estate from the station at the village, Creling, Mr. Parker told them about Pearlbelle Park. Thankfully, Alice managed to, she thought, tactfully bring up the horse situation, which he seemed optimistic about. In fact, his eyes lit up in a way that made her think he loved horses just as much as she did. Alice's excitement grew by leaps and bounds.

Even Nettie's attitude, strangely sour, couldn't dampen her enthusiasm.

The carriage drove up to a three-story, marble-pillared mansion gleaming white in the sunshine. Alice was handed out by a footman. She cast her eyes about wildly, unsure what to take in first. The grand building was so tall that she had to tilt her head back to see the top.

She smiled. She was going to stay in a palace. Oh, who knew what secrets it might hold! Hidden passages, attics full of old relics, basements haunted by ghosts ... There was a world of possibilities.

Alice was looking for Rapunzel's tower, which she knew must be there somewhere, when Nettie put a hand on her shoulder and told her to close her mouth.

They walked into a huge entryway. The ceiling, painted with little baby angels playing golden harps on fluffy clouds, was three stories above Alice's head. There was so much to look at that Alice didn't even notice the white-haired butler who greeted them.

As she was being led down the hall by Mr. Parker, she saw only the walls. The next thing she knew, Alice was standing in a large parlor.

A woman about her mother's age with sable hair and brown eyes stood to greet them. Her large mouth, small nose, and wide eyes gave her a clownish appearance. She walked over and tilted Alice's chin up with a small, white hand.

"Oh my! She doesn't resemble Claire very closely, does she?" asked Miss Lois Elton. She reached behind Alice for Ivy. "Oh, but this one's her mother's mirror image. You're Ivy, aren't you?"

Ivy pulled away from Miss Elton and reached for Nettie.

Nettie took Ivy's hand and said, "Speak when you are spoken to."

"It's all right, Nettie." Miss Elton laughed. "I understand. She's shy. We'll get used to each other. So, you must be Alice."

"Yes, Miss Elton, I'm Alice Christina. And she's Ivy Adeline."

"It's nice to meet you." Miss Elton turned to her cousin. "Here, Steven, have Johnson take their things. I'll show Alice and Ivy to their room now. I want to see their faces when they see my old nursery. Alice, take my hand."

Alice did, and Miss Elton reached for Ivy, who allowed her hand to be taken after a moment of hesitation. Miss Elton led them out of the room. Up some stairs, a quick turn to the right, another flight of stairs, and to the left, they went into the third door. They were in a large, sunny room with light-pink walls and white trim.

"This used to be my nursery," said Miss Elton. "There are two little beds that will fit you nicely, and it's such a cheerful room. I used to have a baby sister—Lydia—who slept here with me." She sighed and patted the pillow of one of the beds, and it almost seemed as if there were tears in her eyes. "And this other room was our playroom." She opened another door leading out of the bedroom. "There are all sorts of toys. I don't know much about children anymore, so I didn't change a thing. I supposed that if this was the way I liked it, I mustn't try to change it."

She walked in front of the fire, and there was a horrific sound somewhere between a screech and a meow. Miss Elton stumbled and only kept herself from falling by catching the mantel. She steadied herself, then began laughing.

Nettie walked in at that moment. "Are you all right, Miss Elton?"

"I stepped on a cat." Miss Elton patted her hair.

"Oh." Nettie crossed the room and looked around before kneeling next to the bed. "Here she is—ouch!" She jerked her hand back and wrung it.

"She scratched me."

"Poor Tiggy! I forgot that she was here." Miss Elton knelt next to the bed and reached under, only to pull her own hand back too. "Stay there if you like." She sighed. "Tiggy was never a very nice cat. I'll see about having a footman come remove her. I found her ranging wild and eating mice in the stables, and fed her, but Tiggy still doesn't like me."

Alice wondered why anyone would keep a cat who behaved so badly. Of course, Kitty could be naughty sometimes, and they loved her.

"O-oh! I almost forgot in all the excitement." Miss Elton whirled to face Nettie. "I do forget things so easily. It's because I have so many things to think about."

Nettie's lips twitched. "Yes, miss."

Miss Elton clasped her hands together. "We had someone arrive here late last night."

Nettie's posture stiffened. "Who? Will they be staying long?"

"I imagine so! All his life, we hope." Miss Elton grinned and practically hopped on her toes. "Philip and Hazel—the Knights, that is—were blessed with a son last night! He's a beautiful, healthy little boy, and they're so proud. Philip would have come down to greet you, but he said he needed to clear his head, so he's out at the stables."

"That is a blessing," Nettie said softly. "Have they decided what to call their child?"

"Yes! Edmond. Isn't that a charming name? Oh, did you know they had actually considered calling him Alice at one point? If he were a girl, I mean. But Philip changed his mind, and so they decided—Goodness, here I am chattering away! I suppose you all ought to rest after your journey. I'll run downstairs and talk to the cook about dinner." Miss Elton turned and ran out of the room.

Nettie smiled at her back, then turned. "Let's get settled in, girls."

"There's a baby?" Ivy's mouth was a perfect *o*. Neither of the girls had ever met a baby before, but they were anxious to.

"Indeed!"

Alice tugged at Nettie's sleeve. "Can we see him?"

"Perhaps—but not just yet, Gracie. Babies need to rest after they arrive ... and so do you! Let's take a nap this afternoon."

But Alice needed to keep her dignity intact. "Just Ivy."

"Then lie on your bed for an hour." Nettie unlocked their trunk. "Shoes off, faces washed. I'll draw the shades."

CHAPTER NINE

W HEN ALICE, IVY, AND Nettie came down after resting, Mr. Knight and Mr. Parker were in the drawing room, a grand expanse of whites and pastels. Alice frankly found it a little boring. Both men rose from their seats.

Mr. Knight spoke before anyone else had time to say a word. "Steven, this one is Alice, isn't she?"

Mr. Parker nodded. "Yes, of course. Alice, this is Mr. Knight. You met him a few months ago at your mother's house, didn't you? He's my cousin and the owner of Pearlbelle."

"Hello, Alice," said Mr. Knight.

Alice glanced at Nettie and took a deep breath. "Thank you for inviting Ivy and me to Pearlbelle, sir. I like it here, or I will, and I think it will make Ivy better."

"I'm sure it will. Country air is the best thing in the world for a weak constitution." Mr. Knight smiled tentatively, as if unsure of himself. "What ... what is it that you like about Pearlbelle?"

"It's pretty." That much was honest. It was a great deal grander than her London home. "I haven't seen a lot of it, but it's much prettier than London. The outside is quite green! And it smells better here, too."

Mr. Knight laughed heartily at this. "I imagine it does. Is there anything you plan to do while you're here, Miss Alice?"

Avoid you. But she knew better than to say that. "I'd like to learn to ride."

"Maybe I could take you riding." Mr. Knight tugged at his collar. "I suppose Mr. Parker has told you about Sugarplum?"

"Yes." But Alice couldn't shake the feeling of wariness. "He says he'll teach me to ride."

"I can help with that." He smiled. "Why don't we go out early tomorrow morning? Ivy, too, if she likes, and we'll try to talk Mr. Parker into coming. I love horses, and certainly I'm a better hand with them than Steven ever will be."

Mr. Parker snorted. "Now see here, Phil! You know very well—"

"Let's not make this another competition."

Alice glanced over her shoulder to see Miss Elton standing in the doorway.

"Nothing wrong with a little friendly competition, Lois," Mr. Knight said. "Steven and I are simply discussing our relative strengths and weaknesses—meaning my strengths and Steven's weaknesses."

"At least I—"

Miss Elton began to laugh. "Now, boys, really! It's going to be horrid having you both in the house if it's going to be a repetition of every holiday growing up."

Mr. Knight heaved a sigh. "Very well, Lois, though I still say that I'm the horse expert in this family, and—"

Mr. Parker gasped in such a dramatic way that Alice wasn't sure it could be real. "How can I be silent when he insists on spreading those lies, Lois?"

Miss Elton raised her eyebrows. "True worth doesn't come from bragging."

Both men stared at her silently for a minute before Mr. Parker spoke.

"I'm going to ignore that excellent advice. It's lovely outside. Alice, Ivy, why don't I show you around the gardens a bit? They're great places to play."

Alice glanced at Nettie who had, like all good servants, effectively blended into the wall. She nodded slightly.

"I'd like that," Alice said. "So would Ivy, but she's too shy to say."

Ivy, who probably also wanted to blend into the wall, took a step toward Nettie. But Alice wasn't going to let her back out, so she grabbed her sister's hand. Ivy would just have to trust her—a walk in the gardens would be lovely.

Mr. Knight cleared his throat. "I must visit Hazel now, but I'll join you in a bit, perhaps." He left the room hastily. Maybe he felt how little Alice cared for him.

Alice and Ivy followed Mr. Parker out of the front door with Miss Elton trailing behind. After a quick glance to confirm that Nettie was watching from a distance, Alice felt confident about throwing herself into admiring flowers and statues and trees.

Mr. Parker made an excellent tour guide, and Alice found she really liked him. Mummy didn't always seem to care for the man, and Nettie hated him—that's what Alice thought anyway. But that didn't mean Alice couldn't like him.

Though it made her wonder ...

"This is my favorite place." Mr. Parker gestured toward a big fountain with multiple layers.

Alice walked slowly around the ornate marble masterpiece. "It's pretty."

"I like the sounds." Ivy had her eyes closed and a dreamy expression on her face. "I'd like one in my bedroom."

Alice laughed aloud. "Oh, how silly, Ivy! Of course you couldn't have a fountain in your bedroom." She paused and cocked her head. "But you could come out here to see this any time."

Mr. Parker nodded. "She's right, Ivy. And if I have anything to say about it, you'll be visiting Pearlbelle Park much more often in the future."

Alice woke with the sunrise and rushed to the window. The sky was the color of her mother's eyes, which was always a sign of a good day to come. Nettie helped her dress in the riding habit Mummy had thoughtfully made and tucked into the trunk, shushing her so Ivy wouldn't be awakened.

"Enjoy yourself, Gracie." Nettie kissed her cheek. "You'll do well."

Alice tugged at Nettie's hand and stepped toward the door. "Come watch me."

Nettie glanced over her shoulder at the bed where the younger child slept. "No—I'll stay with Ivy." She bit her lip. "I hate to leave her alone, and you'll be fine. Trust me. Miss Elton will make sure you're safe."

Now it was Alice's turn to hesitate. *What about Mr. Parker and Mr. Knight? Will they not take care of me?* She longed to understand why Nettie didn't seem to trust much of anyone—except Mummy, of course.

Outside the door, Alice met a maid almost as soon as she entered the hall. The young woman blinked sleepily at her and slipped to the side, her tin pail banging against her leg.

"Sorry," Alice whispered. She wasn't used to servants other than Nettie, Jameson, and Mrs. Bennett, and it was strange to be in a house full of them. Alice had never laid eyes on this particular maid before now. She'd have to visit them downstairs and meet them all.

Though, perhaps she wasn't allowed to do that.

At the top of the stairs, she met Miss Elton, who, though fully dressed in an elegant riding habit with a feather in her cap, had dark circles under her eyes and a pinched expression on her face.

"Good morning, Alice." Her voice was half a sigh. "They're waiting downstairs with the horses. Goodness knows why it must be so early! Riding before breakfast ... what a ridiculous notion."

Alice hurried down the stairs where Mr. Parker and Mr. Knight stood in the foyer.

"And how is Hazel?" Mr. Parker's voice was monotone, and he shifted from side to side impatiently. Alice didn't think Hazel much mattered to him.

Mr. Knight, oblivious to Mr. Parker's disinterest, beamed. "Well, but tired. She's still fighting that cough. And little Ned is beautiful and strong. Now, I wonder what's keeping the girl."

Alice stepped forward with Miss Elton behind her.

"Here the ladies are now." Mr. Parker walked toward Alice with a smile. "The noble steeds are at the door. Allow me to escort you to the mounting block."

Alice placed her hand firmly in Mr. Parker's. She wouldn't be frightened by Nettie's dour attitude. Though, she did glance back over her shoulder to make sure Miss Elton was right behind them.

After all, Nettie was an excellent judge of character.

But, when Alice saw the pony, she lost all doubts.

It was a lovely dappled gray creature just her size with a precious little saddle and its forelock down over its eyes.

"Come pet Sugarplum's nose, Alice." Mr. Parker dropped her hand to take the reins from a stablehand. "She's friendly. And here"—he reached into his pocket—"feed her a sugar cube."

Awed, Alice stepped forward.

"Hold your hand out, palm flat, and place the cube right in the center ... Good girl. Now hold it out where she can see."

Alice extended her hand, unsure exactly what to expect. Sugarplum lowered her head, and Alice felt a slight tickling sensation as the pony lipped the sugar off her palm.

She giggled and bounced back on her heels before realizing perhaps one ought to be calm around majestic beasts. She glanced up worriedly at Mr. Parker.

"It is fun, isn't it?" He smiled. "Here. Let's get you mounted now that you're acquainted with her. You'll be grand friends before you go back to London."

Mr. Parker helped Alice mount and showed her how to hold the reins. In less than a quarter of an hour, Alice was able to start and stop the horse and guide her left and right. At least, usually.

Trotting was a bit of a challenge—but Alice had never backed down from a challenge in her life, and she wasn't going to start now. She held on and followed Mr. Parker's quick instructions as best she could.

Miss Elton, who waited a gorgeous chestnut mare, sighed. "She's doing well enough for us to start out, now, isn't she, Steven? You're just being a perfectionist."

Mr. Parker glared at her. "It's an art, Lois."

"Hmph. She's handling that pony better than I handle Acacia." Miss Elton's brow furrowed. "Let's go. I'm already hungry."

He rolled his eyes but turned back to Alice with a pleasant expression. "You handle her well. I can scarcely believe you haven't ridden before."

"She's a natural," Mr. Knight said with a cheerful grin from where he relaxed on his big gelding's back. "Lois is right; I think she's ready. Are we just going up the hill a bit to show Alice the view?"

"Right." Mr. Parker mounted and turned his horse. "I'll go in front, and both you and Lois need to keep a close eye on her, but I'm not worried."

Alice wiggled with excitement, then reminded herself to keep calm and still so as not to worry Sugarplum. In her heart continued the refrain, *I'm on a horse. I'm an equestrian. A* natural *equestrian. Oh, wouldn't Mummy be proud of me!*

A few minutes later they were up on a big hill overlooking the entire estate. To the south and the west, there were tenant farmers—Mr. Knight remembered the names of most of them and could tell her about their families. To the north, of course, was the big house, the gardens, and, behind, the stables. Further off in the distance was a wood, which Mr. Parker teased might have fairies in it—or at least a pretty little brook he'd take her to sometime. And to the east, there was Creling, the tiny village, with its church steeple rising high above the cobbled streets. The steam of a train chugged its way toward London.

"It's a lovely place." Miss Elton sighed. "I used to think I must leave it, but I haven't had to. Probably never will."

Alice noticed Mr. Parker and Mr. Knight glance at each other. Mr. Parker smirked, and Mr. Knight winced. They probably felt sorry for Miss Elton. After all, her far-off gaze and trembling lips seemed to indicate some sort of sadness.

Alice was starting to wonder if everyone didn't have something to be sad about.

"Well." Mr. Knight cleared his throat. "Let's go back for breakfast now. We don't want to miss it. Cook always works such marvels in the kitchen."

CHAPTER TEN

AFTER BREAKFAST, ALICE WAS allowed a day away from her books so she could explore and get accustomed to her surroundings. She did so alone, as Ivy decided to remain inside with Nettie.

In one of the gardens, Alice plucked a rose, picked off the thorns and leaves on the stem, and tucked it behind her ear. She sat down on a bench and began making a wall out of small, colorful pebbles that she had picked up here and there about the garden.

A hackle-raising growl-and-bark combination began at the other end of the garden and moved swiftly toward her. Alice turned quickly to see a brown-and-white spaniel, hardly any more than a puppy and twice as gawky, running as quickly as he could with his tail between his legs. He was closely pursued by two large hounds. If they caught the puppy, they would surely tear him into a thousand shreds and leave the poor thing to die.

They couldn't do that! She had to fix it somehow.

The dogs chased the puppy into the stables, and Alice ran after them. They raced into an empty stall. The little dog was cornered. Ears laid back, the two hounds slowly approached him, their teeth clenched. The puppy laid his own ears back and growled, baring his teeth.

Alice was powerless to help the little creature. Those hounds were bigger than her, and she couldn't fight them off.

A boy leapt past her, causing Alice to jump against the wall. He was taller than she by a few inches, with shaggy dark-brown hair covered with a floppy gray cap that was a little too big. He wore brown trousers, heavy black boots, and a button-up blue shirt.

The boy hit the hounds on their big, slobbering heads and yelled, "Yah! Go on. Out, you big lugs."

The hounds dove around him and out of the stall, yelping with their tails tucked between their legs.

"You two belong in the kennels, don't ya? Hey, Ingleside!"

A groom about the boy's age popped his head out of another stall.

"You'll take the hounds that just ran out of this stall back to the kennels? I've got to finish with Acacia before I hear about it from Mr. Fennell. I've no time. Please, Ingleside?"

The other boy hesitated. "I'll do it, but you got to finish up North Star."

The puppy's hero nodded. "It's a bargain. The hounds are out in the courtyard."

Ingleside went out the door, and Alice heard him whistling in the yard.

The boy turned to Alice after the groom's departure. "Hallo! Didn't see you there." He walked into the stall and retrieved the puppy. "He's a fine one, just a bit scared. You look worried; don't be. It's fine. He's not bleeding or anything."

Alice nodded and stepped forward. "Is it a boy dog?"

The boy stood with the puppy in his arms and flipped him over. "Right. I'm ... I go by Kirk Manning." He stopped and really looked at her, and Alice realized that his eyes were the greenest she'd ever seen and framed by dark lashes. Didn't seem right that boys always seemed to get the prettiest eyes—at least, this Kirk fellow and Mr. Parker.

Kirk's ears turned red as he looked her up and down, and he abruptly turned back toward the stall he'd come from. "Didn't realize you were from the mansion. Sorry. I thought you might be the new scullery maid before I got a good look at you."

Alice cocked her head and followed him. "That's all right. I like scullery maids, I think." She wasn't sure what made a scullery maid different from a regular one, but they must be nice. Nettie had been a maid, after all, once upon a time.

Kirk Manning gave her an odd look. "I'm a stable boy, you know, and it wouldn't be exactly right for you to ... be here."

Oh, it wasn't, was it? "Who are you to tell me where I ought to be?" She folded her arms in front of her chest. "You're just a stable boy, right?"

A bit of a grin whisked around his lips as he knelt to place the puppy on the floor. The spaniel scurried to the back of the stall and lay there panting. "That's true, I suppose. So stay. See if I care. Only, don't tell 'em I said you could if you get trampled." He really did smile before ducking around the horse he was brushing.

"This is Acacia," she heard him say from behind the mare.

"I know."

Acacia, Miss Elton's horse, was a fine example of horseflesh. She was a beautiful chestnut with gentle brown eyes and a white star on her forehead. Alice looked up into those liquid eyes with admiration and longing. Someday she would have a horse like this. She also instantly knew that Ivy would worship this horse. It was her ideal steed, and she would consider it perfect for any knight in shining armor or princess in silken gowns.

"What will we call him?" Kirk asked

"Hmm?"

"The pup. He needs a name." He ducked around the horse again and knelt in front of the dog. "Here, boy. What's your name?"

Alice shook her head. "He can't answer you."

Kirk glared. "I know that!"

"Then why did you—?"

"How about Warrior. You know, because he wasn't afraid of those hounds who tried to off him."

Off him? What was that? But regardless what Kirk meant, Alice didn't care for it. "That's not a good name at all."

Alice hadn't known until that minute that people, including little boys, could bristle. "Do you have an idea?"

She tapped her finger to her chin and knelt beside Kirk to regard the puppy. "How about Brownie? Because he's brown."

He scoffed. "That's just plain stupid."

Alice pouted. "I saw him first. Shouldn't I get to name him?"

"I rescued him, so I should." Kirk scowled at her. "But I'll be a gentleman, seeing as you're pretty close to a lady. I guess we can call him Brownie
..."

"We don't have to." Alice didn't want him to get away with being noble and leave her in the selfish dust. "Maybe there's a name we can both like."

His eyes brightened. "Champion?"

"Flopsy?"

"Killer?"

"Jackie?"

"Arrow?"

"Chocolate?"

"Oh, for goodness' sake! Even *most* girls aren't *this* sappy."

"I'm not sappy at all. He does look like chocolate!"

After glaring at each other for a solid minute, Kirk broke the silence.

"He was in the stall of a big, old stallion called Open Fire. He's being studded out for a week or so. Why don't we call him that, and you can call him Opie so your girlness will be happy."

Alice wanted to protest, but Opie was a sweet name, and she was done cutting off her nose to spite her face for the day. "All right. Opie it is. What will we do with him?"

"Do with him? I'll keep him. He won't eat much, and he'll keep me company," said Kirk, grinning. "Oh, I don't know your name."

She paused and glanced at her hands. Berck or Chattoway? But now she always seemed to be introduced as the latter, so she'd try that one. "Alice Christina Chattoway."

He wrinkled his nose. "That's long."

She blinked. "You can just call me Alice."

"Good. I'll remember *that*. Come on, I'm done with Acacia. Now for North Star. He's Mr. Parker's horse. The bay here."

Alice followed Kirk into the next stall over. "How old are you?"

He glanced up at her. "Ten. Why?"

She looked down. "I'm only eight."

Kirk grunted. "That's not so little. My little sister's only two." The brush in his hand made circular motions on the stallion's shoulder. "Her name is Lizzy."

Alice nodded and reached up to stroke North Star's shoulder.

After a moment, Kirk turned to look at her. "You still here?"

"Do you want me to leave?" Alice hoped he didn't. Unable to meet his eyes in case he was indeed tired of her company, she knelt down and stroked the ears of the pup who had curled up next to his savior's foot.

He shrugged. "If you get kicked by Star, I'll never hear the end of it." A bit of a smile trembled around his lips before he turned away.

Alice let herself grin as she pulled Opie onto her lap. He *did* like her after all; she was sure of it. And if he didn't, well, she'd have to convince him to.

Alice's eyes strayed listlessly over the soaking landscape that once had been the beautiful Pearlbelle Park gardens. The windowsill was cold under her chin, and she straightened and turned away from the drippy window.

"Why does it have to rain?" She dragged her feet across the room and flopped down on her bed. "I want to go outside."

Nettie glanced up from her knitting. "Why don't you read, Miss Grace?"

"I don't want to read." Alice tossed an arm over her eyes and sighed heavily. "Why does it rain in the summer? I hate it."

Alice felt a gentle touch and lifted her arm to find Ivy leaning over her. "You could play with me." She gestured to dolls and teacups on the floor. "Please?"

But Alice refused to have her bad mood shaken. "Not now, Ivy." And she placed her arm back over her eyes.

There was a knock at the door.

Nettie dropped her yarn and needles in the basket beside her chair and rose. "Come in."

Mr. Knight opened the door and stepped in. He nodded to Nettie before turning to Alice and Ivy.

"My wife was wondering if you might visit her today. She's terribly tired of sitting alone and would like you to meet our baby. Will you come?"

Alice glanced at Nettie, who nodded. After a peek at Ivy, who looked as eager as she, she returned her gaze to Mr. Knight. "We'd like that, sir."

They followed him down the hall to the master chambers, where he paused and looked at them. "Now, girls, you know better than to be rambunctious, don't you? Mrs. Knight is just getting better from an illness, and we don't want to tire her."

Alice puffed out her chest. "I'll be good."

"Me, too." Ivy bounced on her toes.

"I knew you would." He opened the door and gestured for the girls to walk in before him.

The room was lovely and bright despite the gloomy outdoors—multiple lamps flickered, and a fire burned in the grate. Mrs. Knight sat on a chair next to the fire with a blanket tucked around her legs.

"Hazel, you remember Alice and Ivy, don't you?"

"Yes, we met at that party of their mother's." Mrs. Knight cleared her throat and pressed a handkerchief to her lips before returning it to her pocket.

She was paler than Alice remembered, and her light-brown hair was in neat braids. *Why, she looks like a child.*

"I'm glad you could come see me! You're Alice and you're Ivy—did I get it right? Good! Come here; I'm not going to bite y'all!" She motioned to a sofa with her free hand. "I haven't had too many visitors." Her voice was lazy and mild, friendly and sweet.

"Would you like to see my baby? This is Edmond Philip, my little Ned." Mrs. Knight put her hand onto Alice's shoulder and guided the girl over to the side of the bassinet. She drew back the blanket. "There, what do you think of him?"

"He's ... he's so small!" Alice blinked down at a wrinkled pink face and tiny hands tightened into fists. He opened and closed his mouth, making soft smacking sounds.

"Yes, he is, but he'll grow." Mrs. Knight reached down and stroked his cheek. "I don't want him to, of course, but I suppose he must." She jerked her hand back, covered her mouth, and coughed. "You can touch him if you like, but be gentle." She withdrew her handkerchief and wiped her mouth.

Alice touched his soft cheek. "He's so sweet. Ivy, do you see his little hands?"

"Yes." Ivy's mouth was a perfect circle. "He looks like a doll."

"Doesn't he?" Mrs. Knight once again put her handkerchief away and leaned toward her child. "Now, he has Mr. Knight's nose, and probably my ears, and I think he'll have my eyes. But, really, he looks more like Phil."

He looked like a baby to Alice, but she shrugged. "I suppose."

Mr. Knight stepped forward. "I see more of you in him, Hazel, but if you say so."

Alice blinked. Babies looked like their parents, apparently. She didn't look much like her mother, so perhaps ... She swallowed. Mr. Parker seemed the obvious choice to her, based on appearance. But that didn't make sense, did it? Not as much as Mummy disliked him. He couldn't be. Or was he?

She had better do some investigating while she had a chance. She dropped her head back to squint up at him. "It's your baby, Mr. Knight?"

He stared at her for a moment before nodding. "Yes, indeed, Miss Alice. Ned is mine."

Mrs. Knight laughed, but it turned into a cough. "What a silly question," she said after she'd recovered.

"I don't look like my mummy, so I thought—"

"Not all children look like their parents." Mr. Knight cleared his throat.

"Ivy resembles her closely, I thought." Mrs. Knight scooped Ned up and cradled him against her chest. "Alice, why don't you sit down on the sofa, and you can hold him. He's awake now but not fussy. He'll start in a bit, I know, but until then, we can enjoy his sweetness."

But Alice wasn't one for distractions. "Did you want him, Mr. Knight?"

"Ned?" Mr. Knight lowered himself on a chair opposite his wife. "Of course I wanted him."

"Who wouldn't want such a sweet thing?" Mrs. Knight smiled. "If you don't want to hold him, would Ivy like to?"

Ivy nodded, and in no time, she was situated on the sofa with the baby in her arms. Alice's questions continued to swirl about her mind. *Why does a father get to decide if he wants a baby or not? Why can they leave? Why can't fathers be mandatory?*

Alice took a deep breath. She'd better start from the beginning. "Where did Ned come from?"

The sound Mr. Knight made was somewhere between a snort and a gag, and Alice looked up with concern.

"Are you all right?"

"Perfectly well." He ran his hand over his face. "I just think that's a better conversation for another time."

Mrs. Knight motioned Alice to her side. "Don't mind him, honey lamb. Men don't understand these things."

"I—"

She held up her hand. "Shh. What has your mama told you?"

Alice inched toward Mrs. Knight. She felt like a miner who'd finally found a precious gem—a source of information both innocent and kind. "Not much. She says everyone has a mother and a father but they don't always stay. Why is that?"

Mrs. Knight sighed. "I don't know, dear. Why anyone wouldn't stay with a sweet thing like you is beyond me."

Alice didn't know, either. "But if I knew where babies came from, maybe I could understand a bit better how papas just leave and why that's a bad thing."

Mrs. Knight tapped her finger against her lips. "I can see the problem, but I think you ought to have this conversation with your mama." She cleared her throat. "It's a bad thing because only a shiftless, nasty man wouldn't want his wife and children."

Alice scowled. That wasn't her fault. She couldn't make her father want her—especially since she'd never met him. "If that's all, why can't people see me? Why can't I leave the house more often?"

Mrs. Knight sighed. "I don't know why, Alice. The world doesn't choose the right people to punish sometimes."

Alice folded her arms across her chest. "I don't like it."

"I don't, either." Mrs. Knight wrapped her arm around Alice's waist and gave her an awkward hug. "Don't you agree, Phil?"

Alice glanced across the room to find that Mr. Knight had left his seat behind and stood in front of the window. "Mm."

That wasn't much of an answer, but she supposed he agreed.

"Do you think I'll get my father back?" Alice asked. Even if he was shiftless and nasty, she wanted him—or at least she thought so. It seemed like a father could make all the difference in the world.

"I don't know, sugar heart." Mrs. Knight leaned back against the chair. "I don't know. It could be that someday God will bring him back into your life, but even if He doesn't, I'm sure you'll learn more about him in the future."

In the future? Alice wanted to learn about him now. He was her father, after all, and she had a right. Her life would be better if she knew about him, too. Little girls without fathers didn't seem to go far.

"But will people always hate me?"

"I won't." Mrs. Knight gave Alice another hug. "And neither will Mr. Knight or your mother ... It'll be all right. I promise."

Alice nodded, but she wasn't willing to just be all right and not ask questions. "Could Mr. Parker be my papa, though?" That seemed the most obvious answer.

Mrs. Knight was launched into another coughing fit.

Mr. Knight crossed the room to hold her hand. "Are you well? Would you like a glass of water?"

Mrs. Knight jerked her head up and down. "Yes, please." Her voice sounded like a carriage driving over gravel.

Mr. Knight stepped away to get a glass of water, and Alice pressed again. "Mr. Parker. Could he be?"

"I don't know. I don't think so! I hope not." Mrs. Knight accepted the glass Mr. Knight returned with. "Thank you, darling. What do you know of Mr. Parker's character?"

Mr. Knight swallowed. "We're cousins, and I would rather not talk badly of the man."

"But ...?"

He ran a hand over his eyes. "I don't necessarily trust him."

"But do you think ...?" Mrs. Knight fixed her eyes on his face. "And, if so, can he be made to take responsibility."

"I don't think—not definitively." Then he smiled. "But, either way, it's not worth thinking of. Here, Ned's starting to fuss."

Indeed, the baby was making soft whimpering noises, and Ivy looked beyond helpless. Alice rushed to her side, while Mr. Knight lifted the child from her arms.

"I'd best feed him," Mrs. Knight said. "Girls, would you come back to see me soon? It must be almost time for your tea, and I need to take care of Ned, but I want to talk again soon."

Alice bit her lip and nodded. She felt like she was being rushed away after too many questions, but she did like Mrs. Knight. "All right. We'll visit again soon."

CHAPTER ELEVEN

A LICE PUT HER HEAD down and ran. Her legs, throat, and lungs burned, but she pushed harder—yet, she just wasn't fast enough. Kirk Manning could run circles around her, and he almost did, dancing just ahead.

She stumbled to a stop at the crest of the hill and placed her hands on her knees. "It's ... not ... fair." She shoved her hair back with both hands and glared at him. "Your ... legs are ... longer."

"And you're slow." Kirk grinned and flopped down on the lime-green grass. His breaths were regulated.

Alice hated him.

She fell down at his side. When the ache in her chest eased, she propped herself up on her elbow. "Where are we?"

"South of the mansion. Look—you can see Pearlbelle if you stand up. We only left the gate an eighth of a mile ago, though I bet it seems longer to you." He jumped to his feet and reached down to help her up. "Come on."

Alice let him haul her to her feet, still feeling the after effects of their run in her calves. "Where are we going?"

"To my house. It's just over the way, on the road to the village." He shrugged. "I keep telling Mum I'm going to take you over to meet her."

"Oh, all right." Alice glanced up at the gray sky and shivered. The air was heavy and oppressive. "But it might rain."

Kirk squinted upwards for a moment. "No, it won't. It'll hold."

"If you say so." *I'm probably getting a soaking for trusting him, but clothes dry.*

He led her down the hill, which was bare save a scattering of rocks, and along the old cobbled road the carriage traveled on when it came from Creling and the train station. It was a bit worn but still a nice road.

"Does Mr. Knight make sure it stays nice?" she asked.

He gave her a funny look. "Of course. It's his land."

"Oh." Alice glanced about. "How much of this is his land?"

Kirk gestured to the south. "To Creling—almost to the outskirts." Then to the north. "The fence marks that boundary, though it's a ways back. Beyond it belongs to another estate, though their big house is quite a distance northeast."

Alice nodded. The Knights certainly owned a lot more land than she'd know what to do with. "And to the east and west?"

"It's wide." Kirk shrugged. "Don't know exactly how much. Friend of mine works at the stables. Roddy McDonnel's his name, and his family has a tenancy to the west—it's a long walk for Roddy."

Alice blinked. That didn't make sense. "Why doesn't he stay at the stables? You do, right?" She'd thought all servants lived where they worked.

"In our quarters. But he has days off, same as me." Kirk grinned. "You don't know a thing, do you, Alice?"

She stopped and glared. "I do, too! I was just asking a question. You don't have to be so ... so *imperious.*" It was the best word she could think of on short notice.

He scowled. "I'm not ... whatever that is. And you're just a girl."

Just a girl? Mummy had been "just a girl" once—and Nettie and Miss Elton and Mrs. Knight. It was no insult as far as Alice could see. She frowned right back at him. "I'm a *guest* at Pearlbelle Park."

"Well, I live there." He puffed up his chest and continued his walk, leaving Alice huffing by the roadside. "Coming or aren't you?"

"I ... I ..." She scurried to catch up. "I'm a fast learner. Nettie says so. And, anyway, you don't go to school at all."

His swagger paused a moment before continuing. "I don't like school."

"How do you know if you've never tried it?"

"I just know." He pointed up the road. "That's my house."

Though she wanted to keep arguing until her worth was accepted, Alice paused when she saw the house he'd referenced. It was really more of a run-down shack than a house, but it was hard to see through all the laundry hanging about it.

Why, there was almost a maze of laundry. Alice followed Kirk down the road, unsure what all the white sheets, petticoats, and other items drying on all those lines could mean.

Kirk walked up the pathway between the comforters and clothing items to the door, which stood ajar, propped open by an iron. "Coming?"

Alice scurried forward. "Yes. What's all—?"

"Oh, just clothes Mum's washing. She does that as a business, you know. Anything she can get." Kirk stepped forward into the wee cottage.

Alice followed timidly behind.

The inside was a bit dim, especially given there was only one window, which was becurtained. There was also a fire in the grate directly opposite, but it was nothing but coals.

A giant iron pot stood in the middle of the floor and slightly smaller ones hung about the hearth. A table, three chairs, and an ironing board were situated to Alice's left. The floor was wood but badly dented and bruised.

"Mum? Lizzy? Where are you?" Kirk walked across the room. There were two doors leading out of the tiny room.

"Here, Kirk." A slender woman appeared in the doorway, her reddish hair pulled back into a frizzy bun. Alice immediately recognized those bright-green eyes. "Oh, you've brought a friend." And red hands flew to pat her hair. "This must be Miss Alice."

Alice's smile trembled a bit, but she did her best. "Hello, Mrs. Manning. It's nice to meet you."

"It's an absolute pleasure to meet you." Mrs. Manning glanced over her shoulder. "Mr. Manning is ill, or he would meet you, too. And Lizzy—Lizzy is so shy around strangers. She's young, though."

Alice nodded. "I understand. Are you a … a laundress?"

Mrs. Manning glanced about, and a soft chuckle came from her throat. "Yes. Yes, I am. Mr. Manning isn't able to work and hasn't been for several years, so we all do our best. Even Lizzy helps me some. She's a strong girl for her age."

Mrs. Manning had a deep voice for a woman, though it wasn't exactly the kind of voice Alice had expected. She'd expected a voice like Kirk's, that of a poor country tenant. Kirk had a pretty, lyrical way of speaking—but Mrs. Manning's voice was smooth, gentle. Her accent was familiar … quite familiar, though Alice couldn't place it.

"But I'm glad Kirk has made a friend. He doesn't get to go to school anymore, and I know he hasn't much liked it."

Kirk scowled. "Ah, come on, Mum, I don't mind. It's freedom, after all, isn't it?"

"I think an education is—never mind. It doesn't matter now." A tight smile. "Alice, tell me about yourself. You're from London?"

Alice scuffed her toe along the floor. "Yes, ma'am."

"Do you like it there?"

She shook her head. "Not much, but my mummy lives there, and so I'd like to go back soon. But not before I've seen everything at Pearlbelle. I love the country!"

"The country is nice. I grew up in the city myself, and sometimes I miss the noise and the people, but I've been here since a little before Kirk was born now. It's lovely. So peaceful …" She turned away from Alice and walked over to the cupboards. "I wish I had something to offer you, Alice, but I just don't."

"That's all right. It was lunchtime not too long ago."

Kirk smirked. "She calls dinner 'lunch' just like you do sometimes, Mum."

Mrs. Manning smiled. "How nice. Oh, there's Lizzy."

Indeed, a tiny girl had peeked out of the second door. Her eyes flickered over to Alice, then she dashed across the room and buried her face in her mother's skirt.

"There now, darling. This is Kirk's friend." Mrs. Manning scooped her up. "Now, Lizzy, don't be rude."

After a bit more coaxing, Lizzy removed her face from her mother's shoulder just long enough to say, "Hewo."

Mrs. Manning beamed in triumph. "She'll learn. Bit by bit, but she'll learn. Kirk, where's your Opie? Lizzy was looking forward to seeing him."

"Doggy," Lizzy whispered, peeking up from her mother's bodice again.

"I tied him up in the bedroom with Roddy watching. The groundskeeper was around, and he doesn't like Opie much."

Mrs. Manning bit her bottom lip. "Oh dear. If you want, Opie can stay here. You can't lose that job over a dog."

Kirk's face dropped. "I like having him with me. And I don't think much of anyone else cares, especially Mr. Knight. He smiled when he saw Opie following me around the other day."

"Mr. Knight likes dogs," Alice said. She didn't want Opie far from her, either. "If Kirk gets in trouble, I can talk to him."

"Oh, very well. If you're being careful." Mrs. Manning sighed. "I just don't want you getting in trouble, son."

"I won't." Kirk glanced at Alice, then out the door. "Alice thinks it might rain, so maybe we'd better head back."

Alice nodded. "Nettie will worry."

"Very well." Mrs. Manning hitched Lizzy up higher on her hip. "Be sure to come again, Miss Alice."

"I will."

Mr. Parker had promised the girls a picnic not long after they arrived at Pearlbelle. After two weeks of begging and one week of demanding, Alice convinced him to organize it.

Finally, sunshine had beat the clouds back that morning, and the sky shone blue. Even the birds tweeted with unusual ferocity.

Alice spun around on her heel and scowled. "Ivy, come on—you're getting behind."

"She's with Nettie; she'll be fine." Mr. Knight reached a hand out to her. "Walk with me."

Alice shook her head. She wasn't going to hold his hand. Instead, she skirted around him and tugged at Mrs. Knight's sleeve. With her fingers slipped into her friend's hand, she felt better able to enjoy the evening.

"There's the lake!" Miss Elton, who was on Alice's other side, practically skipped. "How I've missed coming down here. This was my childhood—Steven, why don't we have our old friends here anymore?"

Mr. Parker snorted. "They've all grown up and gotten lives, Lois."

Miss Elton glared at him and whipped Ned up onto her shoulder protectively, causing the baby to whimper.

After making sure her son was all right, Mrs. Knight glanced over her shoulder. "Now, Steven. No need to be so morose."

Alice looked, too. Mr. Parker's face brewed like a storm cloud ready to burst. She shrugged, not afraid of him but neither very compassionate. After all, he was a grown-up. Grown-ups should be more in control than he always seemed to be.

"It's more of a pond than a lake." Mr. Knight gestured to the dip in the meadow. The body of water was surrounded by trees and high grasses, but there was a bit of a shoreline, where servants placed a blanket and picnic baskets.

After eating, Mr. Parker coaxed Alice into a rowboat, and they shoved out onto the pond. He seemed to be good at rowing, and Alice commented on this.

"I spent my boyhood here, as Miss Elton said." He smiled. "I used to love coming here. There wasn't a fish in this pond, not naturally, but I think my uncle would have some placed every so often as I've caught a few. They're gone now." Again, his face grew gloomy.

"Did Miss Elton come out with you? Who were your friends?" Alice asked quickly. She didn't want any more sadness. People ought not to wallow. They ought to get out into the world and live their lives.

"Yes, Lois loved it, and actually ... your mother. She'd come here every summer. And Mr. Knight and your uncle, Charles." Mr. Parker lifted the paddle and watched the droplets rain down. "Your mother was a dear friend for many years. Since we were younger than you, I think. She and Miss Elton went to school together, and she'd always spend her holidays at Pearlbelle." He dropped the paddle back in the water and pulled back. "She loved going out on this little pond, you know."

"Oh?" For some reason, Alice could imagine her mother as a girl but not as a boat-rower. That seemed strange. "Why, do you think?"

"I don't know. Rather good fun. Unless your friend tips the boat over." A grin flickered across his face. "That's what I did. She hated me after that, though of course I was eventually forgiven."

Alice scowled. Forgiven? She would never forgive such a grievous offense. "She shouldn't have."

Mr. Parker smirked. "Don't you think forgiveness is a virtue, Alice? Or do you believe anyone, having sinned, is too far gone for repentance and acceptance?"

Alice folded her arms across her chest and leaned against the stern. "I don't know. Some things people do are so dreadful."

"Yes, well." His cheerful expression faded. "I can understand that."

She pushed herself up and cocked her head. "Do you do dreadful things, Mr. Parker?"

He shrugged. "Once or twice, in my boyhood, I did things I am not, and never will be, proud of—I daresay I regret them."

"Like tipping Mummy's boat over?"

His face lightened. "I don't exactly regret that, no. It was a good joke, and I don't think she was truly mad. There were other things." He fixed his eyes on the horizon for a moment. "But you don't think there's really anything a man or anyone can do that puts them beyond redemption, do you?"

Alice wasn't sure about this. It seemed they were having a much more serious conversation than even she had intended—and Alice liked serious conversations very much. Serious conversations were for adults, and she longed to be an adult.

"I don't know." She wiggled on the seat, suddenly feeling as if she did know. "Nettie says there's nothing you can do that will make God not love you, and I guess that's got to be true. Nettie knows everything."

His expression mimed shock. "Oh dear! That's not good news for me."

Alice offered a hesitant smile. "Why?"

"Because Nettie doesn't like me, and if she knows everything, well ..." He sighed heavily and dropped his eyes as if despondent. "I suppose there's no hope for me."

"Oh, I suppose you're not all bad." At least not that she knew of. It was hard to tell with men sometimes, as Alice was quickly learning.

Mr. Parker picked up the oars again and glanced toward the shoreline. "I see they're calling us back. Do you think they'll let us have those tarts now?"

Alice jumped up, causing the boat to rock. She grabbed the edges but nodded eagerly. "Yes! That must be it."

As the sun started to dip toward the horizon and the servants begun picking everything up, Mr. Knight came to sit next to Alice. She licked her fingers from the last remains of her tart and scooted over so he wasn't anywhere near close to her.

For a moment, he was silent, watching her, then he spoke. "I never noticed that chain around your neck, Alice! Is it your mother's?"

She blinked. How did he know that? "Yes, it is." Feeling awkward but obligated, she pulled on the chain and held out the ring at the end. "See—it's her ring."

"Aw." He took the ring in his hand, forcing Alice to scoot closer. "Her birthstone, isn't it? For December?"

Alice nodded and tugged at the chain so he released it. "Yes. Ivy has one for January—that's our birth month, you know."

"So I've heard. It's mine, too." He leaned back in the grass on his elbow like a boy, which made him shorter than her.

She took a deep breath.

"Did you have fun today?"

"Yes."

"Did Ivy? She's such a shy child."

Alice shrugged. "I think she had fun. She likes being out in the world—the country world, I mean. Not London. She hates being out in London."

"Ah." Mr. Knight cocked his head, black eyes pinning her down. "Is Ivy ... She's a great deal quieter than you, isn't she?"

"She is. She was born that way." Alice glared at him. "Doesn't mean she isn't a good sister and a better person."

"Right, right. Of course not. I only wondered ... has your mother thought about seeing that she's taken care of? I mean, a child like that can hardly hope to have a future, and—"

"Ivy has plenty of future! Mummy always says they'll keep each other company."

His brows lowered. "Seems a morose life. Always with your mother. I wonder if there's any way to help her."

Alice's ears perked. Usually when Mr. or Mrs. Lansky talked about Ivy, which wasn't often, they would say things like, "Shouldn't she be put in a home?" or "Can't you see about training her to behave like a regular child?"

Helping wasn't part of the equation in most people's minds when it came to Ivy. Still, Mr. Knight seemed to have the right idea about it.

"Nettie says we can likely help Ivy most by loving and accepting her, and by reassuring her when she's scared. She gets bad nightmares, and sometimes she can't do anything when she's scared—like in London." Alice regarded Mr. Knight closely. "How do you think we could help?"

"I don't know. Perhaps Nettie's right; it's all in loving and caring for the child. But I suppose I would say that ... Ivy's not the first, and surely there has been some research on how a child who is simpler and has such anxieties could be helped." He sat up again, but Alice wasn't afraid of his bigness now. "I think anyone deserves better than to always be scared. I remember I would be frightened of little things when I was young—younger than Ivy, but still."

"Are you ever scared anymore?" Alice almost wouldn't believe that. Big men like him didn't have cause to be scared. They could kill dragons—and there weren't even that many dragons in England anymore, so they surely had nothing to worry about.

"Sometimes." He rose and held out his hand to Alice. "Of things that you wouldn't know about, though."

"Like what? I might know." She was willing to try knowing anything once.

Mr. Knight smiled. "You always think you might know, don't you, Alice?"

Alice nodded. "What, then?"

He laughed. "Well, Miss Persistent, sometimes I'm afraid for my wife and baby Ned. Even though they're safe, I find little nothings to worry about. I want to be a good owner of Pearlbelle, and I'm scared of letting people down. I'm not the most consistent man, and it can be difficult to stay the course. And most of all, I'm afraid of losing my good reputation."

"Oh." Alice bit her bottom lip. She wasn't afraid of any of those things, though if Mummy or Ivy or Nettie were ever unsafe, she'd be frightened, she supposed. And it must be hard to have too many people—servants and tenants and family—counting on you. "That makes sense."

Mr. Knight nodded. "Come now. We'd best head back."

Alice started to solemnly walk down the hill. She paused and looked up at Mr. Knight. He was a grown-up, but sometimes his smile made him seem the fun sort.

She'd try.

Alice tugged at his hand. "Race you back to Miss Hazel?"

He gawked at her for a moment, then laughed aloud. "First one there gets the last strawberry tart?"

Alice started running before he could finish the sentence.

Chapter Twelve

C LAIRE PRETENDED TO EXAMINE her client carefully, though she'd known as soon as the woman entered her shop that the yellow fabric she'd demanded would be murder for her complexion.

But the client was always right. Even when she was horribly wrong.

Claire nodded slowly. "Any shade would complement your brilliant gray eyes, Mrs. Maston." In truth, those gray eyes were squinted and reddened.

"Thank you." The middle-aged woman beamed and twirled in front of the mirror.

"But ... could I suggest a lavender?" Claire turned to a chair behind her, where she'd laid her choice, lifted the soft piece of fabric, and presented it to Mrs. Maston.

"Oh." Mrs. Maston stared at the fabric before accepting it. "It is lovely."

"I could make a beautiful dress in just that style for you." Claire smiled winningly. "Perhaps with this lace trim ..."

In half an hour, Claire had a complete order placed, Mrs. Maston happy, and food for at least the next few weeks. A sense of well-being slid over her as it always did after a successful sale. *I can do this, even by myself. I am strong enough. I don't need anyone but myself ...*

"It seems odd how pleasant you are, Miss Berck, given—" Mrs. Maston pouted. "Oh, I am sorry."

Claire hesitated and narrowed her eyes. "What was that, Mrs. Maston?"

"I'm sorry—I didn't mean to mention it. You're my regular dressmaker, and I do love your work ..." Yet, the trail of her voice indicated that she did indeed want to mention it.

Claire sighed and ignored the heavy feeling in her chest. "Please tell me whatever it is you have to say."

Mrs. Maston tossed her arms up in half-hearted surrender. "Oh, very well. It's only that lately there have been such rumors about you, Miss Berck, that I don't know what to think! Mr. Steven Parker, a former rake, has visited your home multiple times. There have been some unseemly rumors about your relations to a Mr. Charles Chattoway—a respected man of the community, but no less scandalous given your respective backgrounds. And no one really does know where you've come from ..."

Claire smiled through the pain in her heart. It had finally caught up to her. Would there be an easy way around it? Or would this be the final straw that broke the camel's back? Was she to lose her position, her livelihood, her ability to provide for her children?

Her children? Would she lose her children, heaven forbid?

Oh, I can't, Lord.

Another prayer she hadn't planned. But she determined to be calm and suave. Mrs. Maston had only rumors and knew nothing of her children. That would be enough.

"Oh goodness, what horrid rumors." Claire shook her head. "Terrible that people would say such things! Why, can you imagine?"

A bit crestfallen, Mrs. Maston nodded. "Indeed."

"Of course, a respected woman like you realizes it can't be true, but will others?" Claire ran a hand over her face as if distressed. "Oh dear. I'm only a seamstress, really. I don't even know such people as ... was it Mr. Chatt ...?"

"Chattoway. I suppose you wouldn't." Mrs. Maston cocked her head. "But wasn't Mr. Parker's carriage seen ...?"

Stupid, indiscreet man. "I hardly know! I wouldn't recognize his carriage if I saw it. I've never heard of the man."

Mrs. Maston seemed only partially satisfied with this denial, but she fluffed her hair and whirled toward the door. "Thank you for helping me choose a wondrous dress once again, Miss Berck. Oh, one more thing?"

Claire turned back from the counter. "Yes?"

"Do you perhaps have a sweet little niece? Seven or eight, with dark hair?" Mrs. Maston's eyes were narrowed, and Claire knew she'd been sent in deliberately to fish out a scandal. To find out what was really happening. To seek and twist someone's life ... and then report it to her friends.

Let it seep about London through her friends' servants.

Let Claire's reputation at last collapse into nothing. The fragile, fake reputation she'd built around her skill and with her steady wits. All gone.

Some might call it an extreme assessment, but Claire knew London. She knew the rich and the mighty. They were just looking for another life to destroy, another innocent to ruin, another world to collapse.

And then they would watch and judge, peering through their opera glasses at the fire like Nero at his maddest. Gossiping about the downfall.

But she must respond—and quickly, easily. "Why do you ask, Mrs. Maston?"

"Because often was observed a few months ago a small child of that description entering and exiting your house through the back way." Mrs. Maston smiled, too sweet for Claire. "Of course, I have heard this through my maid ... who heard it from others. It's becoming a well-known fact. And now, apparently, according to some, the Knights of Pearlbelle Park have a small ward staying with them, who again matches that same description. And we all know the Knights are cousins to Mr. Parker." Another slow, cruel smirk. "You can imagine my confusion and that of my friends, who are also your clients."

Claire blinked. "How strange. Perhaps our cinder girl has taken her child into our house and left with her on occasion? As for the Knights of Pearlbelle Park, I know nothing of them or of Mr. Parker, as I stated before." She shrugged lightly. "I hate to disappoint you, Mrs. Maston, but I have no story. I was born in London, the daughter of poor parents, like myself. My father was also a seamster before his passing. I live alone, save a few servants." She sighed. "It's a lonely life but a good one nonetheless. I work for all I have."

Mrs. Maston huffed. "Do you expect me to believe that there was really nothing going on?"

"It's your choice what you believe, ma'am. I can only offer honesty to you as what it is—truth. Beyond that is your decision."

Mrs. Maston crossed her arms. "Send word as always when the dress is ready for fitting. This could be the last dress I order with you if rumors prove true."

"They will not." Claire tried to force confidence into her tone, her posture. She held open the door. "Thank you again for your illustrious business, ma'am."

Mrs. Maston shuffled out the door to her waiting carriage, and Claire tried not to cry or scream or throw herself into the glass case in hope of breaking both it and herself.

She had to get the children safe. Away from Pearlbelle, away from London ... and she had to avoid all further contact with her brother, the Knights, or Mr. Parker.

But how?

"Alice, Ivy, look, it's a letter from your mother." Nettie held up a sheet of paper. "Come over here and let me tell you about it."

A bit miffed that she hadn't been allowed to open and read it herself, Alice ran forward and reached for the message.

"No, it's not for little girls, Miss Grace." Nettie folded the letter and slipped it into the pocket of her dress. "Ivy, let me comb out your hair, dearest. I haven't gotten to take care of you yet this morning, have I? And we'll have breakfast in a moment ..."

"The letter, Nettie?" Alice wanted to be patient, but it was so hard when everyone around her was slow as turtles.

"Oh, yes. We're going home now! Isn't that wonderful? We'll probably take the first train tomorrow ..."

Alice's mouth dropped open. Going home? First train tomorrow? This was insanity! "But I thought we were staying at Pearlbelle almost all summer."

"I thought so, too, but Mummy says it's time to come home now." Nettie smiled brightly. "Now, who wants to help me pack?"

"I do," said Ivy.

But Alice didn't want to help pack at all. She wanted to never let anyone pack, because she never wanted to ever leave Pearlbelle Park. It was so beautiful here! She had a pony and a puppy—sort of—and a best friend, and she'd started to like Mr. Parker and Miss Elton and Mrs. Knight ... she loved Mrs. Knight. Even Mr. Knight had started to grow on her.

And now they were leaving? And who knows when they'd be coming back!

This wasn't to be borne.

Her throat felt tight and scratchy as she dressed for the day. She barely touched her breakfast, leading to Nettie's asking if she were all right.

She wasn't all right, and she almost told Nettie so, but there wasn't much she could do. Alice did love and want her Mummy, only ... it would be better if they could all live here. London was dreadful and smelly. She didn't want to go back there.

At last, she was allowed to leave the table, and she ran all the way to the stables. After a brief search, she found Kirk taking a horse out to exercise. She watched without a word as he exercised Acacia.

When he returned the mare to her stall and rubbed her down, Alice still remained silent—and eventually Kirk had to ask why.

Or rather he asked, "What's eating you?"

"What?"

He shrugged and flicked at Acacia's coat. "What's wrong?"

"It's not good news." She patted the mare's nose, then brought her big head down for an on-tiptoes, rather awkward hug.

"Spit it out, then. We can't have bad news inside us forever." He dropped the brushes in a bucket and leaned against the stall door, effectively blocking her exit. "Go on and tell me."

Alice swallowed. It was more difficult getting the hated words out than she'd imagined. Life was too unfair. She'd come to think of Kirk as a combination of brother and future-prince-maybe, and she didn't want to give that up and go home to London. Especially the brother part—as far as she was concerned, princes were optional.

He grinned, probably amused by her facial expression. "Just say it."

She stuck her tongue out at him. "I'm going to! It's just that I'm going back to London, and we're not coming back soon, so I might not see you again."

"Oh, is that all?" He picked up the pail and walked toward the tack room.

Scowling, Alice ran after him. "All? We're friends, aren't we, Kirk? I'm your best friend, aren't I?"

Kirk shrugged and dropped the bucket on the floor. "I suppose. A bit. But that don't mean nothing. You're just a girl."

She folded her arms across her chest. "And you're just a boy, but I like you anyway."

Kirk's eyes flickered up and down her. "I suppose if I had to be with a girl all the time, might as well be one who likes horses and dogs and playing in creeks. But, you know, that don't mean you're special." He raised his chin. "Don't want you getting prideful."

Alice scowled. "*Doesn't*—the first time, I mean—and I am special, but so are you."

He crossed his arms. "I'm not special!"

"You are, too! Anyway, I don't care what you think about yourself or me, because I think you're a good friend. And I love Opie, too—though he's nicer than you'll ever be." To prove her point, she marched down the path between the stables to the room where Opie was tied up and let him out.

The spaniel jumped up and began licking her face.

At least someone cared. She clung to his matted fur and enjoyed the warm puppyness of him.

From somewhere deep inside her came tears, over Kirk's continual boy brusqueness and already missing her pony and feeling disloyal to Mummy and wanting to get to know Mr. Knight and Mr. Parker better ...

Everything crashed down, and Alice cried.

"I mean ... you don't have to ... to *cry* about it."

Alice jumped up and swiftly wiped the tears from her eyes. "I-I wasn't c-crying." Of course, she realized that her thick, shaky voice was tear-filled, but she wouldn't admit that to *him*.

Kirk stepped forward, then stepped back. "I'm sorry. Don't know how to talk to you. Funny, 'cause I mostly spend time with girls—Mum and Lizzy. But, you know, I don't want you to go. I don't have another friend—except Opie, and he drools."

Alice sniffled and rubbed her nose with the back of her sleeve "like a hoodlum," as Nettie would say. "I don't drool much." She offered a tremulous smile.

Kirk grinned back. "Not much." He held out his hand. "Want to wash your face, then go to the creek just once more before you leave? I can get away."

"All right," said Alice.

CHAPTER THIRTEEN

C LAIRE CLUTCHED ALICE CLOSE and kissed her hair. "Darling, I
missed you so much!"

"I missed you to, Mummy." Alice stood on tiptoe to kiss her, then
stepped back and ran off shouting, "Jameson? Mrs. Bennett?"

Claire knelt to kiss and hug Ivy, looking over her head at Nettie. "Thank
you for coming home so quickly. We'll discuss the reasons soon."

"Very well." Nettie stepped aside as their manservant moved through to
collect luggage from the carriage.

She redirected her gaze back down to Ivy. "Did you have a good time in
the country, dear?"

"Yes, but I'm glad I'm home now." Ivy pressed her face against Claire's
shoulder, then moved her head to whisper in her ear. "Mr. Knight is nice,
and so is Mr. Parker and Miss Elton and Mrs. Knight. But I don't like them
much."

Claire smiled. That was just like Ivy. Though her child was convinced
that everyone was quite pleasant, she never took to strangers—part of the
reason it wouldn't do for Ivy to be separated from those she loved.

"Would you ever like to go to Pearlbelle again?"

Ivy hesitated. "Not without you, Mummy."

"Maybe we'll find somewhere else to holiday ... the seaside, perhaps.
Would you like that?" Actually, one option she had considered was moving

to a new town, creating a new alias, and continuing on as before. A beach town might be a nice change.

Even a little beach town in France. The place where she'd gotten her alias, actually—Berck, where she'd married and been happy for one short week. But going there could be risky. The chances of one tourist from nine years ago being recognized were limited, but who knew?

She had to be careful, and there were too many variables to allow any avoidable ones unchecked. The doctor who had tended Ivy was also a source of rumors that might spread, though as of yet, she had heard nothing from that source.

Ivy was enthusiastic about the idea of the seaside, so that was always an option. Claire loved the beach—the crash of the waves, the cry of the seagulls, the wind whipping her hair to and fro ...

His jacket over my shoulders, his eyes on me, his lips on mine.

Claire closed her eyes. She knew better than that.

"Mummy?"

She blinked, then smiled at her child. "Mm—let's get you some tea. Are you hungry?"

Ivy nodded, her head jerking her whole body up and down. *Country air must agree with her.*

"Excellent."

Ivy went off to greet Mrs. Bennett and Jameson, and Claire followed Nettie up to the girls' room. Her chest felt heavy. She knew this would be difficult. No one would hate her proposed plan more than Nettie.

But it must be done.

Claire cleared her throat, and Nettie looked up from unpacking with a bit of a smile flickering around her lips.

"I suppose you know I have a reason for calling you and the girls back early."

Nettie cocked her head. "I guessed it. You rarely do things without cause. I trusted it was a good reason, though, and acted immediately. And I've no fondness for Pearlbelle Park—you know that."

"Yes, I do have a reason." Claire sat on the edge of Alice and Ivy's bed and regarded Nettie. "But first, tell me—how did the journey go?"

"The journey or the visit?" Nettie raised her eyebrows. "The journey went well. Completely uneventful, which is what one wants from traveling, really."

Claire swallowed. "And ... and the visit?"

"Not terribly eventful. Mr. Parker wouldn't leave Alice be." Nettie twitched. His attentions to Alice obviously disturbed her, though Claire wasn't sure why. Steven wasn't a horrible man, even if he wasn't a good one.

"And what of ... everyone else?"

Nettie shrugged. "Alice befriended a stable boy and spent a great deal of time with him and his dog."

"Of course she did." Alice never was one to understand social classes, and she'd been wanting a friend all her life. "But I meant the other residents of Pearlbelle Park."

Nettie lifted one of Alice's dresses from the trunk and smoothed it. "Miss Elton liked them well enough, though she's unaccustomed to children. Mrs. Knight was ever kind, and Mr. Knight ... he tried."

Claire narrowed her eyes. "What does that mean?"

"He's a man." Nettie hung up the first dress and returned for the second. "Alice adored Mrs. Knight and—you've heard of her lying in?"

"Yes." Such rumors trickled into town quickly, and she knew the woman was delivered of a son. "A boy, wasn't it?"

"Edmond. Alice adores him, though I think that has to do with Mrs. Knight's kind treatment of her more than anything. But he does seem to be a sweet babe."

A sweet babe. Of course he was—a sweet babe, an heir, a blessing to his parents. Everything she'd hoped her firstborn son would be.

Claire didn't allow herself to daydream anymore as she used to. She didn't have time for it, and it could only bring pain. Her life was full of variables, but there were no guarantees.

If I can just keep the girls safe, that's all that matters.

She composed herself. "Nettie, come sit. I made a decision while you were gone, and though I won't have you challenging it, I would discuss it with you."

Nettie turned from the closet, and Claire saw fear in her eyes. "What do you mean? What decision would you have made that I would wish to challenge?"

"Sit." She patted the bed beside her. "It's for the best—and you must trust me. But I know you will hate it."

I know I promised you such a thing would not come to pass, and I'm sorry ... Claire didn't want to say that aloud, didn't want to remind herself of the promise she'd made to Nettie eight years ago. *We'll raise them together. It'll be all right; you'll never be separated.*

She would break that promise now, if only for a bit. But she had to save Alice. She had to—didn't she love the child? Nettie's love was that of a mother, yes, but Claire was still the one who made the decisions, the one with authority over Alice's life.

And I'm saving her. God, tell me I'm saving her!

It was the only way, and it wasn't even drastic, at that. Mothers around the world, including her own, had done just what she was doing.

But the risks are so different for me.

Nettie lowered herself onto the bed next to Claire. Her hands were clasped in her lap and her posture straight. "Can you tell me quickly?" Her words were pinched, and Claire knew she'd frightened her.

We've so much to be frightened about, Nettie.

"Remember Miss Selle's?" The boarding school in Norfolk was the most elite a young woman not possessing a title could attend. Claire had spent her girlhood there, from the age of ten through sixteen. That's where Lois Elton and she had become, by Lois's definition, bosom friends.

"Of course." Nettie's posture slumped in relief. "Did one of your friends contact you, perhaps?"

"No—save Lois, I have heard nothing from any of them. Which is exactly what I want, of course." If any of her old schoolmates discovered her, the scandal would be great. Thankfully, a few who did use her dress shop were always confidently handled by her assistant.

Thank God for that.

"Good. Then ...?"

"I've decided Alice ought to go to Miss Selle's Boarding School for Girls."

Nettie's mouth dropped open, and her eyes widened. "I-I ... how? She couldn't! Not as ... forgive me, Claire, but not as your daughter."

Claire's jaw tightened, but so did her resolve. "No, she will not attend as my child but as the young orphan ward of the Eltons. I've already written a letter to Lois requesting she contact the Selles with this request."

"But she couldn't! We would be found out. We risk—"

"We risk everything?" Claire forced a smile to turn the corners of her mouth upward. "We already are, Nettie. You knew that from the first!"

"Yes, but ..." Nettie wrapped her arms around herself. "But I thought I'd be with her." Her eyes turned to Claire, pleading. "Don't make me be without her. I love the child. We can continue keeping her a secret, can't we? Both Alice and Ivy? And what sense does it make to send one and not the other?"

"You know I can't send Ivy to school," Claire snapped. "She wouldn't make it. But Alice would! She'll make friends, as I did, friends who will take her away. Friends who will perhaps offer her a proper presentation. She will be secured of the future she must have. The future she deserves."

Claire could see the bitterness seeping into Nettie's face, her posture. Her chest rose and fell quickly, and her hands were fists at her sides.

"What future does she deserve, then, Claire?" Nettie shot up and spun to face Claire, eyes alight. Claire knew that fire well, and she wouldn't try to smother it. The inferno would have to burn bright enough to extinguish itself. "The illegit—"

"Nettie!"

"No, Claire. You know it's true." Nettie went to the window. "We shouldn't send her away. She'd be open to ridicule. Even if we teach her to use an alias, she's honest—she could never be anything but—and she isn't old enough to be wise about her words. It will get out. We'll lose everything."

"But if she stays, we'll lose everything, too." Claire related the tale of Mrs. Maston and her judgmental friends. "There can be no more Alice. No one knows about Ivy that I'm aware of, and if they do, I have no choice but to keep her here. But Alice will thrive, Nettie. We have to give Alice the chance to thrive."

"W-we would have her for holidays, though?"

The trembling in Nettie's voice made Claire want to reassure her that indeed it was so, that there was nothing to fear. But she couldn't. "Nettie, if we're going to make this work, we need Alice to stay there all year long."

Nettie fell back onto the bed and covered her face with her hands. She didn't move or make a sound for so long that Claire was afraid she'd fainted.

"Nettie?"

"I need a moment."

"We can visit, occasionally, if we're very discreet. Or you could, if you used an assumed name." Claire swallowed. It wouldn't be possible for her to make the journey; there were too many risks involved. "It wouldn't be often, but it would be something. Every few years, perhaps."

Nettie moaned. Claire scooted along the bed and placed a hand lightly on her shoulder.

"It's what's best. I know you're attached to her, and I myself have cried many a time over the last few days." Claire swallowed. The nights always took her by surprise with their empty darkness, but that was neither here nor there. "It's what we have to do."

"I ... I see." Nettie lowered her hands and rested them in her lap again. "You won't hear another protest from me."

Claire examined the tight press of Nettie's lips, the wrinkles on her brow. The lack of protest came at a heavy cost, she could tell. "You can't let Alice know you're frightened for her, either. She cares for your opinion as much as mine. You must know your attitude toward this will make the difference to Alice."

Her maid's head jerked up and down. "I suppose I never should have let myself get this attached. But you know I've always wanted to be a mother,

Claire, and though things have never worked out in that regard—" She stopped herself and sighed. "I'll bear it. I'm sorry—this is such a sacrifice for you, and I'm ... I shouldn't be ..." She rose. "I'll finish unpacking. How soon will she leave?"

"I've only just sent a letter to Lois requesting a reference." Claire also stood and walked toward the door. "With her recommendation, we can do this. An Elton's word will be enough for even the strictest headmistress, and she will help us."

"I've no doubt of it." Nettie removed an armload of stockings from the trunk and dumped them on the bed. She raised her eyes to meet Claire's. "Don't fear for me; I'll be all right. God will give me all the strength I need. And I'll pray for you, too. I know this isn't a decision made without consideration of the price."

Claire nodded and left the room. She knew Nettie disagreed about the cost versus the benefits in this case.

Lord God, please let this be the right decision for us.

Within a fortnight, Alice bid a tearful good-bye to her dear mother and twin. Ivy cried and asked her to stay, not understanding Alice's insistence that she must leave. It wasn't her decision; she never would have chosen to go.

Mummy was resolute to the end, but Alice believed that there were tears in her eyes as she kissed her daughter one last time. "I love you, darling. Be good."

As the carriage drove off to the train station with Alice—and Nettie as chaperone—inside it, she had never felt so lonesome. She looked out the window and watched London go by. The people walking along the cobblestone streets, the bright storefronts, and the carts and carriages seemed boring and blurry. She brushed a hand across her eyes to wipe away the tears, and the sights became visible for a time. She sniffed and sniffed again. Nettie's arm slipped around her, and a handkerchief was pressed into her hand.

"It's going to be all right, Miss Grace." Nettie pressed a kiss to the top of her head. "I'll be with you for the journey. You'll love it there—so many girls your own age! How lovely that will be. And think of what a good education you'll get."

Alice didn't reply. That would mean more crying, and she hated to cry more than anything else. Even so, her throat felt full and her stomach caved.

Why were they making her leave them?

CHAPTER FOURTEEN

T HEY ARRIVED IN HUNSTANTON, Norfolk on a rainy September day. The carriage drove by tall, waving grasses beside a wide strip of beach, which led down to a gray but calm sea.

"Even the weather matches me." Alice pouted. "Sad."

Nettie smiled consolingly and squeezed her hand. "It's going to be all right, Gracie."

"No, it's not."

Nettie didn't reply.

The carriage was dim, though it was only mid-morning, and felt even damper and colder with the curtains open. Alice pulled her shawl closer about her shoulders and stuck her lip out as far as it would go. She had long since ceased to cry in favor of being sullen.

"I believe we will arrive in thirty minutes or so." Nettie had been trying to read since they left the train behind, but the light—or, rather, the lack of—made it impossible. She put the book into one of the bags, touched her hair, and straightened her dress.

"Hunstanton was founded in the eleventh century." Nettie gestured to a little collection of cottages going by through her half-shaded window. "The ruins of St. Edmund's Chapel are located here. St. Edmund supposedly built the village. You know, darling, Edmund the Martyr. Have you studied him?"

Alice scowled, refusing to be interested. "A bit."

"Perhaps you will more now that you're here. There's a river, too. It runs into the North Sea." She gestured out the window. "Did you know that there's also a New Hunstanton? It was developed by a man named Henry Le Strange—I remember the name because your mother thought it was funny—not so very long ago, when I was a girl. It's a beach resort."

Alice crossed her arms across her chest. Even if Mummy had lived here all right for several years, surely Alice wouldn't be able to. And there was nothing, absolutely nothing, interesting about Hunstanton.

"There's an old church that was originally built in the 1300s." Nettie reached over and adjusted Alice's hat. "And in the graveyard, there are soldiers who died in a battle against smugglers on this coast."

That brought her head up, knocking Nettie's hands aside. "Really?"

Nettie laughed. "Yes, really. The smugglers were tried in Thetford a year later, but there was insufficient evidence, and they couldn't secure a conviction."

Alice sighed. "Oh." She had imagined that the smugglers would have some terrible death—burned or hung or cut up into little bits as a warning for further villains—but no, they got off free. And so Alice's conviction that Hunstanton was a terrible place became even firmer.

The carriage stopped in front of a building that was about average in size compared to the house at Pearlbelle Park. However, with two imposing stories, it was large compared to most structures.

The house was a bit back from the road, and short, bright-green grass covered the yard in between the house and the lane. The siding was of brown shakes, wind-beaten and sea-weathered, but somehow still grandiose.

The sign in front read:

Miss Selle's Boarding School for Girls
Founded 1835 by Mr. and Mrs. James Selle

Nettie gestured to the sign as they exited the carriage. "Their daughters are in charge here now, I believe."

As if on cue, a woman opened the door of the house. "I'm expecting a

Miss Alice Elton, accompanied by her nanny, Miss Annette Atwater. You must be them."

"We are." Nettie walked to the porch, motioning for Alice to follow.

Miss Selle had those high cheekbones that are meant for broad, friendly grins, but she gave only a cold smile. Her hair was arranged stylishly, her dress a nauseous spring green in color, and her eyes gray, a bit like Nettie's but harder, firmer.

Alice imagined she was the ideal headmistress except for one thing—she was not old. Why, Miss Selle was only her mother's age. That would have surprised Alice out of her grouchiness if that glare had not already. Miss Selle should have been bent and ugly.

"I'm glad to meet both of you. Won't you come in?" Miss Selle's voice reminded Alice of the metronome Nettie tirelessly set to keep Alice playing her piano pieces at a consistent pace. Not that Nettie could play, as both of them were horrid at anything musical. "The girls are at their lessons now, but in half an hour, they'll be released for a fifteen-minute break. Meanwhile, I'll show you the dormitories. Please come this way to my office."

Her office was small but neat. There were papers scattered on the desk, but that was the only trace of untidiness. She went behind the desk, sat down, picked up a pile, and sifted through the pages to find the desired one.

"These are the forms that Miss Lois Elton filled out on her distant cousin's behalf. I have everything I need, but I was informed you—Miss Atwater, is it?—would be able to handle any details I needed, and I do need a signature to this sheet which is a promise of good conduct."

"I can." Nettie accepted the sheet of paper, scanned it, and wrote her signature on the given line.

Miss Selle took the paper back, set it on top of the others, and stood. "Alice will be sleeping in room eight with two other girls: Georgiana Kingston and Abigail Peabody. Miss Kingston is eight, and Miss Peabody is nine. I believe you will find them very agreeable. Another girl, arriving sometime in the next few days, will also share Alice's room. Her name is Lady Mary

O'Connell, and she is seven."

Nettie blinked. "I had no idea you had so many younger students."

"Indeed. It is an unusual year." She led them out another door from the office, down a hall, and up the stairs. "On this second level are our classrooms. I won't interrupt the teachers just now."

They walked down a long hall lined with closed doors and up another flight of stairs. The third doorway on the left was closed. Miss Selle opened it and led her two companions in.

The room contained four small beds, each with a chest of drawers on one side and some hooks on the other. On the hooks farthest from the door, a coat and a hat hung, both beautifully made. The bed was messy, and a pile of rumpled clothing lay on the floor. The bed next to it was neater. The covers didn't look rumpled, and the hats and coats hung neatly on their hooks. The shoes were tidily arranged under the hooks, where they belonged, instead of thrust under the bed, and two books were stacked beside a small music box. The pair of beds across from them were crisply made and awaiting their new occupants, and the accompanying hooks and chests of drawers appeared ready to hold Alice's and Lady Mary's clothing and outer wear.

"I had a man go out for Miss Elton's things, and I think I hear him on the stairs," Miss Selle continued without a break.

Alice blinked—it would take her a while to get used to being referred to by that name and having to make believe Miss Lois Elton was a cousin of hers. But her mother insisted it was necessary for whatever reason.

An older man, whose hair was touched with gray, walked in, carrying Alice's trunk and bags.

"This is Mr. Thom. He takes care of the garden and does any heavy lifting we require."

After the man left, Miss Selle gestured back toward the door. "The unpacking may be done later. Come. It's time for our break."

They followed Miss Selle out of the room, down two flights of stairs, and onto a large back porch.

"You will meet the servants as time goes on. For now, I'll just introduce you to the teachers and the girls who will be in Alice's group," said Miss Selle. "Ah, here is Miss Kelly."

Indeed, a woman walked out onto the porch, smiled and nodded at Alice and her aunt, and stood slightly behind Miss Selle. Miss Kelly was about Miss Selle's age with light-brown hair and pale-blue eyes full of benevolence.

"Miss Kelly usually works with the younger girls, everyone below fourteen," Miss Selle said.

Miss Kelly nodded.

"Excuse me." Miss Selle turned to Miss Kelly with an air of annoyance. "Well, what's happened *now*?"

"They're still in the schoolroom. I'm having some trouble with keeping order, but—"

Miss Selle frowned. "Have Miss Fabrey help. Bring them down."

Miss Kelly nodded and departed.

A few minutes later, ten girls, aged eight through thirteen, marched out and stood before Alice.

"Good, you're all here!" Miss Selle walked to the first girl and began introducing them.

The girls were all wearing white blouses and brown, tan, or gray skirts. They were simple, without frills or lace, but by no means unbecoming. Alice preferred simpler clothing anyway. Frills and lace got in the way, and unless there was some important occasion, she liked to be plainly dressed.

After Miss Selle introduced the last girl, she dismissed them, and they scattered about the yard.

Miss Fabrey, introduced as working with the older girls, came out a moment later. She was pretty in an exotic way and had an infectious smile. Her mouse-brown eyes were big and bright, and her brown hair curled loosely about a porcelain face. She spoke with a slight French accent.

Alice was also introduced to Miss Schilling, a teacher with light-blonde hair and glasses, both slightly askew. She looked as if she had a bad headache.

Miss Selle had a talk with Nettie and the teachers, while Alice watched her new schoolmates play, unsure if she ought to join them.

What was mother thinking? I would far rather be taught by Nettie!

Nettie kissed Alice's cheeks for the hundredth time, pressing her close. "God keep you, my Gracie," she whispered. "You're going to be all right. Dwell in Him, all right?"

"All right." Alice wiggled free, embarrassed by Nettie's show of affection.

"No—promise me. Read your Bible, pray without ceasing, and make God's will your first priority. Please, Miss Grace. This is all I'll ask of you." Nettie's eyes were full of tears.

Alice patted her cheek. "I promise. Are you sad?"

"A little." She pressed her close again. "But I love you, and I'm s-so excited for you! This is going to be the best thing that ever happened to you. Make friends ... and remember what your mother told you."

Alice swallowed. That was the hard part—remembering all the things she couldn't say. But still, she nodded.

"Your mother loves you more than anything. You can trust her." Nettie squeezed Alice's hand and rose.

Alice watched the carriage bear Nettie away toward the train station and London and home. And Alice stayed behind and told herself that only babies cried, so certainly she would not.

Then she turned and dragged her feet up the steps of the house to where Miss Selle waited. She was led straight to the dinner table, where Miss Kelly greeted her with a gentle smile.

"Come now, you can sit next to me."

After Miss Selle prayed over the meal, they began to eat. Alice wasn't sure what she was putting in her mouth, chewing, and swallowing; she was too busy being quiet and polite.

Collapsing onto her bed that night, Alice was too tired to think so simply fell asleep.

The next morning, Alice ate at the breakfast table with the other girls. They whispered among themselves even though talking was not allowed at meals.

Georgiana leaned close to Alice and whispered, "Behind you, there's the other new girl. The ginger. Arrived late last night."

Alice nodded and glanced back before returning to her plate.

"She's shy, I think," murmured Lady Elizabeth Cromwell, a thirteen-year-old girl with a very pronounced Roman nose.

"How old is she?" asked Miss Lauren Sneed, who was tall and imposing. Alice didn't care for her pinched face and the way her eyes raked over one girl and another as if sizing them up. And she was older than Alice, too, at fifteen.

"Seven. She looks five, though." Lady Elizabeth huffed.

Frances Edwards smirked. "She looks four. I bet she cries herself to sleep."

"Shame on you, Fanny!" Georgiana fixed her glare on the unrepentant ten-year-old. "Don't say that again, or I'll tell the teachers. I think she's a sweet little thing."

At recess that morning, the new girl crept shyly out and sat on the back porch steps, watching the rest of the girls play. Lauren Sneed, Frances Edwards, and Elizabeth Cromwell separated from the rest of them and walked over to the new girl. Alice felt the hair on the back of her neck rise.

Lauren smirked down on the new girl. "You have hair like a carrot."

Lady Mary O'Connell looked down and blushed.

"I think she needs to wash her face," said Frances Edwards. "She has freckles all over her cheeks. And, look now, her face is so rosy!"

"Maybe you need to scrub harder," Lauren suggested. "When was the last time you took a bath? Last month, I'll wager. Ireland is a backwards place. All they do is grow potatoes."

They continued to taunt and tease her. They pulled at her hair and dress. Eventually, the little girl began to sob, and they teased her for that.

The other girls kept playing, not even noticing, but Alice became angrier and angrier until she was afraid she'd burst.

"Leave her alone!" Alice shouted, rushing forward and standing between Lady Mary and her three torturers.

"Alice Elton, go back and play." Lauren stepped toward her, shoulders thrown back. "We're just having a little fun. This is none of your business."

"I'm not going to let you make fun of this poor little girl just because she's scared of you. And you know why she's scared of you, Lauren Sneed? Because you are mean!"

"Oh, go on and play." Lauren pushed Alice away from her.

Fury rose in her chest. How dare Lauren Sneed touch her! Furthermore, how dare she tell her to go on and play? She was a big girl, yes, but that didn't mean she could treat people badly. Alice was about ready to fly at the girl when something stopped her.

Be good. Make God's will your first priority.

Alice swallowed. She knew very well that reacting in anger wouldn't do. So she grabbed Mary's hand and marched away, ignoring Lauren's taunts. Underneath an old tree, she turned to her new friend, and they regarded each other quietly.

"Thank you."

"You're welcome, Mary."

"Please ... not Mary." She had a rollicking brogue that Alice found herself liking.

"What do you mean?"

"Call me Cassidy—Cassie, if you like. 'Tis ... *it is* my mother's maiden name, and it became a part of mine—Mary Cassidy O'Connell."

CHAPTER FIFTEEN

Six Months Later
London, England

"I LOVE YOU, AND I want to be with you. Is that so unreasonable?" Tom Jameson's voice echoed off the walls of the empty kitchen, and Claire placed her hand on the doorframe and waited on the stairs to see how her maid would respond.

Nettie's sigh was audible through the door. "No, it's not unreasonable. I just ... you know all the reasons, darling. I've told you all, and it's difficult for me. I'm less sure of my place here than ever, and I need to know my future before—"

"But, Nettie, if I am your future, then can't we just have a go at it? I know you, and I know myself. We're ready for this. You've kept me waiting six months."

Claire was glad he kept his tone tender, or she would have been obligated to march into the kitchen and give her manservant his notice. But, as it was, she held back, waiting for Nettie's reply.

"I'm sorry, Tom. I really am." She heard Nettie shuffle across the room to the stove. "I don't want to rush into things because I'm grieving. You've kept me going without Alice, but ... I'll always be loyal to Claire and Ivy, and if we should have Alice back in our lives for whatever reason, to her, too."

Good, for you mean more than anything to me, Nettie Atwater.

"But surely you're allowed a smidgeon of happiness! If this is from God—and I must believe it is—we shouldn't hesitate. We should dive right in."

Claire had never thought much about Jameson, and she certainly hadn't thought much about Jameson and Nettie. But now she was, and, to her shame, she realized she'd been ignoring the obvious.

Nettie had fallen in love somehow. Claire wanted to say six months was quick, but she was in no position to judge. Five days was incredibly quick, but Claire knew her own heart. At least she thought so.

And Nettie was sure to have considered the pros and cons thoroughly.

Yes, overall, Claire wasn't displeased. Jameson was a nice sort, and it would seem Nettie had entrusted him with her past—and probably Claire's, too—and he was still here. His presence alone made him a better man than some she knew.

The little, bitter stab of jealousy was easily ignored. She stepped back to give Nettie and Jameson time to discuss the matter on their own.

Though, if she were the only impediment, she would gladly give her blessing. Nettie deserved happiness.

Nettie arrived in Claire's room half an hour later, slightly flushed. She made no mention of the conversation with Jameson, but Claire decided it was time to nudge.

"Do you perhaps have something you'd like to discuss tonight, Nettie?"

Nettie moaned. "I knew you'd find out sooner or later." She sank down next to the hearth. "I suppose I knew I'd have to tell you."

"*Have* to tell me?" Claire frowned. "I wouldn't say it's a 'have to,' but if you want to, you're welcome to." After all, she wasn't about to force Nettie to confide in her. That was Nettie's decision. She could *not* confide in her lifelong friend if she chose.

A smile flickered around Nettie's lips. "Of course I'll tell you. I'm in love ..." She hesitated. "Yes, I'll say that. I'm in love with Tom Jameson. He's a good man, who has been pursuing me quietly for years and made his intentions clear of late. He ... he knows everything, Claire, even things about you, which perhaps were not mine to share. But it was a part of the same story."

Claire nodded. She trusted Nettie's discretion completely on that point. "That's fine. Do you ... that is, have you been able to arrive at an understanding?"

Another of those soft smiles. "With your permission, we would be married at the end of this month. I think I've waited long enough, and I'm—Well, when it comes to Tom, I'm ready."

"Good." Claire struggled with her impulses for a moment, then rose, crossed the room, and pulled Nettie into a hug. "I'm glad for you."

Nettie's arms tightened. "Thank you, Claire." There were tears in her voice. "You don't know what this means to me after ... after everything. God has truly blessed me."

Claire released her. "If only God could bless me as He has you." The words were out before she could stop them, petty and selfish as they sounded. Claire didn't mean it like that, but they were out, and she could not call them back.

But Nettie didn't seem offended. "I agree, Claire. But I will continue to pray that God will bless you. The question is, will you seek out His blessings in your day-to-day life and hope for a better future—or will you live with death instead of eternity waiting to greet you?"

Claire swallowed. At this moment, the question seemed more pressing. She knew nothing of what her life on earth would be like. Everything was uncertainty. "I-I don't know."

"If you ever do, let me know. I can walk you through it." Nettie cocked her head. "Claire, I've been praying for you since I could breathe, and I have seen God calling to you again and again. There must come a breaking point where you can no longer resist His love. I suppose I need to be more patient for that moment—I get frustrated with God's pacing, often. But that's just how life is ... waiting and waiting. So I'll wait, and I'll pray."

Claire didn't feel like shushing her maid tonight. She simply met her eyes. "I admit it's been ... well, I can't stop thinking of it lately. But I need more time."

Nettie nodded. The respect written on her face was new, and Claire relished it. Nettie quit the room, leaving Claire alone with her thoughts.

Claire's day could not have been worse. Three of her orders were cancelled without explanation, leaving her with half-finished dresses to try to salvage. She had to return part of the payment, scramble to think of ways to repurpose the fabric, and assure her frightened seamstresses that it wasn't their fault.

Women walked past the shop, elegant in their finery, small groups of them chatting together behind their hands. Their glances through her windows proved their trains of thought.

The gossip that had flagged in September seemed brought back to life, and Claire wasn't sure why. Perhaps one of Mrs. Maston's friends had reignited it. But what mattered most was not *how* but *what* to do next.

Her feet dragged as she left her shop behind, and when she reached her house, she went straight to her room, changed into a leisure dress, and had her dinner on a tray. Nettie sat by the fireplace, chatted about her life-to-be with Jameson, and kept Claire distracted from her own worries.

Thankfully, Alice's tuition was paid for through this year, and after that, she'd manage it somehow—or beg Lois Elton to help.

There were other expenses, but that was the biggest one. Not all her clients had deserted her. Surely there would be enough to support herself, Ivy, and Nettie—and Jameson, it would seem. She couldn't just compel him to leave should they be unable to pay him. Not without losing Nettie.

Whatever happened, Claire must not lose her business. It was all she had left save Ivy, and she wouldn't have Ivy if she couldn't support her.

"But is it worth the risk?" Nettie's voice crashed through her thoughts like a steam engine arriving at its destination.

"Hmm?"

"Claire." Nettie fake-scowled. "I shared my deepest fears, and you're off in dreamland."

"Sorry." Claire hadn't meant to drift off to the degree where she wasn't listening, but she'd focused now. "I know your deepest fears." *Abandonment. Abuse. Losing a child to miscarriage.* All things anyone had a right to be afraid of. "What about them?"

"Never mind. I think it is worth the risk—all the risks." Nettie turned her gaze back to the hearth. "Anything is worth the risk for children."

Claire agreed. Anything, *anything* for her children.

There was a quiet rap at the door. Mrs. Bennett had since gone home, so Claire felt confident to say, "Come in, Jameson."

He opened the door and peeked in. "Pardon me for bothering you at this hour, Miss Berck, but there's a man to see you—Mr. Parker."

Claire hadn't meant for an audible sigh to escape, but it did just the same. "I see. Well, show him to the drawing room, if you haven't already. I'll be down in five minutes."

Jameson departed without another word, and Nettie rose. "Should I come with you? I don't trust that man, Claire."

She shrugged. "I don't, either, but I can handle him. Stay nearby. I'll see what he wants and send him away with as much haste as possible."

Mr. Parker rose when she entered the drawing room, and crossed the room toward her, hat in hand, smiling brilliantly. He stopped when she held out her hand.

"Let's sit, Steven. What is it now?"

He shifted his hat from hand to hand. "You don't seem very happy to see me."

"I'm not. You've caused me more trouble than you know." Claire lowered herself onto a chair and gestured to one opposite her. "Let's hear it."

Mr. Parker faked a pout. "I can see I'm not wanted, and I understand that, but I don't see why you must assume I'm up to something."

"You're always up to something." Claire refrained from folding her arms protectively about herself. "So what is it?"

He sank onto the chair, his posture far too relaxed for a man who again threatened her reputation with this late-night visit. "I simply want to talk. About ... about Alice."

"Alice?" Claire raised her eyebrows. "What of her?"

"I worry for her." He shifted on his chair, and his eyes flickered about the room. "I found out from Lois that she's attending some finishing school to the north."

"Miss Selle's Boarding School for Girls. She can remain there until she's seventeen." Claire swallowed.

Hopefully, some of Alice's holidays would be happily spent at friends' estates. That was what she hoped for—it was how she'd spent many a holiday as a child. Pearlbelle Park, Lois Elton and her family, feeling a thousand times more wanted there than she ever had at home.

She shook off the memories. "I believe it will teach people to think of her as a poor ward of the Eltons, cement their opinion of her good standing, at least as far as legitimacy goes, and make her many good friends. In time, one of them must offer to introduce her to society, and that will secure her future."

"I see." Mr. Parker cocked his head. "That's not going to work for you, but I appreciate your thoughts. Now, let me offer an alternate solution."

Claire blinked. She'd put months into her plan, and now Mr. Parker thought that his outside opinion was going to take its place? No. He'd better mind his own business. "I don't need—"

"Yes, you need my help! I know about your clients. They're dropping like flies! Er, not literally." He winked. "But I know you need money for tuition as well as to support yourself. How will you manage that without orders?"

Claire swallowed. She wasn't sure of that, of course, but somehow it would work out. "That's hardly any of your business."

"I think it is. At least, I want it to be." His dark eyes met hers evenly. "Allow me to help. My offer is this: take Alice out of school, shelter yourself and your children at Pearlbelle for the summer, and let all this gossip die down."

Claire raised her eyebrows. That would never work. "Won't my sudden disappearance only make them gossip more?"

"Only if you don't have a reason … only if it seems like you're fleeing. And I can help you cover that up. I've averted many a scandal in my day."

Claire opened her mouth to ask him to elaborate, then shut it. She didn't want to know. "Very well. I can withdraw Alice for a period of time if I assure the headmistress she'll continue her education. We'll spend perhaps a month at Pearlbelle Park, if the Knights are amiable to the proposition. However, things must return to how they were before. And we must not keep in contact—you'll destroy me." *Everything you touch turns to flames.*

"Well … that'll do for now." He stood. "The Knights are amiable and would love to have Alice and Ivy at Pearlbelle again. You'll be included in the invitation—I can encourage them to send a formal one, if you wish."

Claire nodded. "Yes. Please have them do that." She, too, rose and fixed her eyes steadily on the man before her. "It will just be a month, though, and after that, I can tolerate no changes. I know what I want, and I know how to secure happiness for my own child."

Steven cocked his head. "It wasn't the children I was worrying about so much as you. What of your happiness, Claire?"

She shrugged. "That's hardly important." *At the very least, I'm unwilling to think of it.* She doubted she'd ever be perfectly happy again, though her children might bring her some comfort.

"Hmm." He stepped toward the door. "I believe you to be deserving of happiness, Claire. But I know you don't, so I forgive you your resistance to the idea. Let's all hope for happy endings, now, and see if they don't come."

Claire chuckled. "You were always an optimist."

"A realist. If you keep grasping for contentment, you're sure to find it." He bowed slightly and exited the room.

Grasping for contentment seemed a bad description. Contentment, to Claire, came when one was able to stop grasping. But it was like Steven Parker to put it that way.

And now he's embroiled you in another scheme. Who knows what he has in mind? Claire shuddered at the thought. But a few months away from London would be good for her—and probably for the girls, as well.

Perhaps it wouldn't hurt if Alice came to visit her family from time to time. If they were very careful, at least.

Chapter Sixteen

May 1871

T HOUGH ALICE LOVED HER friend Cassie more than anything, and though she didn't exactly mind learning, she still found Miss Selle's Boarding School for Girls tiresome. Worse yet, this past year she had spent all her holidays there, even Christmas. Really, it was unfair. Other girls came and went with the seasons. Other girls didn't have to live at Miss Selle's all year round. Other girls, Alice dared to think in her poutiest moments, had families who loved them.

Oh, Alice did know that her mother and Nettie both loved her very much. But it was hard to see when they'd practically abandoned her at a boarding school in Norfolk since September. Yes, they'd done it because "she needed a decent education" and "the friends she'd make at Miss Selle's would last a lifetime." Though those things were all very well and good, Alice's fierce loyalty told her something more important—that protecting her family came first. And how could she protect them from Norfolk?

Then a letter came in the mail for Miss Selle informing her that there'd been a change of plans. Alice would be going home for at least a month. The letter was written by Miss Lois Elton, but Alice could read between the lines. She was going home to see Mummy.

Alice packed everything hours before Nettie was supposed to arrive, then lingered about the house, underfoot. A few teachers scolded her half-heartedly, but they probably knew of her excitement and restlessness.

Nettie was on her way! Alice would go home to London. Her mother and sister would be there. Nothing could possibly be better.

"Miss Alice, your nanny is here for you."

Then Alice dashed out the front door, and Nettie hugged her tight—laughing, crying, telling her she was coming home, and stroking her hair because Alice was crying, too.

Jameson was there, too. He helped Alice into the hired carriage and then, much to Alice's shock, hopped in after Nettie.

Nettie caught Alice gawking at him and reprimanded her for staring. Alice found her eyes attracted to Nettie's left hand. She was wearing a ring.

"Nettie!" She blinked as if the ring might disappear, a figment of her imagination, but it didn't. "Are you ... you and Jameson ...?"

Nettie blushed. "Gracie, Jameson and I are engaged—Tuesday last." She glanced at Jameson and smiled. "But we want your permission, of course."

Alice glanced from grown-up to grown-up. *My permission?* She suddenly felt herself gifted with all the power she'd always wanted, and it was tempting to say *no.* "Would you ... would you leave us, Nettie?"

Nettie opened her mouth to reply, but Jameson beat her to it. "Of course not! Leave you, Miss Alice? Neither of us would. We'll stay with you as long as you need us."

Nettie nodded. "Exactly. You've no need to fear losing us, Gracie. Things have changed a bit but not much."

Alice furrowed her brow. "How much is 'a bit'?"

Nettie and Jameson both laughed and glanced at each other. Jealousy oozed its way into Alice's soul. How dare they look at each other like that?

Adults always cast such secretive looks at each other, and Alice hated it, but she'd thought at least Nettie was immune to such tomfoolery.

"Well?" She raised her chin and glared them down. She might not be an adult, and secretive glances would never be her forte, but now she'd lived nine years. That was enough for people to begin taking her seriously.

Nettie couldn't seem to stop smiling, but she did meet Alice's eyes evenly. "Gracie, I know this will be a difficult transition for you, but I love Tom—Jameson—and I love you, too. Nothing really is going to change except that now I will be happier than I have been in a long time. Surely you don't mind that."

Alice hesitated. She did want Nettie to be happy. But at what cost? What if Nettie couldn't love her as much? What if she moved far away? She snuggled against Nettie's side and glared at Jameson. She'd liked him so much before, but he had turned out to be a betrayer of the worst sort.

Nettie kissed the top of her head. "Well, no matter what, I'll always love you, Gracie, and I think Tom feels the same. Don't you, dear?"

Tom Jameson nodded. "I do, Miss Alice."

"See?" Nettie gave her a hug. "Does that set your mind at ease?"

It didn't, but Alice shrugged. "I guess." She wiggled from side to side on the seat. "Would it really make you that happy?"

"It would."

Alice took a deep breath. Could she really give up Nettie? Not all of her, she supposed, but a bit more of her time, a bit more of her love?

Claire barely restrained herself from running out into the alley and collecting Alice in her arms, but she managed to wait until the hired hack had disappeared around the corner and Alice stood in the kitchen to smother

her in love.

"Darling, darling, I'm so glad you're safely home." She pressed kisses all over her face, then drew back. "Look at you! You're inches taller. Did you miss me? Did you learn a great deal? And did you make any friends?"

Alice stuck out her bottom lip. "I can't answer everything at once, Mummy."

Claire laughed. "That's my girl. Tell me you missed me, at least."

Her face crumpled. "Yes." Alice's voice lowered. "I don't understand why I had to go away when I love you so. Don't you know you need me here?"

Claire squeezed her hand. "I do know. But you did learn lots of wonderful things, didn't you? And you did make friends?"

Alice glanced away. "I suppose I did. But—"

"Shush." Claire tapped Alice's lips. "I know what's best. But you'll be here for a few days, and then ... guess where we're going?" She rose from her knees and smiled. This would be a treat for Alice.

"Where?"

"Pearlbelle Park!"

The smile started small but soon spread like wildfire across Alice's face. "Really?"

"Would I lie to you?"

Claire laughed as Alice began hopping up and down.

"When do we leave?" Alice asked. "Will Mrs. Knight still be there? How big will Ned be after a year? Will they have all the same stable boys? Can I have a puppy this time—Mr. Knight said ..." And on and on.

Claire did her best to answer the questions, but Alice was not easily satisfied. Still, she'd made her daughter happy. The trip would be torture, but Alice wanted it. And a reprieve from London, perhaps, was worth it.

Alice leapt out of the carriage and landed in Mr. Parker's arms.

He laughed and swung her up in the air. "My, how you've grown!" He set her down and stepped back. "You're a good two inches taller, I think."

Alice beamed. Her height definitely pleased her, and she was glad he'd noticed. "You've gotten shorter."

He laughed deep in his belly before turning to greet her mother and Ivy. Alice ran forward into Mrs. Knight's arms.

"Look at you! So grown-up." Mrs. Knight leaned back and cupped Alice's face with her hands. "I missed you, sweetheart. Now, let's get you up to your room and settled in. Oh, and here is sweet little Ivy—and Miss Chattoway! Oh, it's been a while, hasn't it?"

Mummy stepped forward. Even Alice could tell her smile was pasted on. "It has, Mrs. Knight. Thank you for your generosity in allowing us to visit Pearlbelle Park."

"Of course!" Mrs. Knight gestured toward the house. "Alice and Ivy will have the same room as their previous visit, and your chamber will be near theirs, unless you prefer—"

"No, that will do well, thank you." Mummy placed her hands on Alice's shoulders. "We would love to get settled, if you don't mind."

"Oh, yes." Mrs. Knight turned toward the door, nearly jostling into her husband. "There you are, Phil. Is everything arranged for our guests' rooms?"

"It is." Mr. Knight stepped forward slightly. "Alice, Ivy, Miss Chattoway. It's lovely to have you here."

"The pleasure is mine." Mummy forced the words out, though. Alice sighed. Couldn't everyone just live life without a lot of worrying?

After Nettie unpacked Alice and Ivy's clothes and saw that they were presentable, they scurried over to Mummy's room.

"There you are, darlings." She kissed them both in turn. Her eyes were a bit teary.

Alice frowned. "Are you all right, Mummy?"

"Yes, I am."

But Alice didn't believe her for a moment. Her face showed too much sadness for "all right." The only thing Alice could do about that was try to help make her happy again, so she gave her a big hug.

"Thank you, Alice." Mummy squeezed her shoulder, then stepped back. "Now, Mrs. Knight asked us to come to her private chambers to play with Ned for a bit. Won't that be fun?"

Alice and Ivy both nodded. Ned was a dear fellow, and Alice had missed him. She'd always wanted a baby in the house, and he was such a cuddly one.

Mrs. Knight was sitting in a chair near the window, watching little Ned playing on the floor with some blocks. In one hand, she held a book, which she laid aside as Mummy, Ivy, and Alice entered.

"Oh, hello there! You're just in time. Young ladies, I think Ned needs help buildin' that tower, though all he really wants to do is knock it over." She rose and gestured to the chair. "Miss Chattoway, you could sit with me, if you'd like."

Alice hurried over to play with Ned, but she kept one ear tuned to the adults' conversation. One never knew what could be gleaned when you weren't supposed to be listening.

"Did you find your rooms all right?" Mrs. Knight asked.

"They're perfect." Mummy perched on the edge of her chair. "There's a lovely view of the gardens from my window."

"Oh, good! I thought you might like that room. It's so light. I love light—can't stand the darkness."

Mummy smiled slightly. "Darkness is dreary."

The adults didn't speak for a minute. Ned collapsed the tower Alice and Ivy had created, and they scurried to pick up the blocks and begin again.

"Ned can almost walk," Mrs. Knight said. "I'm so proud of him. He's a dear boy, and Phil and I are very blessed with him."

"Yes." As Mummy spoke, Alice felt her mother's eyes on her and quickly focused in on the blocks. "Children are always a blessing."

"No matter the circumstances." Mrs. Knight's voice was firm. A silence, and she forced the next words out. "Miss Chattoway, I've been wanting to ask you a few questions that are, actually, extremely personal. I know I have no right to ask, but could you tell me … what I mean is … well, really, I wanted to ask …"

"About Alice and Ivy's father, I presume?" Mummy sighed.

Alice went stiff. She mustn't let Mummy know she was listening. She had to focus on the blocks, on Ned.

Mrs. Knight nodded and lowered her voice, but not enough. "Alice told me last year that she … she was worried about you and the circumstances surrounding her conception." She blushed bright pink and dropped her eyes.

"She feels that something is amiss in her life, yes," Claire confirmed. "She is aware that everyone has a father, yet she has never so much as heard his name. I'm not comfortable telling you who he is, but I will tell you some of the details about our brief marriage, if you would like to hear them."

"I would." Mrs. Knight said the words quickly and a bit overloud.

Ned knocked over another tower, and Alice pretended not to be distracted by the adults' conversation.

"I don't know exactly how to begin."

Alice's ears strained to hear her mother's low words.

"Simply enough, I met and fell for him when I was seventeen years old. He said he cared for me, so I agreed to elope with him to France—a little town on the coast. My alias, Berck, is the name of the town, you see. A week afterward, my father found us and dragged me away from him. I found out later I was with child. That's all there was to it."

The silence that followed stretched on forever. Alice tried not to cry, but it was very hard. Her throat was tight, her eyes were watering, and she knew her mother didn't want her to know what she'd just heard.

How convenient it was to be a child—and yet sometimes the things one heard were so frightening. She swallowed again and again, trying to keep the lumps down.

Below the confusion and the pain was a sense of relief ... that she knew the story and that her father hadn't abandoned her, not exactly. They'd been separated, like in some novel Nettie would read. But he hadn't just left.

Thank you, God. I didn't want him to just leave.

Mrs. Knight dabbed at her eyes. "He didn't come for you?"

"No, he didn't." Mummy's voice was quick and measured.

"Why not keep up hope? Perhaps he'll come still. He could be delayed; he might not know where you are." Mrs. Knight cocked her head. "Give me his name, and I'll help you find him. That would give you closure at least."

"No, I'm certain that the best way is to try to forget. Over time, the hurting will stop. Life isn't all depression." Mummy's eyes again flickered over to Alice and Ivy. "I, too, have been blessed."

"Yes, Alice and Ivy must be great comforts to you. Nevertheless, it must be difficult," Mrs. Knight murmured. "If there is anything Phil and I can do for you, we would be happy to."

"I'll tell you if there is anything." Mummy stood. "Speaking of the girls, I must see Alice and Ivy to their tea. It's near time, and they must be hungry."

On cue, Alice stood and dragged Ivy to her feet.

"God bless you and keep you," Mrs. Knight said. She looked like Alice felt—emotional, still a bit confused, and wanting to comfort Mummy.

Mummy sighed. "He does. I believe that there have been times of late when He is the only Thing keeping me on my feet."

Alice refrained from asking about that. She prayed for Mummy all the time, but she wasn't sure she was a Christian. It was all very confusing how Mummy could seem to understand a bit about God and yet miss so much about His love and grace.

"I'm glad. He's always gotten me safely through my trials." Mrs. Knight rose to walk them to the door but paused when Mummy didn't move.

Mummy raised her eyebrows a notch. "Your trials?"

"Yes." Mrs. Knight smiled, but it trembled. "Wars are always horrible, but when they're fought between countrymen, they're despicable. I lost a lot more than I believed was possible. Thankfully, Phil was there when I needed him."

"I see." Mummy pressed her lips together. "I'm sorry."

"Don't be. It's all in the past, and nothing can ever change it. We have only the present to work with, the future to hope for. No use lingering on the past."

Mummy cocked her head. "Yes. You're right," she said softly. "No use lingering in the past."

Chapter Seventeen

"K IRK?" ALICE PEEKED AROUND the corner of the horse stall.

Her friend jumped a foot in the air, startling Jupiter, a big bay gelding. After the horse calmed down, Kirk turned to her with a scowl.

"Will you stop sneaking up on me?"

"Sorry. You knew I was here." She folded her arms across her chest. "Anyway, I didn't know Jupiter was so jumpy."

He glared at her for another moment, then picked up a brush. "I could've been stepped on or something."

"Well, I'm sorry. You didn't say hello or anything." Alice expected more of a welcome after nearly a year apart from her first real friend. "Did you miss me?"

Kirk coughed. "No."

What? Of course he had. Alice placed her hands on her hips. "What do you mean?"

He just rolled his eyes and went back to brushing the horse.

"I didn't miss you, either." She upended a bucket and sat on it. "How've you been?"

"All right, I suppose. You?"

"I had to go to boarding school, which I hated, except the friends I made." She paused. "I made lots of friends."

He hesitated. "Girl friends?"

"Yes."

"Oh. Who cares about a lot of giggly girls?"

"They're not giggly!" Alice jumped to her feet. "They were very nice girls."

"Even very nice girls are giggly." Kirk turned to the door. "I'm done here. Let's move on to the next stall."

Alice stepped aside as he moved past her, then stamped her foot to get his attention. "You don't know that."

"Hmph." He glanced over his shoulder. "Say, do you know everything people are saying about you?"

Alice blinked, her anger disappearing and confusion taking its place. "What do you mean?" People were talking about her again? Of course she'd heard whispers between her mother and Nettie about how people liked to talk—but about her? And why?

Kirk shrugged. "At first us servants weren't sure what to think of you, but now that you're here a second year, we wonder." He blushed. "I wouldn't gossip about you, Alice. But others are, and I think you should know."

Her hands felt cold and clammy. "Wh-what are they gossiping about?"

Kirk cocked his head and stared at her. "I want you to know, all right, because you're my friend. Mum says rumors and gossip are just as bad as bullets sometimes—I mean, they hurt people the same way. And you should know."

Heart racing, Alice nodded. "All right."

"They say you're maybe not anyone's child. I mean, you don't have a father. And that makes you ... well, you know. Then your mother is not a lady."

"But she is a lady." Of course she was. How dare anyone say otherwise? "She's the most perfect lady who ever existed."

"I know that." Kirk held up his hands. "It's just other people who say it. I don't believe it, and neither does Mum, all right?"

"A-all right." Alice took a deep breath. "Go on. What else?"

"Just that. They say perhaps ... perhaps Miss Chattoway ran off with a servant here at Pearlbelle nine years ago. The staff changed a lot back then—Mr. Elton was mighty temperamental. Or you're Mr. Parker's child. And they say terrible things about Nettie." Kirk shrugged. "You don't need to hear. I think they're just jealous. And of you, too, and Miss Chattoway."

Alice swallowed the lump in her throat. "I suppose so. Wh-what do people think happened? Do you know who my father is, Kirk? Or does your mother?"

Kirk shook his head. "Mum didn't say if she does know, and anyway, she never knew much of what was happening at Pearlbelle Park back then. And I was too small. But people say that Miss Chattoway ran off with someone and then he left."

"I heard her say that. My grandfather separated them, and my father didn't ... he didn't come back." Alice wrapped her arms around herself. "Why didn't he come back? Why wouldn't he love me?"

"Maybe he didn't know." Kirk rubbed the back of his neck. "Or maybe he was just a bad person. Mum says our parents don't reflect on who we are. Though, of course, my parents aren't bad at all."

Alice nodded. "My mummy isn't bad. Nettie says God is my heavenly Father and that's all that matters, but I would like my father to be nice. I guess maybe that's not possible."

Kirk shrugged. "It wouldn't be your fault." He stepped into the next stall and began grooming the horse within. "I need to get him tacked up. Mr. Parker's going for an afternoon ride, and it's nearly time."

"Oh!" Alice started. "I'd better get changed. I'm going with him." She started to run off, but Kirk called her back.

"Don't worry about what people say, all right?" He opened and closed his hands and shuffled his feet. "I-I don't think it's good to fuss. You're a good person. You know, for a girl."

Alice smiled. "Right. For a girl."

"Don't put pressure on the bit; you don't want to ruin her mouth."

Alice loosened her grip on the reins and patted Sugarplum's neck. A slight shift forward was all she needed to set the pony in motion; she barely needed to move to guide her left and right. Still, it seemed foolish to trust the horse to obey such subtle commands.

"That's it." Mr. Parker smiled down at her. "Sugarplum is sensitive. You don't have to yank her about."

Alice sighed. Maybe being a great equestrian still sat beyond her reach after all. There seemed to be so much to learn.

The Pearlbelle Park grounds stretched out below them. Everything looked and smelled green and fresh. Alice took big gulps of the cool air.

Mr. Parker smiled. "Do you like it out here, Alice? At Pearlbelle?"

"I do." Everything about the place appealed to her. Nettie said wealth often corrupted, but Alice didn't think the grandeur of Pearlbelle Park was really wicked. The servants seemed to be fairly treated, and the tenants' homes didn't look like anything one might see in a Dickens novel.

"Pearlbelle has been my home for so long." Mr. Parker's dark eyes were distant. "Strange how inheritance works. The estate was never entailed, so Uncle John was able to simply give it to his more worthy nephew." He glanced sideways at Alice. "And now Ned will receive all the benefits of the firstborn. Though, you're not a boy, so I suppose it makes little difference."

Alice blinked. "If I were a boy, what difference would it make?"

He cleared his throat. "Let's head back to the stables." A slight movement sent his horse trotting down the hill.

Hmm? Before Alice hadn't been too curious, but now she wondered. What did Ned and she have in common? Unless …

"Mr. Parker." Alice kept her voice as firm as possible. When he didn't turn, she urged Sugarplum to follow him.

He slowed North Star to a walk at the bottom of the hill, and Alice drew up alongside him. Her chest was tight; her breath came in shallow pants. Questions swirled about her brain, and she struggled to articulate them.

"Mr. Parker." She forced her hands to hold the reins gently. "Mr. Parker, is Mr. Knight my father? Is that why, if I were a boy, I should have ... should have received the benefits of the firstborn?"

Mr. Parker leaned back in his saddle, and his horse slowed on cue. "Alice, you're asking me more than I ought to tell you. I said too much."

"But am I?" Her eyes blurred with tears, but she watched him steadily. "Is Mr. Knight my father?"

"Alice ... to the best of my knowledge, yes."

Sugarplum wasn't exactly capable of a full gallop. Her fastest gait was a somewhat-hurried trot. But Alice made her keep to that pace all the way to the stables. She left the pony with a groomsman and ran all the way into the house.

Hasty searching and a few questions of bemused servants led her to her mother. She sat at a desk in the library, penning a letter. Alice watched for a minute, her stomach a well-kneaded lump of bread dough.

At last, her mother put down her pen and glanced over her shoulder. "Alice?" Mummy's eyes flickered over her face, and she held out her hands. "Come here. What's wrong?"

Alice dashed across the room and into her arms. "Mummy, I ... Mr. Parker said ... Mummy, I'm so scared ... I don't know ... if he ... was telling ... the truth." And if it was the truth, what did that mean?

Papas shouldn't be married to anyone but one's mummy. Alice was sure of that. And furthermore, one's brothers shouldn't have their own mummy. How could this have happened? Why weren't they all a family? It was impossible to have more than one family.

Yet, Alice's Papa seemed to have two. And he had abandoned the first one.

"Shush, shush ..." Mummy rubbed slow circles on Alice's back. "It's all right. You're all right. Shush, darling. Breathe, then tell me all about it." Her voice was soft and soothing, and Alice wanted to make believe that everything *was* all right.

But it didn't *feel* all right, and the truth had done nothing but make her nauseous. It was an ugly truth, not the imaginary one of a Prince Charming on his white steed coming to rescue them.

This Prince Charming had another princess. This Prince Charming had another life. In fact, Alice wasn't sure he was a prince at all. A prince didn't abandon his princess.

"Mummy, Mr. Parker said that Mr. Knight is my father. But how can that be? Mummy, Mr. Knight already has a princess and a baby, and ... and we can't have him, too, can we?"

Mummy went stiff. "When did he say that to you?"

"J-just now." Alice drew back and searched her mother's face. "It's not true ... is it?"

Mummy's eyes met hers. They were glazed, like the ripples in glass visible only when sunlight hit them at an angle. "Alice, let's go to your room with Ivy and Nettie. We need to talk." She rose and walked toward the door.

Alice didn't want to talk. She wanted comfort. But Mummy's quick, jerky motions—so confident—did offer a bit of reassurance, and she ran after her.

In the nursery, Mummy took a seat on a chair by the fireplace and drew Ivy onto her lap. The room's cheerful atmosphere seemed dim now. Alice snuggled against Nettie's side and was drawn down on her lap like a child. But for once, she didn't mind.

"I've decided it's time to tell Alice and Ivy about their father."

Every muscle in Nettie's body tensed. Alice reached up and twisted her fingers through the maid's brown hair, mussing it from its perfect bun.

The childish gesture brought a small amount of comfort to Alice, and Nettie slowly allowed herself to relax.

"Are you sure?"

"I'm very sure. Mr. Parker decided to tell Alice the truth—"

Again Nettie stiffened. "What truth?"

Mummy's eyes were hard. "The only truth there is. That Mr. Knight is her father."

Nettie didn't reply.

"Ivy, do you understand, darling?"

Ivy blinked. "I don't need a father. I have you and Nettie and Jameson and Mrs. Bennett. And Uncle Charlie, too, sometimes."

Mummy sighed. "Nevertheless, you have a father, and it's best for you to know who he is. After this, we'll have to leave Pearlbelle—"

Alice gasped. "But, Mummy!"

"Alice." Her firm voice allowed for no arguments. "We will have to leave Pearlbelle. I doubt we'll see Mr. Knight again, or anyone here. It simply must be that way now that you know. I don't know what we're going to do yet; however, leaving Pearlbelle is the only natural step."

Alice swallowed. *How horrible.* Why did knowing who her father was come at such an expense? It wasn't fair. *Especially since it's Mr. Knight.*

"I-I don't want to leave." She stood and glared at her mother. "I shouldn't have to. We were supposed to be here a month. I have friends here, and a pony, and I can be outside. Why do we have to leave?"

Mummy sighed. "Alice, don't make this difficult. You were all questions for so long, and now that I'm willing to answer some of them, you're distracted. Listen. Your father is Mr. Knight. He owns Pearlbelle Park. He is married. Now that you know, there's too much at risk. We couldn't possibly stay."

But how could they leave? Alice needed to talk to Mr. Knight. Maybe she'd be able to convince him to mend his evil ways. But how could he? Mrs. Knight needed him, too, and little Ned.

Pearlbelle Park needed him, for that matter.

But now we need him, too. Or we always did, and I just didn't know it.

The unfairness leeched into Alice's heart, and she lowered herself back on Nettie's lap. "I don't like this at all." Unbidden, tears welled, and she let them fall on Nettie's shoulder. "I don't like this. I want ... I want to go home."

Good-bye to Pearlbelle Park. Good-bye to Mr. Knight and his villainy. Good-bye to Sugarplum and Kirk and Mr. Parker.

"Shh, Gracie." Nettie kissed her cheek. "It's going to be all right. Your mummy and I will take care of you. And perhaps Uncle Charlie will have to help some if gossip gets out, but maybe it won't. God still loves us, remember?"

Alice shook her head. She didn't know anything now.

"Perhaps we can talk about it later." Alice heard rather than saw Mummy set Ivy aside and rise. "For now, I'll begin packing. Nettie, you're welcome to ... to sit for a time."

Nettie nodded, her head close to Alice's. "I will. Ivy, come sit with me. We'll have a story—"

"I don't want a story." Alice sobbed.

"Shush, now. No need to talk back." Nettie stroked her hair. "You'll be all right, Miss Grace. God has us in His hands."

Chapter Eighteen

"Mr. Knight, if I might have a word ...?"

He turned and blinked at her like a man just woken from a long sleep. "Miss Chattoway? I ... I suppose so." There was guilt in his eyes. She didn't know how it wasn't visible to everyone who looked at him, much less his wife, who she believed knew nothing of her husband's past.

"Would your study do?" She gestured to the room he'd hurried toward right after lunch. Perhaps, between Alice's tearful face and Mr. Parker's nervousness, he'd guessed what she wished to talk with him about.

It was all out now, more or less. Admitting it to her child made Claire feel exposed, and now, for the first time, she must discuss it with him.

With Phil. He was supposed to be her Phil, but he belonged to someone else. She swallowed down the bile in her throat and followed him into his office.

"Will you take a seat?" He gestured to the chair across from his at the desk. "How may I help you?"

She lowered herself onto the chair and placed her hands palm down on the arms. A grand chair, a grand study, a grand house. *Mine. This is all supposed to be mine.*

But it wasn't. It wouldn't be. It couldn't be.

"I've told my children the truth. About you. You're ... you're their father." She forced the words out through the lump in her throat, despite the dryness of her mouth. "Steven told Alice enough that I had to confirm it. We'll be leaving within the hour. But I thought you should know that they know the ... the truth."

Most of the truth. No child could ever fully comprehend the details. Claire didn't understand exactly what had happened, either. Something terrible to change her lover into the man who sat before her.

Weak. Unwilling to admit his own guilt.

His face twisted as if in pain—pain he deserved but which she seemed to have suffered the lion's share of.

He's my husband

It's been annulled. He's wed to another.

I love him.

You mustn't. It's wrong.

Why hasn't he suffered as I have?

Because he's a man. They don't have to suffer if they don't want to.

Frustrated with her own thoughts, she clasped her hands in her lap. Another moment. She'd give the wretch another moment to explain himself. Then she'd be gone.

But I need to see him again.

You hate him.

I can't.

You must.

It wasn't fair, but it was true.

His eyes remained glued to a distant point above her head as he answered. "I see."

Claire swallowed. That was it? After nearly a decade of waiting, after her patience, after her heartbreak, after her steady belief in his fidelity in the face of undeniable doubts?

"I was faithful." She whispered the words, afraid to utter them but not daring to remain silent. "I waited. I thought you'd come. All these years, I thought you'd come." She stood, and her voice raised to a fever pitch. "How dare you? How dare you abandon me after all your promises, after standing before God and man and marrying me?" She pounded her fist on the desk. "How dare you!"

Philip was on his feet then, but he leaned back, as if a bit afraid of her. "Keep your voice down," he hissed. "Do you want the servants—"

"I don't care if they hear! They should know what you are. You didn't come. I can't blame you for the annulment, as I know that was all my father's doing. But I can blame you for abandoning me for nine years with no word before returning with an American bride on your arm. How dare you show your face in England after what you've done."

He cleared his throat, played with his cravat. "Claire—"

"Don't address me so familiarly."

"Miss Chattoway, I apologize if my behavior to you seems—"

"*Seems.*"

"If it is reprehensible, I am sorry." He placed his hands on the desk and leaned forward. "I did wait six years, but after that, it seemed expedient to marry. I know I have duties to this land, and I couldn't stay away. I can't imagine what you mean by 'abandoning' you as you were the one who called things off, but—"

"Me, call things off?" She stared at him, mouth partially open, then snapped it shut. "I never said or did anything ..."

"The letters." He folded his hands across his chest and glowered at her, like she were the villain. "The letters. I presume you sent them before you knew about the children, but nonetheless, you did send them—"

"You received letters." She fell back onto the chair. "What do you think I said to you?"

"Well, not you, directly. Your mother, of course, but by your command. You must remember, surely. You didn't want to see me again; you thought it would be best if we forgot about the whole unfortunate incident." He took his seat. "If I had known about the children, I would have come, of course. I suppose you had difficulty contacting me once you knew you were with child—but you must see I had to get away. I didn't think I had a chance in society after ..."

Claire dropped her eyes to her lap and tried to breathe. Her thoughts swirled helplessly about her brain, harried birds seeking a perch and finding none. "I never wrote you such a letter or asked anyone else to." Her own voice sounded thick as pudding. "I never would have. I was in love with you and remained so for much of your absence. And I wanted you to return to me until I learned you had remarried."

Philip didn't reply. The silence in the room stretched on interminably, and at last, she rose.

"I'm returning to London. I'm not sure what my next action will be, but you can rest assured I will be provided for. My brother already offers me some support, and I have friends. I think it's best if we cut ties."

"I trusted your mother." He sounded so defeated, and she couldn't look at him. "I thought you said she was a good woman."

She wrapped her arms around herself, but nothing was going to make this easier. "Yes, she is. A good woman completely under the control of my father."

"I see." She heard him stand. "I think, finally, I do see. Is there anything I can do? My hands are tied, but if there is anything—"

"There is nothing. Not at present." Claire wouldn't close the door. She'd leave a crack in case of emergency. But, for the most part, she needed separation and time to think.

Yes, he should have come to her anyway. Any sane man could see through her parents' lies. But he'd taken the easy way out. That was like him.

But, if he was sincere, it made a difference.

She turned to leave, then paused. "Will you tell your wife? She seems a sweet woman and undeserving of the lies."

"I only want to spare her the painful truth." He shuffled behind her, probably ill at ease with the idea of confessing all to the current Mrs. Knight. "It's not easy."

"Nothing's easy. Please—promise me you'll be honest."

Another silence. "I will."

"Thank you." She quit the room and rushed up the stairs to finish packing.

London

Nettie's gray eyes met hers evenly. "You're sure that's what he said?"

"I'm sure! If only I'd known. I'd have … have done something. Found a way to contact him sooner." Yet, Claire knew such a thing would have been impossible. For nine months, she'd been a prisoner in her father's house, barely allowed to leave her room. Contacting the man who had been her husband for one short week was impossible. Both Nettie and she, as well as any servants who might have aided them, had been helpless.

"Mm." Nettie shifted from her seat next to the fire. "Well, at any rate, it's over. The girls know. We're finding a way to get on with our lives. God willing, your business is secure. All that matters now is doing our best with the situation we've been given."

Claire sighed and leaned back against her pillow. She stared at the ceiling above her. There was a crack running diagonally that she'd never wanted to get fixed, and it wasn't in the budget now. "The poor girls. They'll never know a father."

"Jameson is a father figure in their life anyway."

"It's not the same." Claire bit the inside of her left cheek. "Alice doesn't care for him, I don't think. Well, she likes him, but she's mistrustful since he stole you away."

Nettie chuckled. "I'm still here. I suppose it's like having a stepfather to her. It feels strange. I don't believe any child really wants their parent to remarry."

"Well, she can rest easy. I never will." Claire followed the ceiling crack's path all the way to the opposite wall with her eyes. She really ought to get it repaired. Though, how did one repair cracks in ceilings? She wasn't sure.

"I don't think Alice is missing much. Surely, in hindsight, some flaws in

Mr. Knight's character have become apparent," Nettie murmured.

"'Some' is a gentle word." Claire smiled at the ceiling. "But that doesn't mean he would be a horrible father. Surely there are some good things about him."

"'Some' is a gentle word in that case, too, Claire. He might be a cheerful, pleasant father, but beyond that? Do you really want him involved with the girls? Alice is especially impressionable, I think."

Alice, impressionable? Claire supposed she was. Philip probably wasn't the best influence. She didn't feel that she knew him anymore. But of course, it didn't matter if she knew him or not as he would never be a part of Alice's and Ivy's lives.

"You're right, of course." She picked at the coverlet, working a thread loose with her fingertips. "I'm just shaken."

"I know. I can understand that. Life is undependable. But God isn't. I wish you could see that." Like a broken clock stuck on the same time for eternity, Nettie circled back to her favorite subject with the ease of someone who never truly left it. "There is such comfort in Him."

"Perhaps."

Before Nettie could reply, there was a rap at the door.

Saved by random coincidence. "Who is it?"

"Jameson, Miss Berck."

Claire sat up and drew her dressing gown's sash tighter about her waist. "Come in."

The door opened, and Jameson peeked in. "There's a message for you, miss. The man is in the hall waiting; he's ridden hard."

Her pulse spiked. "Where is he from?"

"He didn't say. Only that it was urgent."

Nettie took the letter from Jameson and delivered it to Claire's hand. She fingered the paper. No return address. Nothing about the exterior that might betray its contents. Her name—Miss Claire Marie Chattoway—was written on the back in a hand that seemed vaguely familiar. Not familiar enough to identify the sender, though.

She broke the plain, unadorned seal and began to read.

Starboard Hall

July 22, 1871

Dear Claire,

I doubt you expected to hear from me any time soon, and, honestly, I am very sorry for the fact. Lately, things have been a bit clearer, and I wish I'd tried to contact you sooner. But, frankly, it was impossible for so many reasons.

Charlie gave me your address. He is here, and your sister will be soon, with her husband and baby. I had no idea that you had kept in contact, much less that he'd offered any monetary support to you, so it was a surprise, but I'm glad.

I know he wasn't able to do much more than a tiny stipend from his allowance, and I know his father had forbidden both him and Christina from visiting you. I'm proud of him. He did what I should have.

I suppose I'll tell it to you quickly—your father has died. He passed in his sleep a week ago. I don't think you could come to Yorkshire in time for the funeral. However, I want you to come as soon as possible.

Claire, I'm your mother. I know I've done a poor job at it for many years, but you must understand that things have been difficult for me. Still, that is no excuse for my behavior. I know I played a huge part in the ruination of what could have been a happy life for you. Your father convinced me it was the only way, and I never could speak against him.

But, in hindsight, I admit my error, and I ask your forgiveness. I doubt I can receive it, but at least come to Starboard. Bring the children—Alice and Ivy, isn't it? And, of course, Nettie. This is your home; please don't feel that you must stay away now that your father is gone.

I will do what I can to make this a livable atmosphere for you. Charlie will be here from now on, I think, and when he marries, he'll bring his bride. But it will just be us and the servants until then.

I think it's a safer atmosphere than London. We don't have any visitors; your father had become a hermit in recent years, and I never was good with people.

I can't imagine a city to be a good place for children to grow up, and

Charlie tells me you've been dealing with some unsavory rumors of late. Even the truth would be so horrific to anyone in London. Here, people are kinder, and you are welcome to be a widow, if that makes it easier.

In summary, I'll await your reply, your return, or your silence. I accept whatever you decide as a fair response. No more manipulation. That's over now.

I'll pray that you may find it in your heart to forgive me, but if that's not possible, I at least will wish you the best in all your endeavors.

Sincerely,
Nora Chattoway

Claire set the letter facedown on the bed and dropped back against her pillow to stare at the crack in the ceiling again. *Father dead? Mother repentant and wanting me back at Starboard Hall?* Her thoughts threatened to give her a headache.

"What is it, Claire?"

"Read it—I don't mind."

There was a rustling as Nettie took up the papers and began to read them. "What will you do?"

Trembling, she wrapped her arms around herself and closed her eyes. Everything had changed now. "I'm not sure."

CHAPTER NINETEEN

Yorkshire, England
August 1871

T HEY ARRIVED AT STARBOARD Hall, a large castle perched like a gargoyle on the top of a hill, late at night a week later. Alice didn't get a good look at the place until they stepped out of the carriage. The clouds coating the sky, the rain pouring down without cessation, and the darkness punctuated by a glow coming from a few of the windows gave it the look of a mansion from a gothic novel.

The inside didn't have a cheerful effect on one's soul, either. It was dark and shadowy. Ivy shivered and hid her face in her mother's skirts, and Alice wished she could do the same. Instead, she grasped Nettie's hand, but she drew away to direct the servants on their luggage.

"Come this way, please," the butler said in a low, creaking voice, and the little group followed him through a gloomy hallway and up a creaking flight of stairs.

"The place has really fallen apart." Mummy ran her hand along the banister then displayed her glove, now coated in gray. "Have they dismissed a great many servants, Emerson?"

"Yes, miss." The man glanced over his shoulder. "But Master Charles—Mr. Chattoway—hopes to hire a new staff."

"I see." Mummy looked perplexed. "How strange."

"Mr. Charles Chattoway and Mrs. Chattoway are waiting in Mrs. Chattoway's private room." Emerson gestured to a door with soft light emerging from underneath.

Nettie squeezed Alice's shoulder. "It will be good to get warm again. What an odd summer storm this is!"

"Indeed." Mummy's face blanched as Emerson opened the door.

The four entered the room. An old woman sat on a chair by a roaring fire. She had hair which must once have been blonde and great brown eyes. Uncle Charlie stood to her right. He'd grown a beard—which Alice thought looked ridiculous—since she had last seen him.

"Hello." Grandmother Chattoway stood. "I was afraid you wouldn't come. I can't tell you how glad I am to see you ... all of you."

Mummy's eyes were wide. "I-I suppose I am to have my old room, Mother?"

"Why, yes." Alice's grandmother blinked and shuffled forward, then stopped. Alice thought she looked like a half-awake kitten. "Yes, and your daughters can have the room across from yours. That will leave Charlie his room, and Christy hers when she comes with her family. She has a child now."

"You mentioned it in your letter—a boy?"

"Yes. They've named him Benedict. I've met him once. He's a sweet child." Grandmother twisted her hands together. "Well, anyway. It's late. I suppose I shouldn't keep you."

Mummy's expression softened slightly. "Thank you. We'll talk in the morning. Alice, Ivy, say good night to your grandmother."

"Good night," Alice whispered, and Ivy echoed her.

After leaving the room, they walked down more twisty passages to the wing opposite. There they were led into another room, the fire already lit and a lamp burning on the table.

In the flickering firelight, Alice made out a large bed with blue curtains surrounding it. The covers of the bed were turned back and the curtains half let down.

"Girls, come here by the fire; you must be cold after walking through those halls." Mummy removed their wraps and draped them over the end of the bed. "Nettie will be up soon, and we'll have some warm milk before bed. Look, there's water here—let's wash our faces."

Emerson and a second manservant arrived, carrying the first trunk between them. Jameson wasn't far behind them with the remainder of their luggage, and Nettie arrived from the kitchen. In no time at all, Alice and Ivy were washed, nightgowned, and tucked into a big bed across the hall.

"There now." Mummy sat on the edge of the bed. "I'll see you both in the morning, but for now, let's all get a good night's rest."

"Is Grandmother nice, Mummy?" Ivy whispered.

"Of course, darling." Mummy smiled and smoothed Ivy's hair back from her face. "I wouldn't have brought you here otherwise."

Alice frowned. "It doesn't seem like a nice place, though." The whole house was covered in gloom and dust, neither of which she much cared for. Besides, hadn't her grandmother played a part in separating her parents? Though it probably wasn't all her fault, Alice couldn't help blaming her for it. At least in part.

"It isn't, but soon it will be. Sunlight makes everything look better, and your Uncle Charlie will hire a brand-new staff. They'll make everything clean and cheery." Mummy reached over the coverlet and squeezed Alice's hand. "Don't worry, darling. We might not stay long. I wanted to see your grandmother and Starboard Hall again. I would rather live in the country, I think, or at least not in London. But we'll see."

"Oh, all right." Alice supposed she could allow for that. "Will Nettie come in and pray?"

"She will indeed—and bring some milk for you. But I'll turn down the lamp for now." Mummy rose and adjusted the light. "Sleep well, darlings."

Breakfast the next morning promised to be awkward, but Claire arrived downstairs early, Alice and Ivy blinking and yawning behind her. Charlie was there with his newspaper and tea. He already had sunk into the role of master of the house—though, of course, he could never be cruel, and he wasn't much of an eccentric, either. He'd never be like their father in those regards.

Mrs. Chattoway also came down for breakfast, an event which surprised Claire. She was used to her mother's taking the first meal of her day in her room, seldom appearing before ten. Though her father had always called it 'laziness' or 'elegance,' Claire believed it was an attempt to have a few minutes to herself. Mr. Chattoway seldom let his wife out of his sight.

"After breakfast, perhaps we could talk?" Mrs. Chattoway met Claire's eyes. "I think we ought to discuss future plans."

"Of course." Hopefully they'd be able to arrive at an agreement—although, that would depend on her mother. "Charlie, why don't you take the girls on a tour while we chat?"

Her brother blinked. "Why?"

"Because they've not seen Starboard before, and I believe they would like to." She glared at him. "Don't be difficult."

He harrumphed and hid behind his newspaper, but Claire knew he would do as she'd asked. Charlie wasn't overly familiar with children, but the girls always loved him when he visited. It wasn't often, but his attention was always welcome—and his gifts even more so.

When they finished eating, Claire stood and followed her mother out of the room. She led the way to a chamber Claire was only vaguely familiar with—her father's office.

It wasn't such a horrifying room when the thick curtains were thrown back and the windows open to the garden. However, the scents of tobacco and old books lingered, both of which held unpleasant memories. Claire wrinkled her nose.

"Take a seat, will you?"

Claire wrapped her arms about herself. "At the desk?"

Mrs. Chattoway glanced at the solemn oak furniture, the great chair behind it, and the smaller chairs in front of it. "No, let's sit by the fireplace. But I have something for you ..." She went behind the desk and opened a drawer. "Please take a seat."

Claire's father had never invited her to sit in front of the fireplace. She had sometimes been relegated to one of the seats across the desk, like her father was meeting with a subordinate. Though, more often than not, she'd been forced to stand like a servant rather than sit. Comfort was never his priority.

Claire lowered herself onto a large chair with intricately carved arms. The leather gave way under her backside, and she sank into it, surprised by the softness.

"These belong to you." She looked up to find her mother extending a bundle of papers tied together with twine. "I found them when going through your father's things. They are the letters from Mr. Philip Knight."

Claire stared at the letters. "What?"

Mrs. Chattoway nodded. "I didn't mean for this to happen, Claire. I should have defended you. If you will give me another chance, I will try to do better."

Claire swallowed and untied the string, letting the letters fall in her lap. There were perhaps a dozen of them, all with her name on them in his hand. She swallowed. He had written. He'd not done enough, no, but at least, in his own way, he'd made a small effort to contact her.

Of course, it was a useless effort. Of course, he should have known better. But, if he believed Mrs. Chattoway to be on their side at the time, perhaps he had trusted in that.

No more excuses.

She gathered the missives up again and pushed aside her thoughts. She'd think about them later.

"Thank you, Mother." Claire retied the string and set the bundle on a side table. "I appreciate having these. I don't know if I'll read them or not—that's not a man I need to remember anymore. He belongs to another woman, and I want to keep my thoughts honorable."

"It's not as if you can forget him completely, I suppose." Mrs. Chattoway lowered herself onto the chair opposite Claire. "Have you decided if you will let him see your daughters occasionally? Or is he even interested?"

"I'm not sure; I haven't worked it out yet. Alice seems to think he's the villain in her fairy tale. I want to avoid seeing him as much as possible. He cannot take them from me, and allowing him to visit can only bring pain." She was a bit afraid of her attachment to him. What if it reared its ugly head once more?

"You'd see him more often in London, possibly. Here in Yorkshire, it'd be safer." Mrs. Chattoway cleared her throat. "I don't want to rush you, but I do want to make amends. You are more than welcome here—you are wanted, and so are your children."

A lump rose in Claire's throat. "Th-thank you. Of late, rumors have leaked out. I'm afraid people will find out who I am. Perhaps it's time to find a new home, somewhere I won't be in the public eye."

As isolated as Starboard Hall was, and as few as the Chattoways' acquaintances had become, it would be ideal. A safe place for the girls to grow up, and she'd find a way for them to marry well. With Chattoway backing, how could she not?

"Live here, then. The estate has gone to Charlie, and he would never want you to leave. When he finds a wife, well, we'll conquer that challenge when it comes. But I doubt Charlie will marry anyone who wouldn't accept you. I know he cares more about a woman's character than anything—he has often told me so."

Claire bobbed her head up and down. *Yes, Charlie will always take care of me, even if he isn't an openly emotional man.* He tended to show up at the crises of her life, offering what she needed to get on, and trusting her to take care of the rest. Some might find it uncaring, but Charlie understood her need for space—and her need to remain as anonymous as possible. He'd had to keep his distance or she'd have been found out.

"Thank you for your offer. I would love to accept. I think I'll sell or simply close my shop in London." As soon as she said the words, a huge weight lifted off her shoulders, and she straightened in her chair. "I can't tell you how grateful I am."

Mrs. Chattoway visibly struggled to hold back tears. "I'm more grateful than you ever could be, Claire. I've missed you—and I've regretted every action I let your father perpetrate. The man mistreated us both, but you especially. I became frightened when you left, frightened harm would come to you, or that I'd hear years later that you'd died in a gutter somewhere. But still, I thanked God that you escaped! I almost wished, some days, that I had been so lucky."

Mr. Chattoway did tend to ruin every life he touched. Claire rose and knelt beside her mother's chair. "Perhaps I shouldn't have left. I saw it as the only way to save my children. But, maybe, if I had been a better daughter, you might have seen there was something worth protecting. Still, I don't believe any of us had a chance while he lived. Even Charlie was tied down by his manipulation."

"Don't make excuses." Mrs. Chattoway squeezed her daughter's shoulder. "Not for me. I lived here in relative luxury while you struggled for your life. Do you know how proud I am of you? I didn't know you were Miss Berck. I have friends who speak so highly of you! I almost fainted when Charlie told me. How did you manage?"

"I'm not sure." Luck? Hard work? Nettie? So many factors had contributed. Truly, knowing the upper class well had helped her majorly. Her maid believed God was responsible, and it almost seemed the most plausible reason. "I'm glad you're able to be proud of me. I know I've made some mistakes. I should ask your forgiveness for the way I treated you when I was a girl. You understand why, of course, but that doesn't excuse my behavior."

Mrs. Chattoway didn't reply. Claire knew she didn't believe the apology to be her due. Her mother rose. "Well. I for one would like to really meet my grandchildren. I've never gotten to, and I'm sure they're sweet girls."

"All right." Claire stood and stepped back. "I know they're somewhat unsure what to expect, so I'll talk to them first, if you don't mind."

"Of course not." Mrs. Chattoway cocked her head. "Has Nettie been able to see her mother yet?"

"Er, no. I'm not sure she has." Nettie's mother lived in the nearby village, but it was still a bit of a walk. "Which reminds me—my maid is married to a man named Tom Jameson. He traveled with us. Will we find him something to do at Starboard? He's fairly adaptable, Nettie says."

"I'm sure we can find something." Mrs. Chattoway smiled. "Let's not worry about it now. I think the priorities should be getting to know each other and settling in."

Claire picked up the bundle of letters from the side table. "Very well, then. I'll probably call the girls to my room and talk with them briefly about the situation. Nettie, as well, since this impacts her life."

"I think you'll find the children out in the garden." Mrs. Chattoway gestured toward the window—in the distance, Charlie's head was visible above some overgrown hedges. "He must be introducing them to the wonders of weeds. We really do need to hire a gardener."

Claire laughed. "I suppose so. I'll go fetch them." She stepped toward the door, then turned and faced her mother. "I do forgive you. It's not easy for me, but I do."

Outside, she hurried across the lawn to where Charlie stood with the girls. His posture loosened when he saw her.

"There's your mother now. Why don't you go greet her?"

The girls had probably been bothering him with a thousand questions. Claire smiled and waved. "Alice, Ivy, I need to talk to you both."

Alice's face went from open and laughing to closed and solemn in an instant. She ran over to Claire and took her hand. "Mummy, what is it?"

Claire blinked. *Does she think something's happened again? Something that might cause me pain?* This world had turned her daughter into a pessimist. "Everything's fine. I just want to talk about our living arrangement. Charlie, you should stay, too."

Alice's posture slumped. "Are we going to stay here?"

Claire cocked her head and tilted Alice's chin up to see her face. "You mean you don't want to? Darling, this is a lovely place. We're going to fix it up, and it'll be our home. Why, we could even get you a pony, if the budget holds out—couldn't we, Charlie?"

"Of course." He lowered himself onto a nearby bench which chose that moment to shift. He jumped to his feet. "Though, let's make sure everything gets fixed first."

"Naturally." Claire raised her eyebrows. "This is ridiculous, even for Father. Didn't he realize that these repairs would cost more if he waited?"

"Father didn't notice much of anything for the last few years." Charlie took Ivy's hand and led her over to where Claire stood. "I'm glad you're staying. It'll be just you and me and Mother."

"And me and Ivy!" Alice said. "But what about Mrs. Bennett, Mummy?"

Claire laughed. She knew what her daughter was really worried about. "We'll make sure Mrs. Bennett delivers Kitty safely to Starboard. After that, we'll offer her a position at Starboard, if one is available—which I believe it will be—or give her an excellent reference that allows her to move on to a better position. All right?"

Alice placed a finger to her lips and cocked her head. "All right. What about our house?"

"Uncle Charlie will sell it for us."

Charlie coughed. "I will?"

"You will." Claire smiled at him. "I have to close my dress shop, too, so we'll probably travel to London together."

Charlie grunted and walked toward the house.

Claire watched him hurry across the overgrown lawn. "We'll have to convince Uncle Charlie to help us. He can be a grouch." She whirled back to her children, affecting a cheery attitude. "How does that sound, darlings? Living at Starboard will be lovely, won't it?"

Ivy nodded, smiling in a mime of her mother's expression. Alice nodded slowly.

It's going to be harder to convince Alice this is a good idea. Claire was determined to, nonetheless. "We'll have a real home, where we won't have to hide you." She bent and kissed both of their cheeks. "Come back to the house now. Your grandmother wants to meet you."

Alice's eyes brightened. "Is she nice now?"

"Yes." But Claire wouldn't entirely open her heart until she was sure.

Not with anyone. Never again.

Chapter Twenty

October 1871

"So it's decided. Alice will go back to Miss Selle's after the New Year." Charlie shifted Ivy against his shoulder where she'd slumped, tired from a long day exploring the recesses of a forgotten attic with Alice.

Claire had to smile. Her brother stubbornly pretended not to like the girls, but they crawled all over him now. "Yes, I think that will be lovely. I know she has friends there, and she needs the schooling."

Alice folded her arms across her chest. "I don't need to go to school."

"But it's only for part of the year now!" At least, that was their plan. "You'll come home for holidays, and you can use your real name, too." For a great deal of money, one could buy almost anything. Charlie's pocketbook had assured Alice's safety at the school. Alice simply had to pretend she was his ward rather than his niece.

The expression on Alice's face said that that wasn't too great of a comfort, but she would enjoy being back with her friends. Claire had enjoyed school herself, but it took a bit of adjustment for any child.

Charlie stood, lifting Ivy with him. "It's almost bedtime, isn't it?"

Indeed, it was—past time, in fact. She followed her brother upstairs. Alice, of course, was never cheerful about sleep, but at least she didn't whine.

In the bedroom, Charlie laid Ivy on her bed and tiptoed out of the room. Claire knelt and removed her shoes and stockings, then loosened her dress. That would do until she got Alice settled.

"But who will take care of Kitty and Truffle when I go to school?" Alice whispered.

"Shush. Don't wake your sister. Wash your face and hands."

Alice did as she was told, and Claire laid out her nightgown. There were servants who could perform such tasks, yes, but Claire appreciated a bit of quiet time with her daughters in the evenings. Afterward, Nettie would stay until they fell asleep, but these minutes belonged to her.

Ivy stirred enough to be nightgowned and tucked in, then fell right back asleep. Claire pressed a kiss to her brow and returned to Alice. She felt that they were healthily tired—she'd always put a great deal of stock in country air and regular exercise, and it had made her girls rosy and hearty.

Claire perched on the edge of Alice's bed. "To answer your question, darling, Ivy and I will take good care of Kitty, and the stablehands will make sure Truffle is exercised and loved until you come home. All right?"

Alice sighed. "All right."

"You're going to have a wonderful time." Claire leaned over and kissed her. "You'll see Cassie and Georgiana and Abby."

"I know." Alice flopped back on the pillow. "I just don't like being away from you. I'm afraid—" She stopped, and Claire could see her jaw clench.

"What are you afraid of?"

"That you won't want me anymore."

Claire blinked. She could honestly say that was the last thing in the world she had imagined Alice thinking. "What do you mean, darling? Of course I'll want you! I love you so much." Hadn't she told Alice that every day of her life? What reason did the child have to doubt her love?

Unless Parker had said more than Alice let on. That was a distinct possibility. But she didn't think that was the case, or it surely would have come out by now.

"I don't know." Alice wiggled her body from side to side and looked at her hands. "You sent me away before and forgot about me, is all. That was what you wanted, right? For everyone to forget about me?"

Was that what Alice thought?

"Darling, it was because I loved you—for your own protection. I wanted you to be safe, because there are people who would hurt you if they could. But now you're safe, and now you can come home all the time. I'm making sure of it. I wish you'd told me you've felt like this!" What a burden for a little child to bear for so many months—no, a year now. Her throat tightened, and she gathered Alice close and hugged her tight.

Alice sniffled. "I'm sorry. I wasn't sure of anything. My father didn't want me, and I know I don't come from a good place. You know, because ... because you're not ..."

Claire could finish the sentence for her. *Married. Because I'm not married.* "That doesn't have anything to do with you. And we were married, even if ... Things have changed, but you don't need to doubt that you were a wanted child. Nettie would say that God planned you." If only she had the words Nettie always did in these situations.

As if in answer to a call, there was a light rap at the door.

Claire glanced over her shoulder to find her maid standing there, head cocked. She motioned her over, and Nettie crossed the room and sat on the opposite side of the bed.

Alice wiped her eyes and turned to Nettie. "I was wanted, wasn't I?"

"Yes, Gracie." Nettie's gray eyes were tear-filled as she nodded. "You were wanted. You *are* wanted! You were wanted since before time by God. You were wanted from the first moment your mother knew you existed. You weren't a mistake, and never for a moment were you regretted."

How did Nettie know? Claire rubbed small circles on Alice's back, but even knowing the issue, even having had the conversation with Alice, she still didn't know what to say.

I love you more than words can possibly say. I can't begin to put voice to my feelings. Please believe I do care despite my silence. Words she had wanted to say to another person many years ago, words she had been unable to voice *... Perhaps if I had, he would have fought for me.*

"Your mother and I both love you," Nettie said. "I'm sorry you're frightened, but you don't have to be. You're a special girl, Gracie."

Gracie. Special nickname, special girl.

Claire summoned up her courage and spoke again. "Nettie's right, darling. And we won't forget about you any time soon! I love you." She cleared her throat and leaned back. "Now it's about time for bed. In the morning, we'll plan our after-Christmas trip to London. We'll get you a brand-new wardrobe for your next term."

Alice's eyes brightened slightly. "With you?"

"Yes."

Alice sat up. "Will Nettie come? And what about Uncle Charlie? What kind of clothes? Pretty clothes?"

Claire and Nettie both laughed softly. "Slow down, darling. You'll wake up Ivy! No, and yes, and of course I'll get you pretty clothes! Only the best for my girl."

Alice tossed her arms out. "That'll be nice. Can I pick some things? Like a new hat?"

"Within reason." Claire kissed her cheek and pulled the coverlet up to her chin. "Remember, we're living off your Uncle Charlie now, and we can't stretch his generosity too far."

Alice raised her eyebrows. "Uncle Charlie says I can have whatever I want as long as I keep quiet."

Claire stifled another laugh and rose. "We'll see about that. Nettie will pray with you now. I'll see you in the morning, darling."

Her daughter pushed herself up on her elbows once again, eyes worried. "Couldn't you stay? Nettie wouldn't mind, would you, Nettie?"

Claire was fairly certain Nettie smirked. "Mind if your mother stays while we pray? Not at all. In fact, I welcome it."

Trapped by motherhood. She lowered herself back down on the edge of the bed. "Very well. Let's ... begin."

Nettie placed a hand on Alice's shoulder and motioned for Claire to do the same—some strange connection ritual, probably. She also imitated Nettie in closing her eyes and bowing her head.

"Father God, thank You for keeping us safely through another day." Nettie paused for a moment, then continued. "Thank You for our good health in this family and for our safety here at Starboard. Thank You for giving us a lovely day exploring the attic and spending time with Uncle Charlie. We ask that You keep us all safe—Alice, Ivy, Mummy, Jameson, Mrs. Bennett, Grandmother, Uncle Charlie, Aunt Christy, and her family."

"And Truffle and Kitty," Alice whispered.

"Yes, we definitely want them to be safe, too." There was a smile in Nettie's voice. "Please let Alice's trip and her time at Miss Selle's be uneventful in the best way, and let them have a wonderful time. Especially Uncle Charlie, because we know how much he likes shopping for dresses."

Alice giggled. "Not very much."

"No, not very much. But I pray he has a lovely trip with his girls even so." Nettie took a deep breath. "And I also have a prayer for myself, which You know."

Claire's throat tightened. *Oh, Nettie... can't the girls be enough?* She never would give up that dream, and Claire couldn't blame her. Not that Claire wanted or expected more children herself, but Nettie ought to have a baby to raise as her own. She certainly had done an excellent job with Alice and Ivy.

Alice didn't question Nettie's special request, surprisingly—perhaps it was a frequent request. Claire didn't doubt it.

Nettie moved on. "Lord, I pray for Mummy. I know she's resistant to the idea of You. We can't know what's in her heart. But I do pray that You find a way to work in her soul and bring her to You. I know it will bring her deep and abiding comfort, and I know there's nothing that can separate her from Your love save her own stubbornness. Your will be done.

"Keep Alice through the night and may she only have pleasant dreams. In Jesus's name I pray, amen."

"Amen," Alice echoed.

Claire added her own voice in a half-mumble, but there was no conviction to it. She raised her eyes to Nettie's, but her friend's gaze was too intense for her liking. She stood and cleared her throat.

"Well. I'll leave you now. Sweet dreams, Alice."

"Sweet dreams, Mummy."

Outside the door, she stood still in the dark, cold hallway for a moment, gaining her bearings. Nettie's sincerity and strength had always been obvious to Claire, but it never ceased to amaze her, nonetheless.

If I were Nettie, could I have faith in God if He allowed what happened to her to happen to me?

The answer was clear: never. Claire couldn't imagine herself going on with life, let alone thriving. Even now, everything felt so difficult.

Something about Nettie, that special something that Claire couldn't imagine possessing herself, made her different.

If the difference was Jesus, well ...

But no. Claire wouldn't think about it. Not tonight. Some other time, perhaps, when she wasn't so tired. When she wasn't so hurt.

London
December 1871

"Now twirl for me!"

Alice obliged, pirouetting in front of a mirror at a haberdashery. The ribbons trailing off the hat twirled with her, blue and white sails behind her. She giggled, causing the young shop girl to giggle, causing Mummy to smile.

Anything that made Mummy smile was good as far as Alice was concerned.

"That one, I think, and the more basic ... yes, the second-to-last we tried.

You've set aside the ones I chose, haven't you?" In no time, the hats were boxed, and Mummy and Alice added more parcels to their carriage.

Uncle Charlie, who was halfway through *Great Expectations*, glanced at the new boxes. "Is that it?"

"One last stop. Gloves and fans. For me, not for Alice." Mummy arranged her skirts and regarded her brother closely. "You're not angry? I couldn't resist another, but she needed something basic, too."

"Mm. Whatever." Uncle Charlie flipped a page. "Our expenses are few. It's not like we'll be hosting any house parties soon."

Mummy smiled. "And Alice will have such lovely clothes for school!"

Uncle Charlie raised his eyebrows at her over the book. "For church and perhaps a holiday or two. They have uniforms, you realize."

Mummy shrugged. "She'll be the best-dressed student at church."

He chuckled and went back to his reading.

Mummy turned to Alice. "Should we see about finding a bakery, perhaps? Or a sweet shop? I think we need a treat."

Uncle Charlie groaned.

"Oh, he'll be as glad as us. I'll tell you a secret, darling—your uncle has a sweet tooth."

"And an empty pocketbook." But he smiled as he returned to the depths of Dickens.

The carriage rolled to a stop again, and Uncle Charlie stepped down to help the ladies out before returning to the carriage and his waiting book. In no time, they'd completed their purchases and exited the shop.

"Miss Chattoway!"

Mummy paused and glanced over her shoulder, then went to the window of a carriage. "Mrs. Knight?" Her tone was a great deal more inquisitive, and Alice soon saw why.

Mrs. Knight had plainly lost a great deal of weight and color since Alice had seen her last. Great dark circles underlined her eyes, her cheeks seemed to sink into her head, and she was pale as a sheet.

"Yes." Her smile consumed her entire face, and she looked a bit more like herself. Alice relaxed slightly. It *was* her friend—only she wasn't feeling well. "H-how are you?"

"I'm well." Mummy shifted the box she held from hand to hand. "Are you ... well?"

"Oh, you sound like Phil." Mrs. Knight slumped back in the carriage, then pushed herself forward again. "I'm not, exactly. This cough is horrible. But I'm just havin' a servant do some shoppin' for me, and I wanted the air."

"I see." Mummy glanced down at Alice. "Be sure to rest when you get home, Mrs. Knight. If you don't mind my saying so, Mr. Knight might be right if he's concerned for your health. That cough still hasn't left you?"

Mrs. Knight huffed and didn't reply to Mummy. Instead, she looked down at Alice. "I would pull you right up in this carriage and hug you, sweetling, but I'm afraid this li'l cold might be contagious, so I won't. How have you been?"

"I've been wonderful. How—I mean, I hope you get better soon, Mrs. Knight!" Alice reached up and touched her hand.

"Thank you, Alice. I hope I'll be better soon, too. Ned's runnin' around like a li'l puppy, all trouble and putting everythin' in his mouth, and I can't keep up just now. Now, what are you two doin' in London?"

Alice glanced at Mummy. She didn't say anything, so Alice felt free to reply. "We're getting me new outfits before I go back to boarding school. Uncle Charlie is with us—we're going to get a sweet after this!"

"Candy? Oh, how fun." Mrs. Knight squeezed Alice's hand, then let it go and withdrew her own into the carriage. "Perhaps I should let y'all go on with that. I don't want to let a sick, old girl like me get in the way."

Sick, old girl? Well, she was sick and a girl, but she wasn't old. Alice felt an impulsive need to comfort her. "You still have a pretty smile, at least."

Mummy squeezed Alice's shoulder hard—apparently that wasn't exactly a proper comment—but Mrs. Knight laughed. Or she tried to. It turned into a hacking cough.

In a moment, she recovered, leaning back against the seat as if exhausted. "I really must go home now." Her voice was a faint whisper, and her eyes were strangely bright. "But y'all should come to tea this afternoon at our house. Do you know the address? The Eltons have owned the place for years, I hear."

Alice looked up eagerly, seeking confirmation. She missed Mrs. Knight, even if her husband was awful, and it would be nice to see Ned again.

Mummy's eyes widened. "I ... I don't know if we should interfere. You plainly need your rest—"

"Oh, honey, I'll be right as rain by tonight. I'll get a bit of a nap this afternoon, and I miss havin' people around. I haven't gotten to go to any parties in practically forever. Tell me you will come!"

A look passed between Mummy and Mrs. Knight that Alice couldn't identify. But, in the end, Mummy looked down first.

Mummy nodded, her head bobbing up and down like a sideways pendulum, although Alice supposed pendulums didn't work that way. "Yes. We'll come."

"Good, good! I'll expect you two and your brother at four, if that's all right. We'll have a marvelous time. I'll make sure the maid brings Ned down for a bit, too, so we can all see him." Mrs. Knight sighed. "There's my maid now. Four?"

"Yes, four." Mummy placed a hand on Alice's shoulder. "Thank you for the kind invitation."

"Oh, don't mention it."

As soon as the maid stepped into the carriage and settled against the seat opposite Mrs. Knight, the carriage lurched forward, and in no time, it had disappeared in the traffic.

Mummy and Alice walked back to their own conveyance, where Uncle Charlie greeted them with a disgusted look. However, after the situation was explained, he was a great deal more understanding and agreed to accompany them to tea at the Knights'.

CHAPTER TWENTY-ONE

C LAIRE TOOK A DEEP breath as a footman helped her down from the carriage. The Eltons' London house towered above her, and her soul wanted to cringe and run away. She didn't allow her eyes to linger too long, however, but instead forged on. Up the steps, into the foyer, and on to the parlor, Alice's hand grasped tightly in her own.

Mrs. Knight reclined on a sofa, her feet propped up, and Mr. Knight lingered nearby. When Claire, Alice, and Charlie entered the room, Mr. Knight rose and took two steps toward them before stopping.

Even in the low lamplight, Claire could make out beads of sweat on his forehead, and his hair stood up as if he'd run his hands through it. Dreadful habit. But at least she knew he was as concerned about this meeting as she.

I shouldn't have come. I shouldn't be here. I don't want him to think I've come back into his life. This should be over now. It's meant to be over!

Yet, there was no turning back now. She greeted them both kindly, focusing her attention mostly on Mrs. Knight. The woman looked as bad as she had that afternoon. Her complexion had taken on a waxy tone, and every so often, she'd stop talking to deal with another coughing fit.

Claire and Charlie glanced at each other. Mrs. Knight's condition was certainly worsening. This would be the last time Claire let Alice in this house, definitely—though her child was strong, she couldn't resist consumption. Alice was too young and the disease too deadly.

Still, Mrs. Knight remained cheerful and Mr. Knight silent.

Claire did her best to respond in a calm but friendly manner. She wasn't sure what her position was—and she wasn't at all sure what Mrs. Knight thought of her. As for the woman's husband, Claire couldn't care less. Indifference, it would seem, and perhaps a touch of irritation, would be her companions this afternoon.

After tea was over, the servants whisked everything away, and Claire began to look for an escape. The sooner she got out of this situation, the better. Yes, Alice seemed to be enjoying herself, but for how long? Surely she knew what a strange tea party this was. Surely the hatred toward Mr. Knight must still exist—her daughter hadn't spoken his name more than two or three times since she found out the truth.

A servant brought down Ned, and Mrs. Knight rose on shaky feet.

Mr. Knight jumped up and helped her. "Love, why don't you sit down?" His voice was quiet but firm. "Let them bring Ned to you, and then the others can play with him. Please, for my sake."

"N-no." She struggled for breath, then seemed to calm herself. "I'm fine, honey. I th-thought Mr. Chattoway and Alice and Ned and I could all go outside to the garden. Just a bit of fresh air would do me wonders."

"It's rained this afternoon, and you're already ill. Please—" He pulled at her arm, urging her to sit.

Claire stood, too. "Yes, Mrs. Knight, please. Don't take any risks."

Mr. Knight glanced at her, then back to his wife. "You're pushing yourself too far. You ought to have rested tonight, but you insisted on this party. However, this really must be the last time. You know—"

"What the doctor said?" Mrs. Knight shrugged. "I'm fine, Phil. Really, I am. Now, I'll sit and watch Alice play with Ned for half an hour. What will that hurt? I want you to stay here and have a nice chat with Miss Chattoway and then come out to us when you're all done. How's that?"

All the color left Mr. Knight's skin, making him as ghostly as his wife. "I hardly think that's necessary." He spoke the words through gritted teeth, sounding like how Claire felt.

Uncomfortable. Afraid. Irritated. Loath to have the conversation Mrs.

Knight suggested.

"You'll thank me. Please." She squeezed his arm and tottered away from him. Charlie grabbed her arm and sent Claire a worried look, but she felt helpless to protest, to make a scene in front of Alice.

Her daughter ran off happily, naive to the emotions in her mother's chest.

The door clicked shut, and Claire turned to face her former husband. She met his gaze this time and told herself to remain firm.

Mr. Knight cleared his throat. "She's a master manipulator at times." He made a sharp gesture toward the furniture. "Please. Sit. Let's ... She told me that she would like us to speak to each other, and what about, but I didn't think she would carry through. Yet, now that she has, I agree that perhaps exchanging a few words in a controlled situation might be ... might be best."

Claire lowered herself onto an uncomfortable but stylish chair. "I see. She knows all, then?"

"All. I spared no details." He took a seat and gripped his trouser legs. "I should have told her from the first, but I was afraid, and I admit I didn't think it would come back to me. I thought you would be married again by now, and I certainly didn't think ... I didn't expect the consequences."

Anger flashed hot, causing her vision to go red for a moment. "My children are not consequences, Mr. Knight. They are blessings. Unearned, God-given, impossibly undeserved blessings." *How so much good can come out of evil is beyond me.* She didn't say the last aloud, but she felt it. Claire's life seemed pulled out of a cheap novel, and the effect was demoralizing. *God, you couldn't want me, could you?*

He started to stand but remained seated. "I'm sorry. I didn't mean for my phrasing to offend you. I only meant that, of course, your life has changed because of the children. For the better in some ways, yes, but you were removed from your position and forced to work for your own living. You should never have been forced that low, Miss Chattoway. You succeeded, of course, because you must. But a lady shouldn't have to do such a thing.

"I consider it to be entirely my fault. I will not even mention your parents' part in it, as it is insignificant to my own behavior, my own weaknesses." He paused and looked away for a long moment before turning back and meeting her eyes. "It's a complicated issue, but I want you to know that I am apologetic, and I do not place the blame on your head as I had thought to originally.

"My pride got the best of me, and I thought I couldn't beg. I'd written so many letters and not received a reply, and I thought if I continued begging, it would only serve to further humiliate me. In addition, my country had launched itself into a civil war not long after our brief marriage—not even weeks after—and it was a welcome escape."

Claire blinked. "I didn't know—" She stopped herself. "I only mean to say, I didn't know you were in the army in America."

"Briefly, yes. Three years. I was shot through the shoulder." He rolled his right arm as if the memory brought a pang, and she had to coax herself out of sympathy.

She wouldn't be concerned. She wouldn't.

Still, she owed him basic courtesy, as a lady. "I see. I'm sorry."

He flushed. "It was of no consequence. The fact remains that I have caused a great deal of trouble for you, and for our children, and I apologize."

Trouble. Children. Apologize. Yes, he could say "sorry" all he wanted to—but Claire didn't think it was within her to forgive him. If that was what he was asking. She wasn't sure. Perhaps he only wanted an opportunity to say how sorry he was.

Unlikely. Nobody wanted to offer something for nothing. Yet, neither was Claire willing to take words and exchange them for something as precious as forgiveness. He'd wounded her, and it would be some time before she could look at him without revulsion.

If she ever saw him again.

The bittersweetness of it hit her again. Yes, the separation would be good for her—and doubtless good for his family and him. But what of her children? What of the rest of her life? What of memories she must toss away?

Forgive him.

Claire swallowed hard and turned her face away. She wasn't sure where the voice came from, only that it was insistent.

You should forgive him. The bitterness is eating you alive. So forgive him.

"I can't." She didn't realize until they were spoken that the words had come out aloud, but the look on Mr. Knight's face confirmed that, indeed, she had voiced her thoughts. He must think her insane.

"You can't what?"

Claire wrapped her arms around herself and shuddered. "Forgive you. I can't forgive you. I don't know if I'll ever be able to. I loved you for so long, and the betrayal hurt. And, for some time now, the bitterness has grown and grown, and now I fear I'll never be able to be around you without feeling the pain."

Mr. Knight remained silent. He stood after a bit and walked to the window. When the silence had stretched on for what seemed like eternity, he spoke. "Alice seems to be taking to Ned again. You can see them playing in the garden here. He's a cheerful little fellow."

"I-I've noticed." She, too, rose and walked to his side. "He's a lovely boy. I'm glad for you. I won't allow Alice and Ivy to interfere with your family … I promise. Your name will never be associated with them."

His Adam's apple bobbed. "What if I want my name to be associated with them? What if … what if I'd like to see them from time to time?" He turned to face her, and she stepped back. "I love them, Claire. I know it's not fair for me to interfere—it's the last thing they need. But I want you to know that my aid is there, financial or otherwise. Of course, Hazel would have to be involved …" He faced the window again. "No more secrets."

Claire shrugged. She needed those secrets to keep people from spitting in her face on the street. At least in part. But she supposed if she were married, she would keep nothing from her spouse. That, she could approve of. "Very well. I'll contact you if I ever need help."

"But more than that—I'd like to see them from time to time." He cleared his throat, and his eyes snaked sideways at her. "Hazel agrees. We would both be honored if we were allowed to be part of their lives."

Claire watched his face. "You mean that?" There were no lies in his eyes, but men could hide their true nature deeper than what one could see. She knew that now. "It's not just duty or pride?" Not that it mattered. He couldn't be very involved—the children were hers. Still, she felt a need to justify her mistrust in him, and it was hard to do that if his feelings for the girls were sincere.

"Of course not!" His fingers gripped the sill until his knuckles turned white. "But I suppose I've given you no reason to believe otherwise. You must simply take my word for it. Can you imagine knowing you had a child—children—and not being able to spend time with them because of your own actions?"

No, Claire couldn't. She would never allow such a thing to happen. But then, hadn't she separated herself from Alice for her own good by sending her to boarding school? And hadn't she experienced guilt for bringing Alice and Ivy into a world where they could be so hated?

"I can see how that would be difficult," she admitted. *Not as difficult as being abandoned by the man you love ... but difficult.* "If you like, we can find a way for you to meet—sometimes. I'm not sure Alice wants to see you."

Mr. Knight nodded. "I understand why." Claire thought there was genuine repentance in his eyes. But, again, eyes often told stories hearts didn't echo. "I'll let her make the decisions. You needn't worry about me forcing myself on her."

Claire almost laughed at his choice of words—though, perhaps it was tasteless to laugh. Certainly she couldn't tell him the reason why, at any rate. "Very well. As long as you are gentle. She isn't sensitive, not exactly, but I won't have you getting her hopes up. She cares very deeply."

"I can see that." He gestured toward the door. "Let's go see them now. I won't risk any feelings of mistrust from my wife. Not personal, you understand—I believe 'once bitten, twice shy.'" Mr. Knight's entire face flamed red. "I only meant ... I only meant that I don't want to cause another round of gossip. I'd like to save both of our reputations further damage. Y-you understand?"

She dropped her eyes. "Yes. I understood you." He wasn't the vengeful sort, and she didn't believe him exactly capable of that type of barb. "I agree. If we are above reproach, there can be no gossip. So let us be."

He nodded and held the door for her. "Thank you," he murmured. "Thank you for being so reasonable."

Had she any choice but to be? Would throwing a fit help? Probably not. And perhaps forgiveness was the path to follow. She'd seen bitterness erode good people—and she'd seen joy in those who triumphed over it.

If Nettie could move on, Claire could, too. Maybe God would look favorably on her. Half-forgotten verses from a childhood of routine study drifted to her consciousness about forgiveness: "Even as God for Christ's sake hath forgiven you."

She wordlessly followed Mr. Knight to the garden.

Ned squealed and launched himself into Alice's arms, causing them both to tumble back on the grass. She managed to stand and pick him up, though he was almost too heavy for her. She set him down again and directed his attention to some pretty flowers.

"Why don't you pick some for me, Neddie?" Mrs. Knight said. Her voice was an airy whisper, and Alice hoped she could breathe all right.

Ned set himself enthusiastically to the task and, in no time, returned and handed his mother a crushed fistful of flowers, all plucked off just below the blooms. Alice would have to give him some flower-picking lessons.

Mrs. Knight tried to stand from her seat on a bench, then sat down quickly and coughed. "This cold has made me weaker than a newborn." She coughed again—and again and again.

Alice clutched Ned close and watched, a bit afraid. No one could cough that much and still have their insides in the proper places. At least, Alice didn't think so.

"Mrs. Knight, should I get you anything?" Uncle Charlie stepped forward, eyes dark. His hand rested lightly on her lower back as she bent over and clutched her handkerchief to her mouth.

"I'm fine." Mrs. Knight coughed out the words, muffled in her hand, rather than said them. "It's just a cold. I'll be fine ..." She pulled away from Uncle Charlie, and Alice saw dull red stains on the cloth in her hand.

Mrs. Knight swayed on her feet and tumbled to the ground.

Alice shrieked as Uncle Charlie rushed to catch her.

CHAPTER TWENTY-TWO

C LAIRE'S HEELS ECHOED IN the large foyer as she approached her brother. His eyes, questions swimming in them, met hers.

"The doctor will be here soon. Mrs. Knight's resting." Claire glanced down at her daughter, cowering behind Charlie's legs. "I'm sure she'll get better, Alice. Don't worry. Uncle Charlie's going to take you home, and I'll come as soon as I can."

Charlie blinked. "You're not coming?"

Claire shook her head. "No ... not yet." She was the only woman in the house save the servants, and Mrs. Knight didn't know them. If Claire were in her place, she would want another woman around—one she knew. Not that Mrs. Knight and she would ever be friends, but any woman was better than none at all.

"Very well." Charlie sighed and placed a hand on Alice's shoulder, nudging her toward the door. "Hurry home."

"I'll try to." But she didn't want to leave the Knights alone. Perhaps it was guilt—or perhaps it was pity—that compelled her to stay, but both were equally convincing.

The doctor arrived not half an hour later, and Claire did her best not to get in the way. However, even from the corner where she stood, she could see the worried look in his eyes. It wasn't good. Of course it wasn't good—it was consumption. The illness seldom allowed the bearer to not be, well, consumed.

At last, the doctor stepped toward the door and gestured for Mr. Knight to follow him. With glazed eyes and slumped shoulders, he looked like a man going to his death sentence.

Perhaps he's going to hear his wife's.

"Claire?" His monotone voice broke into her thoughts. "Would you come?"

She shifted from foot to foot. He wanted her to hear the probably grim news the doctor had to impart to him? It wasn't her place. "I—"

"Please. Hazel is resting now, and it'll only be a minute." He turned to the door, and Claire followed.

"It's not good." The doctor shifted his black bag from hand to hand but met Mr. Knight's eyes evenly. "She's very ill. The consumption is in advanced stages, and she certainly should have sought treatment before."

Mr. Knight's fists clenched. Claire could feel the tension emanating from him. "I know. I tried to convince her to slow down, but she always insisted she was fine. I-I had no idea until these last weeks that it was bad at all. But she wouldn't listen to the last doctor we spoke to ..."

Claire knew guilt, and this man was swamped with it. He had reason to be. She stood there quietly, awaiting the rest of the doctor's diagnosis.

"I understand that she believes she is well, but you can easily tell she's fading fast." The doctor cleared his throat. "Consumption can move quickly once it reaches this stage. It's possible she only has a few days ... or she could recover. It's an unpredictable disease."

Mr. Knight continued to open and close his hands. "Is there nothing you can do?"

"It's beyond me." The doctor sighed. "I'll do all I can, but she must fight it herself. Her life rests in God's hands, not mine and not yours. I'm very sorry."

Mr. Knight remained where he was after the doctor left, head hanging, eyes closed, every inch of him defeated. The silence was thicker than his wife's accent.

"We ought to go back in and sit with Hazel," Claire said. *Don't let your grief cause you to waste what may be your last hours with her, Phil. You're better than that. I know you are.*

Like a stone giant coming to life, he shook and turned back to the door. His hand on the knob, he paused. "Thank you for standing with me."

She had done and said nothing, but still, she nodded. "Never mind that. Go to her. I'll come in a moment—she'll want to be bathed, perhaps, but it'll wait."

Mr. Knight hurried through the door, and she waited in the hallway for ten minutes before rapping on the door.

"Come in."

Claire slipped through the doorway and approached the bed, where Hazel lay propped up against several pillows. Claire focused her attention on the invalid, taking her hand and squeezing it. "What can I do for you? I thought you might want to clean up a bit."

"No ... not yet." Hazel's groggy voice rattled through her chest. "I think I'd like to sleep for a while."

She drifted to sleep moments later, and Claire took a chair a distance away, while Philip huddled by the bedside. Claire let her mind wander as the minutes ticked on. Should she leave? But what if Hazel was approaching a crisis—Claire didn't want Philip to be alone in that case. She didn't want Hazel to be alone, for that matter. Philip was anything but a nurse.

"I feel as if I'm being punished." His words broke the silence like glass shattering.

Claire raised her eyes to look at him, but his were fastened on Hazel's sleeping form. "It's not your fault. You did what you could. About ... about Hazel, I mean."

Philip's head swayed from side to side. "No. Not that. It's ... if I had done more, been a better man, not told her a lie, perhaps God would have taken pity on me. Perhaps He wouldn't take her, too."

Claire swallowed. She often felt that God punished her for faults not her own. But it wasn't true. It couldn't be. If it were, then surely everyone would be continually punished, for Claire knew no perfect men or women.

"Nettie has always told me God doesn't punish us in that way exactly." She stood and went to the window, uncomfortable with sitting still as she spoke. "She says His ways are beyond comprehension. He has a plan—that's what Nettie says." *And Nettie is almost always right.*

She glanced over her shoulder to see a weak smile on his lips before he spoke. "Nettie seems to be a wise woman. I believe Hazel would say the same thing—that this is not my fault, or our fault, and that God has dealt graciously with us always. Perhaps there are some areas of my faith that need strengthened. It's difficult to trust, in these circumstances."

Claire raised her eyebrows to hear him speak so openly of God and faith. When she'd known him, he'd told her he was "barely a Christian"—and Claire willingly fell under that definition, too.

But who could live with Hazel Knight and not be at least a bit converted? Claire felt the same way about Nettie from time to time. Philip seemed sincere. Lost, yes, but he wasn't lying. She was almost sure of it.

"In the end, I suppose God *has* dealt graciously with me. I have a son. I have Hazel still. Perhaps I can even become close to Alice and Ivy. And you are not mad at me." He met her eyes. "I must believe Hazel will recover. Surely He wouldn't take her."

Claire didn't respond. God had spared Ivy many times, though other people, other things had left her life. She now had a safe home, an adoring brother, a loving mother, and her precious children. She, in truth, had been blessed beyond measure.

But how did one reconcile such a loss, if it came to that? A child, a spouse, any loved one? Life would seem empty without those special people—and yet, those left behind must keep on living. How could one cope?

Hazel's eyelashes fluttered. "Phil?"

"I'm here, darling." He clutched her hand. "What can I do for you?"

Her chest shuddered. "I'm fine. I-I ..." She broke off into another coughing fit, and Claire rushed forward to help hold her so she could breathe. After she seemed to struggle for breath, Philip rose.

"I'm going to fetch the doctor again. He might be able to clear your lungs." He glanced back at the bed when he was halfway out the door.

"You'll be all right while I'm gone?"

Hazel nodded, and he rushed out.

A few minutes of silence passed. Claire fussed about the room, brought Hazel water, fluffed the pillows behind her back, and played with the curtains.

"Claire?" Hazel panted the words out rather than said them.

She rushed back to the bedside. "Yes?"

"I'm dying, aren't I? I'm dying. That's what the doctor said to you and Phil … that I'm dying." She turned her face away.

"Oh, Hazel, we don't know that." Claire wrung her hands together. Likely as it was, deciding that one was going to die could only hasten the end. She wanted Hazel to have every chance. They weren't exactly friends, but Hazel was the innocent in the mess Philip and Claire had made.

God, could you spare her?

She sighed at the prayer that once again escaped before she could stop it. But it was true—God ought to let Hazel live a happy life, at least.

"It's all right," Hazel rasped. "God … God won't let anything happen to me unless it's His will. But if He decides it's time, I'm ready."

Claire shuddered. Ready to die? How could anyone be ready for that? Claire certainly wasn't. The idea of death was frightening—the ultimate end. She wasn't sure what she believed exactly as far as Heaven or Hell, but she didn't want to face either.

"You must keep fighting." She again shifted the pillows, as if making Hazel more comfortable would keep her from death. "Ned and Mr. Knight need you. If you truly believe God is merciful, surely you don't believe He'll allow you to die."

Hazel struggled to sit up but couldn't manage it. Still, her eyes bore into Claire's. "That's not how He works. He is merciful. He sent His Son to take our place on the cross, to die for our sins. No matter what happens, He has already paid the price for me, and I am as safe in His hands on earth as I am in Heaven." She closed her eyes. "I don't believe you are a Christian, Miss Chattoway, but I hope you will become one. I could not hope to bear any of this without God, nor would I want to."

Claire sighed. She could hardly bear her life, but God couldn't be the solution. How many times had she cried out and been unanswered? If God was there, if He loved her, then her life wouldn't be like this.

God can take my pain but won't. The thought, which had weaved in and out of her mind for years, came to the surface once again. She turned her face to the window.

"'And God shall wipe away all tears from their eyes; and there shall be no more death, neither sorrow, nor crying, neither shall there be any more pain: for the former things are passed away.'" Claire glanced over her shoulder to find Hazel smiling faintly at her. "Revelation 21:4. It's a favorite. Also, Romans 5:3-5 and 2 Corinthians 4:17-18. My Bible's in the drawer by the bed. Would you get it?"

Claire slid open the drawer, startled by the loud rattle of wood against wood. She reached in and withdrew the thick black book with a leather cover. "Hazel Leeanne Bailey" was written inside the cover in loopy but childish script. Below was a list of births and deaths and marriages, a record Claire's own father had kept in his Bible, too.

However, she guessed Hazel's Bible-keeping was a great deal less hypocritical than Claire's father's. More than that, she knew Hazel was a true Christian. Her behavior confirmed it in every minute Claire was with her.

"Romans 5:3-5," Hazel prompted.

Claire slid her fingers through the delicate pages until she found the book and then the passage. Standing by the window to capture the last of the afternoon light—a servant would hopefully arrive soon to refresh the fire and light the lamps—she read aloud: "'And not only so, but we glory in tribulations also: knowing that tribulation worketh patience; and patience, experience; and experience, hope: and hope maketh not ashamed; because the love of God is shed abroad in our hearts by the Holy Ghost which is given unto us.' I don't really want to learn anything, though. I just want to be happy."

Hazel shrugged. "2 Corinthians 4:17-18."

Again, she found the verses. "'For our light affliction, which is but for a moment, worketh for us a far more exceeding and eternal weight of glory;

while we look not at the things which are seen, but at the things which are not seen: for the things which are seen are temporal; but the things which are not seen are eternal.'"

Claire had no argument to that, so she pressed her lips together and sank back onto her chair. They remained quiet until Mr. Knight returned with the doctor, Hazel's choppy breaths the only sound in the room.

CHAPTER TWENTY-THREE

December 31, 1871

C LAIRE SLUMPED AGAINST THE wall outside the Knights' bedchamber and pressed both hands to her abdomen, eyes closed, breath ragged. A feeling of emptiness took over her soul from her heart to her mind to her stomach. The numbness was welcome but also fortunate. It kept her from feeling too strongly.

When she arrived that afternoon to check in on Hazel, the doctor was there looking grim. With the crisis approaching, she couldn't leave. The next several hours had been agonizing. Hazel's breathing caused an echoing ache in Claire's chest. It got to the point where she just wanted it to be over for the other woman's sake. Her suffering was painful to watch. At last, her breathing had stopped, and Claire had slipped out of the room to leave Philip by himself.

She now ran her hands over her face and sighed. Hazel was so young, and she had so much to live for.

Poor Ned! He'd have to be raised without a mother. She pitied the little chap.

God, how could You let this happen to such a good woman? A woman who trusted in You?

There were no answers in the dark hallway. She leaned against the door and listened. Mr. Knight's sobs broke through the solid wood, corroding her ears like acid. She couldn't go to him. Anyone else in this world was more qualified to comfort him than she, so she must remain silent.

Claire stepped away from the door and walked down the hallway. The desire to go home, hold her child, and perhaps weep overwhelmed her, and she made haste to do so.

When she arrived, Charlie met her inside the door; he must have been waiting in his office, which sat off the foyer of his London house.

"Is it over, then?"

"Yes." She removed her gloves and clasped and unclasped her hands, stretching them. "It took so long, Charlie. She suffered much toward the end, and those there had, of course, to suffer with her."

Charlie nodded. "I'm sorry. She seemed to be a kind and noble woman. But she is in a much better place now, at least."

Claire supposed she was. "She's deserving of Heaven." A woman who loved her husband, her child, and her God. Kind, unopinionated, a good hostess, and sweeter than sugar. "I don't understand why God took her, but I do know that she deserves some sort of paradise after death."

Charlie gestured to the door of his office. "Tea before bed? Cook's still up, or was fifteen minutes ago."

Claire followed him into his private room and took a seat by the fireplace. The flickering flames allowed warmth to seep into her bones, and she relaxed against the leather of the chair. A servant came with a tray, and Charlie slipped a warm cup of tea into her fingers.

"Thank you," she murmured. "I appreciate it. Sorry if I'm not very talkative tonight."

"Don't mention it. I have something to say, though, actually." Charlie lowered himself onto the chair opposite her and smiled. "You mentioned Hazel Knight was, in your eyes, worthy of Heaven. But I want to tell you that none of us are. None of us are without sin. It is only the blood of Jesus Christ that gives us passage to eternity, that keeps us from Hell."

So, somehow Nettie's faith had reached her brother. Not that, she supposed, she had ever asked about his spiritual state before.

"I've heard that said. But I'm not sure I believe." Yet, her faith in her lack of faith had been so thoroughly shaken that she wanted to believe. She desired the peace and poise Nettie possessed. She longed for Hazel's positivity and kind heart. And she wanted to be strong and sure of herself like her brother. Even her mother's loving attitude and her daughter's persistency were attractive to her.

Christianity had ceased to be mindless and begun to make sense. God must exist. He must play into mortals' lives. And He must care about Claire's life.

"I can see you're close, Claire. I wish I could be the one to shove you over the proverbial cliff, but that lies in God's hands. Still, I would encourage you to seek Him. He's there. He loves you. And He will give you comfort and strength beyond anything you can imagine." Charlie took a sip of his tea, wrinkled his nose, and set it on the table between them. "Well. That's lukewarm. Is yours hot?"

"Barely." She placed her cup beside his, her mind churning over his words. "It's late. I imagine whoever poured it wasn't thinking, and I don't mind."

"Mm." Charlie leaned back on his chair and scratched his chin. "I'm trying to think what else I ought to say to you. I'm not as good about talking about my faith as I'd like. But I do believe, and I want to share it with you. Only through God can you find true joy."

Joy.

She'd often heard Nettie say the word instead of happiness as a way of indicating true contentment, true well-being. Joy, Nettie said, was something no one could ever take away from her, something that not even the greatest tragedy could remove from her soul. Joy was more than happiness in that it was interior and did not depend on what happened to you or how people treated you. Joy belonged only to God. Joy was the only way to be truly happy.

"I want joy," Claire whispered. "I want to experience joy in this horrible world. But, Charlie, how can I trust a God Who—?"

"Who gave you two beautiful children, a brother who adores you, a mother who wants to make you happy at the cost of her reputation, even if it means social isolation, and, of course, Who sent His Son to die on the cross for your sins? I know. It's hard for me to trust a God Who would be so generous, too. What does He want from us?" Charlie grinned at her. "You'll be shocked to find that in exchange for making the ultimate sacrifice, all He wants is your heart."

"Hardly worth winning." Claire rolled her eyes. "It's been cracked too many times and, I fear, is rather bitter."

"God doesn't see you that way. He's offering you a new life." Charlie rose and moved to her side. His hands covered hers. "Sister, it is such an incredible gift. Forgiveness, purity, His Spirit, eternity ..."

Claire looked away. Her thoughts swirled, her mind too full to settle on any one thought. *He loves me. He wants me. He has given Himself up for me. I have only to accept. I could have such joy. If only I give up myself. If only I surrender.*

She rose. "I'll think about what you've said. For now, I need some time to myself. But thank you, Charlie. Talking to you has ... has helped."

"I'm glad." He bent and kissed her cheek. "I love you, Claire, even if I don't say it often, and I'll pray for you tonight."

Did he sense that, like Hazel, she'd neared a crisis? Only through this death, she would gain life. If only ... if only she could really believe. How could she be sure?

Perhaps there wasn't a way to be perfectly sure. She gripped the banister hard as she ascended the stairway. At the top, she veered off her usual path to peek into the room where Alice slept, curled up on her side like always. She bent and kissed her child's cheek, fingered her hair, and straightened the comforter. A servant had doubtless helped Charlie get her settled, and they had done well, but she imagined Alice's face slackened further at her touch.

"I love you." She breathed the words, quieter than a whisper, and left the room behind.

In her own chamber, she undressed herself. There was lukewarm water in the pitcher, and she poured it and washed her face and hands. Her face in the mirror seemed pale, and the dark circles under her eyes stood out.

She sighed and tilted her head from side to side. Crow's feet at the corners of her eyes—her children made her laugh too hard. But otherwise, she still saw the same woman in the mirror she'd always seen.

Did she like that woman? Not exactly, no. Claire didn't think she was a bad person. She'd told some lies, for her children's safety, but surely that was permissible. Overall, she tried to be a good woman. Perhaps she tended toward mistrust and bitterness, but that was to be understood, wasn't it?

She picked up her hairbrush and stroked until her arms were tired. This helped distract her from her thoughts, from the reality that she'd watched a woman die tonight.

I don't like myself, she admitted. *I suppose no one is perfect, but I could be better. And no matter how good or bad I am, I need help to get through this life. Help I can't find within me.*

Claire's views on life felt shaken. She lay on her bed in silence, the darkness surrounding her. And somehow in that darkness, she found a light she hadn't expected.

And in that light, Claire died.

Alice's eyes popped open. For less than a second, she was confused about her surroundings, then she remembered she was at her uncle Charlie's house in London, that Mummy had kept them there longer than usual because Mrs. Knight was sick ... and that it was her own birthday.

She hopped out of bed and grabbed her robe and slippers. Shuddering in the cold, she ran all the way down the dim hallway to her mother's room.

"Mummy!" Alice launched herself onto the bed and threw herself on her mother. "Get up! It's my birthday—I'm ten."

Mummy moaned. "Alice, what time is it?" She laughed and pulled her into a hug, nonetheless. "Happy birthday, darling. I love you."

Alice sat back on her heels and grinned. "What are we doing today?"

"Dinner, of course, and Uncle Charlie and I bought you some presents." She rose and walked to her vanity. "It's hardly five, darling. But I understand you're excited. I wonder if Ivy's up."

Alice felt a twinge of guilt but assured herself at that Ivy was probably having the time of her life, spoiled by Nettie, Jameson, and Grandmother. "I think she's all right."

"I hope so." Mummy smiled. "I do have a birthday present for you. And one for Nettie and Ivy, too, when we see them."

Alice narrowed her eyes. "Nettie's birthday was forever ago, Mummy."

"Well, it'll be a belated one. It is belated on so many counts!" Mummy returned to the bed, hairbrush in hand. "Turn around."

Alice flopped over the bed and submitted to being brushed within an inch of her life. "What is it?" Of course she didn't really expect her mother to respond. She'd have to unwrap whatever it was before she could know.

But her mother did respond. "Well, last night I became a Christian."

For a moment, Alice didn't even breathe. Then she let it out in a whoosh. "Mummy, you can't say that because you know it'll make me happy. You have to actually believe."

Mummy laughed so hard that Alice had to turn to glare at her. This wasn't a matter to be taken so lightly.

"It's not funny!"

"I didn't think it was." Mummy pulled Alice closer and kissed her cheek. "Darling, I'm being sincere. Of course, I have a lot to learn—perhaps you can teach me some of it—but I am now a child of God, same as you and Nettie."

Alice blinked. Could it be true? "Really, Mummy?"

"Really."

Her heart did a double flip, and she hugged Mummy close and kissed her cheek. "I'm so glad! Now we can be in Heaven together!" She giggled and bounced back on the bed. "How did you decide?"

"I feel as if ..." Mummy's face grew dim. "You're ten now? So old. Old enough to hear this kind of news and be a brave girl."

Alice's emotions were as flighty as sparrows today—a moment ago, she'd been ecstatic, and now her soul felt colder than the ground. Mummy wasn't one to look sad over anything. "What is it?"

"Mrs. Knight had to go to Heaven last night, Alice."

Her mind mulled over the words, and she swallowed hard, trying not to feel sick. "I-I thought she'd get better." Alice slumped against her mother. "I wanted her to get better."

"I know." Mummy pulled Alice into the tightest, best sort of hug that made her feel a little better. Not as much as it would have a few years ago, but still, there was safety in a mother's arms as nowhere else. "I'm sorry, darling. I know."

Too numb to cry, Alice cuddled against Mummy's side and closed her eyes tight.

CHAPTER TWENTY-FOUR

Seven Months Later
July 1872
London, England

A LICE HAD AN ENTIRE fortnight away from Miss Selle's. Though it wasn't much in the general scheme of things, it was enough for her mother to whisk her away from Norfolk to London to see her family.

She liked school. It greatly improved the more time one was at it—mostly because the homesickness got better and one came to an understanding with one's teachers—and she found most of the work fairly easy. Nettie had seen to it that Alice was a bit ahead of her years. Now Alice saw the benefits of how hard her nanny pushed her.

Nevertheless, holidays were rare and prized, and none more precious than those spent with those she loved—and everyone was waiting at Uncle Charlie's London house to hug and kiss her when she arrived.

As she hugged Ivy and kissed her mother and was exclaimed over by practically everyone, she said a prayer of gratitude for her aunt Christy. Alice hadn't even known she existed until last year, and she seemed like a very silly woman. But, if she hadn't had another baby, all her loved ones wouldn't be in the same city all at once for the christening.

It was a little girl, and Grandmother said she was "a charming little thing." Alice wondered if she was at all like Aunt Christy's other baby, who was nearly a year old and grunted and pointed and threw tantrums.

No baby, Alice found, was quite like Ned. Still, she was determined to love them all despite their obstinacy.

Later that afternoon, they arrived at Aunt Christy's big, fancy house and were instantly ushered to the second-time mother's chambers. Alice didn't understand at all at first—if Aunt Christy were sick, as women always seemed to get after babies came, why would they visit her?

It didn't taken Alice long to understand, however. Aunt Christy wanted to talk.

She moaned about her poor, sore body and how fussy her baby was and how unsympathetic her husband—who, as far as Alice could tell, was bearing her patiently—was and how little her friends cared about how she was dying. For Aunt Christy was convinced she was dying.

Alice felt a bit concerned—surely no one would go as far as to completely invent an illness for attention—but then she saw Mummy and Uncle Charlie. Every other sentence, they'd glance at each other and smirk.

Yes, Aunt Christy was definitely being ridiculous.

As the adults and a lost-looking Ivy clustered around Aunt Christy's bedside, Alice noticed Nettie motioning her toward the adjoining room. The door which was cracked open. She tiptoed away and joined Nettie in the dim room.

A cradle sat in the middle, and Nettie stood over it. "This is your little cousin Arabella. Isn't she pretty?"

Alice placed her feet carefully as she moved across the room. The little face, surrounded in white frills, was indeed very pretty—rosy with a tiny button nose and a puckered mouth. "I like her. Why doesn't Aunt Christy talk about Arabella instead of her poor, aching head?"

Nettie chuckled softly and squeezed Alice's shoulder. "Some women are like that, Miss Grace. See that you don't ever become one, or you'll drive your husband mad, your friends away, and your family to hating you. Choose joy."

Alice nodded and reached out to touch a tiny fist balled on top of the coverlet Arabella was tucked beneath. "Well, I like babies, and I think I'll have a dozen, so I won't complain."

"Good." Nettie sighed. "Not every woman can have a dozen babies, Gracie. I doubt I will, though I would like them. And my mother just had me—well, the rest had to go to Heaven."

Alice looked up at Nettie, hating the sudden sadness in her eyes. "I didn't know you had brothers and sisters. I'm sorry."

"Well, I never got to meet them. Some women don't get to meet their babies—and some sisters, too. Sometimes God takes them up to Heaven before they've even arrived. We don't know why, but ..." Nettie blinked like she was trying not to cry. "It seems to happen a lot in my family."

"Oh." Alice wiggled her feet from side to side. This wasn't a nice conversation at all. "Did it ever happen to you?"

Nettie's face twisted. "No. Not exactly. But it could. I'd actually like you to pray for that, Alice—that we could have a baby come to live on earth with us. Jameson and me, I mean. Oh my, this isn't at all what I meant to say." She laughed under her breath and pulled a handkerchief out to dab her eyes. "I'm scared, Gracie, is all. Sorry. Can we start over?"

Alice raised her eyebrows. "Start what over?" She didn't know what they'd begun or why.

"This conversation." Nettie knelt and placed her hands on Alice's shoulders, looking up at her now. "You're so tall! Now, what I meant to say was, Jameson and I are expecting to have a baby this December. But God has to do it for us. He might decide to take the baby before it comes. We think He won't or He already would have, but God has His own ways of working. Now, wouldn't it be lovely to have our own little baby in five months—almost like having a little brother or sister for you?" Nettie's eyes flickered over Alice's face, and she knew that the answer was important to Nettie.

Still, this nonsense couldn't go on. She was ten years old, for heaven's sake!

Alice crossed her arms over her chest. "Nettie, are you with child?"

The sound her former nanny made was somewhere between a laugh and a cough. "Alice Chattoway! Whatever am I going to do with you? I remember very distinctly informing you that babies came from God, and we were going to keep to that until you were at least twelve." She folded her arms. "Now, who told you otherwise?"

"Uncle Charlie," Alice admitted. "He had to explain, you see, so I could help him breed his hounds some."

Nettie moaned and ran a hand over her face. "Men! Barring Tom, of course, they're all fools. Now's not the time, but I don't doubt he told you some things that didn't make a lot of sense."

Alice shrugged. It made a lot more sense than babies appearing out of the clouds. "Well, anyway." She placed her lips close to Nettie's ear and whispered, "Are you afraid your baby will die? Because I can pray it won't."

Nettie nodded, a barely perceptible jerk. "I am afraid. But God is taking care of us either way, and we must trust in Him."

Alice swallowed and gave Nettie a hug. Not long afterward, everyone wanted little Arabella, and Alice stepped back. And she did pray for Nettie and her baby, because it had never occurred to her before that God could take someone before they arrived.

"I'm actually here to see Miss Alice and Miss Ivy Chattoway." The tenor voice echoed about the foyer of Uncle Charlie's house, and Alice cowered at the top of the stairs.

"I'll ask Miss Chattoway if ... if ..." The butler was plainly a bit befuddled by Mr. Knight's requesting an audience with the girls. "If the children are at home."

As the butler shuffled off to find Mummy, Alice eased down the stairs.

Mr. Knight stood with his back to her, and he jumped a bit when she said his name. He whirled to face her. "Alice?" A smile lit up his face, then faded. "I don't imagine your mother knows you're here. I wanted to give her the option ..."

Alice generally didn't believe in giving parents options, but that was beside the point. She cocked her head. "You came to see Ivy and me? Why?"

Mr. Knight took a step toward her, then stopped, worried his hat about in his hands, and watched her. "Because I missed you."

Nonsense. Alice folded her arms over her chest. "You can't miss someone you hardly know. Why did you really come?"

"I want to know you." Mr. Knight glanced around, up the stairs and to the door of the parlor. He continued fidgeting, and Alice didn't like the way he couldn't seem to settle.

"Let's sit." She backed up, lowered herself down on one of the steps, and brought her knees up to her chest. When he hesitated, she patted a spot beside her on the stair.

He chuckled and crossed the room, then dropped down next to her. "Your mother will kill us both."

Alice raised her eyebrows. "Well, she won't kill *me*." Mr. Knight? Sometimes Alice hoped she would; other times, she wanted him to like her.

There were a lot of feelings involved, and it was awfully difficult navigating them.

"I honestly think she should sometimes." He sighed. "Alice, I've made a wreck of our lives, haven't I? And now I've lost everything."

"Not everything." Alice rocked back and forth thoughtfully. "You still have Ned. And ... and me. I suppose."

He shook his head. "I don't, really. You're not mine. I suppose I do have Ned, but now I have to raise him alone." A dry little laugh escaped his lips. "I loved my wife. It stings as much now as it did seven months ago. And yet ..." He sighed. "I want to be with you, Alice, and with Ivy. How can I manage that?"

If he thought Alice knew the answer, he was dead wrong. "I don't know." All she knew was that he'd hurt Mummy, and left them, and no explanation on earth was enough to make up for that.

But he was still her father, and a part of her wanted him more than anything in the world.

"I don't know, either." Mr. Knight scratched his chin. "But God knows. I sinned and made mistakes and lost myself in so many things, but He was there through it all and has forgiven me. I'm trying to find out what He would have me do now."

Alice swallowed. He was talking to God? Well, what could she say to that? She hadn't imagined anyone so villainous would actually pray.

"After Mrs. Knight died, I went to Pearlbelle Park with Ned, and I spent all my time out with him in the gardens and the fields. I'd watch him play and try to make sense of things. Just me, Ned, and God."

Alice could understand why he might like that. It definitely sounded pleasant—and most of all, it sounded like the best way to spend one's time. "Did you learn anything?"

"A lot of things. Too many to name." He smiled at her. "But I still haven't found the secret of making a bad situation good. I only know that I must trust."

"But you wouldn't marry Mummy, would you?" She wrinkled her nose. That was a bit too forward. "What I mean to say is, well, that's what *some* people might want." Alice almost wanted it, too, on some days.

On others, she wanted him to leave. Leave and never come back.

"I'm not sure." He placed his hands palms up on his knees. "The decision doesn't lie with me. I'd like very much for us to be the best of friends either way, though."

Alice's insides flopped. "I ... I don't know if I can." Was he safe? Was he telling the truth about spending time with God? Would he leave again ... or was he here for good?

Too many variables.

"Perhaps we'll let it sit for a time. We don't have to rush." Mr. Knight stood and brushed off his trousers. "I have all the time in the world."

Alice placed a hand on her chin. "I do, too, I suppose."

"Good." He glanced up the stairs. "Oh, there are your mother and Ivy."

Alice jumped to her feet and grinned up at Mummy. "I wasn't sitting on the stairs," she clarified with a bit of a grin. "I was ... resting for a moment."

But Mummy didn't laugh at her. Her eyes were glued to his face. "Mr. Knight."

He bowed. "Miss Chattoway."

"What ... that is to say, we appreciate your visit." She glanced down and placed a hand on Ivy's shoulder. "Will you come to the drawing room?"

"Of course."

In no time, they were all perched on the edge of their chairs.

"I only wanted to see Alice and Ivy." Alice noticed his hands kept clasping and reclasping on his trouser legs. "I didn't mean to disturb you—or force a conversation with Alice."

Mummy shook her head, eyes flickering over to Alice affectionately. "Mr. Knight, you couldn't *force* a conversation with Alice. She'll do what she will. I've never known such an obstinate child."

Obstinate? She wasn't obstinate—she knew how to get things done. "Mummy—"

"Shush, darling." She didn't even look at Alice but kept her eyes on Mr. Knight. "Have you been in London long, sir?"

"A few days. I was surprised to find you here, too, though I suppose Alice has a fortnight holiday." He glanced toward the door as if half-expecting to be booted out of it, but he remained on his seat. "I'd like your permission to visit Alice and Ivy from time to time."

"You have it." Miss Chattoway rose. "If you'll excuse me, I remembered—that is, I should attend to ... other things."

"Oh." He rose hastily. "I should be on my way, too. But I'll see you ... sometime."

"Yes. Sometime."

In a whirlwind of activity, he was gone. Alice hurried upstairs to watch his carriage leave from the window.

Why do adults always have to make everything so awkward?

CHAPTER TWENTY-FIVE

Five Months Later
December 1871

"I WANT TO GET Mummy a new comb," Alice said, slipping her fingers into Uncle Charlie's hand against the rush of Christmas shoppers on the London street. "I think Ivy would like ribbons. Do you think that's too silly?"

"No, I don't think any gift is too silly." Uncle Charlie jerked her to the side so they wouldn't be run over by a cart. "There now. The shop we want is across the street. Though, I doubt we'll survive the trip across."

"Perhaps we could go over a ways down."

"That's probably wisest."

They began wading through the crowd once again, jostled at every side. They rested by a lamppost for a moment before continuing on.

"Alice? Mr. Chattoway?" It might have been five months, but Alice wasn't about to forget that gentle tenor.

Mr. Knight stood behind them, Ned sitting in the crook of his arm. Behind him, a manservant trailed, his arms full of packages.

"Christmas shopping?" Uncle Charlie said.

"Indeed." He shifted Ned to his other arm. "Miss Elton is having a dress fitted, and I thought Ned and I could see what there was while we waited.

Of course, we found a great many things—I enjoy buying presents."

Uncle Charlie, who liked nothing more than to express his dislike of shopping, grunted. "Yes, well ... Alice does, too."

Alice admitted she was glad to see Mr. Knight but wished it weren't here, where they could barely talk. He'd written her a number of letters since they'd met last, and it made her want to be his friend.

More than that, be his daughter.

But how could she be if she never got to spend any time with him? If random meetings on the street and letters were all she could count on, how would they become close?

An idea blossomed in her brain, and it was out of her mouth before she could stop it.

"You'll be alone, then, for Christmas, won't you, Mr. Knight? Or practically? With Mrs. Knight gone and only Miss Elton and Mr. Parker for company. And Ned, of course."

Mr. Knight blinked, and his eyes flickered helplessly to Uncle Charlie's face.

"Well, it's true, isn't it?" Alice glanced between the two men, who shuffled from foot to foot as if unsure how to respond.

"I suppose it is, Alice. But my cousins and I are friends, and of course I have Ned." He bounced the boy on his arm, causing him to squeal and giggle.

"But still ... wouldn't it be better to have the burden of hosting Christmas off you?" Here Alice nudged Uncle Charlie in the ribs.

He glared at her and rubbed his side. "This is a dangerous part of London."

Mr. Knight chuckled. "Indeed. I'm not searching for an invitation, though, Mr. Chattoway. This is Alice's invention."

"It's a good invention!" Alice turned pleading eyes to Uncle Charlie. "I think we ought to take care of widowers and orphans. It's in the Bible."

"I think that's *widows* and orphans, Alice." Uncle Charlie squeezed her shoulder. "But, truly, Mr. Knight, you would be welcome at Starboard Hall. I believe we ought to try to foster a relationship between our families."

Mr. Knight shook his head. "We couldn't impose. Besides, Steven and Lois would tear each other apart left alone that long—it wouldn't do." He glanced over the throng. "It's starting to clear up. Where are you off to?"

"Oliver's. Alice has a few trinkets she wants to purchase." Uncle Charlie glanced at his watch. "We must go. But, really, you should come to Starboard. We have plenty of room and plenty of cheer. Mr. Parker and Miss Elton would both be welcome."

Mr. Knight hesitated, caressing his son's chubby leg. "I would, but I fear Miss Chattoway might not want ... might not appreciate my presence in her home."

"Oh, bosh. Claire won't mind! But, if you want, I'll have her send the invitation. We're leaving for Starboard tomorrow morning. You should expect an official invitation in the mail soon."

Mr. Knight struggled to keep his face straight. "Oh! Well, in that case, I'll ... I'll consider it. Of course, my cousins would have to be consulted, too ..."

"Of course."

Once they were off in the crowd, Uncle Charlie glanced down at Alice with a wry smile. "Well, little miss. It lies with you to convince your mother. I doubt it'll be much of a task for you. Mr. Knight can say whatever he pleases, but it's clear the invitation was a welcome one. You're a master, Alice—but not even slightly subtle."

Alice pretended not to know what he was talking about.

Starboard Hall

Claire stared at her brother, but no matter how long she stared, the words that came out of his mouth didn't change.

"You want me to invite Mr. Knight and company to Starboard? Myself? A personal invitation?" *No. Never.* He'd read a thousand things into it that she didn't want to say, especially less than a year after his wife's death.

Not that it made any difference how long it'd been, because Claire wasn't interested in him. Forgiveness seemed far beyond her grasp, and she was unsure if God even allowed them a new start. *We're too far gone, aren't we?*

"I don't see why that's a problem." Charlie leaned casually against the doorway of his office, where she'd tucked herself away to wrap presents. He seemed to think he was asking her to do something simple, something one did every day.

Something that was not inviting her former husband—the father of her children—and his family to her brother's estate for Christmas.

"Mr. Knight wouldn't come unless you allowed it." Charlie examined his fingernails, innocent as a newborn kitten but with a great deal more claw control. "Alice wants him to come, I think. She suggested it."

This gets better and better. "Charlie, you can't expect me to want that man here—and for Christmas, of all things! I get so little time with Alice now, and Nettie's having a baby within the week, and Christy is coming ..." She ran her hand over her face as if that could rub away all her worries. "It's going to be stressful as it is."

"I know. So why not add one more stressful thing?" He shrugged. "I'm warning you. Alice is biding her time, but she'll ask."

Claire sighed. Of course she would. And though Claire was skilled in the art of telling Alice *no*, her daughter's determination and follow-through didn't make it easy. It meant direct conflict—there was no putting Alice off easily.

"I'll leave you to your presents." He backed out of the door, and it clicked shut behind him.

Claire sat still for a moment, then checked to make sure everything Alice shouldn't see were wrapped. She had an idea that after Alice had finished visiting with Nettie, she would be coming down to make the request. Claire was glad Charlie had warned her—she still wasn't sure of her answer.

Then there was a light rap on the door. "Mummy? Can I come in?"

She set a bundle of tangled ribbons aside. "Yes, darling."

The door eased open, and Alice peeked around it. "It's funny—I don't like secrets, but I do like being surprised about Christmas. I wouldn't want to know ahead of time!"

Claire laughed and motioned her over to the desk. "Everything is well-hidden. This is for your aunt Christy. Come help me find the perfect box."

Alice banged the door shut behind her and began digging through the boxes. "Of course, I have a reason for being here, Mummy."

"Mm." Never a surprise. Claire grabbed a piece of paper to write a little note for her sister. "Go on, then."

Alice picked out a few boxes that seemed about the right size for the Dickens book Claire had bought for Christy. "I thought we could invite Mr. Knight and his family to Starboard for Christmas. We met him in London, and he seemed lonely. And poor little Ned hasn't any mother or *real* family like us. So, really, it'd be our Christian duty."

Christian duty? That was taking it a bit far. Claire set her pen back in the inkwell and placed her hands palms up on the desk. "Don't you feel that would be a bit awkward?"

"Awkward?" Alice placed a flat box on the desk in front of Claire. "Why would it be awkward?"

The innocence was both feigned and unrealistic. "*Alice.*"

The puppy-dog eyes came out. "But I miss him! And Ned. And Mr. Parker and Miss Elton aren't bad, either."

She wants this. It would make her happy. But how could Claire consent to such a thing? Mr. Knight wanted her invitation, as Charlie had said, but it made no sense for her to be the one to invite him. They had a history, after all, and not one she wanted to dredge up. Especially as everyone would doubtless read far too much into it.

Still, she had no true reason to not want him here. He was still in mourning for his wife. Nothing would happen. Nothing could happen.

Can I forgive him? God, is that what You want of me? But surely I can't have him back. No, of course not—there isn't that much grace for us.

But Alice wanted to spend more time with her father. A natural feeling—not one Claire ought to squash.

She stood and took the package from Alice. "I have one condition."

Alice's face brightened. "All right."

"You send the invitation. You may say that I allowed it, but it must be from you." Claire tied a bow with the ribbon she'd selected for the package. "Will you do that?"

"I will." Alice grinned and bounced on her toes. "I'm so excited! Can I write it now?"

"There's paper and pen on the desk." She placed the package in a pile with the other ones. "While you begin that, I'm going to talk to Nettie." Though as of yet there were no obvious signs of labor, her maid would plainly give birth soon, and Claire made a habit of checking in with her every few hours.

Alice hopped onto Uncle Charlie's chair and shoved it forward. "I'll see you in a bit. You'll read it for me and make sure it looks all right, won't you?"

That much Claire could do. In fact, she'd appreciate knowing what was said. She didn't want Alice implying anything that wasn't true—and she did believe her child, almost eleven already, to be capable of it. "Yes, of course."

Claire quit the room and hurried up the stairs to her maid's chamber. For now, she'd placed her not far from her own room. A breach of custom, yes, but she'd been close to Nettie so many years ago, when Alice and Ivy had been born—how could she offer anything less in the woman's time of need?

Nettie was up again. Of course she was. Thankfully, this time she remained in her room, though not in her bed as the doctor had ordered. Instead, she sat on a chair near the window with a book.

"Nettie!" Claire pointed at the bed. "What did I say?"

"I'm fine." Nettie set her book down. "It's going to be soon, but I'd rather be active and make it sooner. Though, of course I can't, because of these absurd restrictions."

"Not absurd. Just cautionary." Claire took a seat on the edge of the bed. "How do you feel?"

"Fine. Impatient! No pains since last night." Nettie struggled to rise, and Claire hurried to her side. "I really am all right—or I will be when I have my baby in my arms." Her eyes shone. "I don't know if I ought to be afraid of being this happy or if I should accept it for the miracle it is."

"I say enjoy it." Claire smiled. "God has blessed you. Don't doubt Him!"

Nettie shrugged. "I don't. Myself, though? Goodness, I can't stop."

"Oh, nonsense. You've already been a mother." Claire picked up the book. "You're really going to tell your child you read *From the Earth to the Moon* on the very eve of her birth? A French novel, Nettie."

"It's going to be a boy this time." Nettie did manage to get to her feet then. "At least it's not in its original language. Hopefully it won't turn my child too continental." She paused, then laughed. "You almost got away with that because I'm tired. Claire, you conceived in France."

She chuckled. "That I did. But I didn't tell you why I came up. I wanted to see you, but I also wanted to share the latest thing Alice has talked me into."

"Oh dear. Now what?"

"She's inviting Mr. Knight, Mr. Parker, Miss Elton, and little Ned to Starboard for Christmas." Claire shook her head, a bit incredulous about it still. "She met him in London, and he seemed to want an invitation but implied that he would only accept with my permission. And she has it, of course. She couldn't not." Alice really could be a statesman if she were a boy. She stood to be a powerful woman even so, and Claire only hoped she had the ability to curb her daughter's enthusiasm before she went too far.

Still, on this point, she could afford to be lenient.

Nettie didn't reply. Perhaps she didn't approve of Claire's parenting of Alice. It wouldn't be the first time—Claire tended to trade leniency for love. It was a bad habit, one she struggled to break, but she felt a delicate balance was needed with Alice.

Nettie, on the other hand, believed that to love was often to deny, especially in the case of a mother. She never hesitated to tell Alice *no*.

Claire turned to find Nettie pale, clinging to the back of the chair with distant eyes.

"Nettie?" *Have the pains started again?* "Nettie, is it the baby?"

"I-I'm not sure."

Claire took Nettie's arm and led her to the bed. "Now, lie down. I asked the doctor to stop by this afternoon and see if everything is going well ..."

"That's not necessary." Nettie placed her hands protectively over her stomach all the same. Unlike most women, she hadn't grown much larger than her usual petite size since she'd conceived. "The baby's fine. It's going to be a while."

How could she be sure? Claire never had been—childbirth was as much a mystery to her now as it had been a dozen years ago. Well, almost. "Is there any ... any pain?"

"Some. Occasionally. I'm ... I'm sorry. I suppose I was in another world." She ran her hands over her face, twitched from side to side. "I apologize. I must have scared you."

Why is she acting so strange? Claire supposed all women close to child-birth had the right to act a bit oddly. "Can I get you anything?"

Nettie shook her head. "No, no. I ... I'm surprised you allowed Mr. Knight to come here."

"Yes, well." She gritted out a smile. "Alice is persuasive, as you know. So now we'll have quite the crowd for Christmas." A bit of understanding dawned on her. "I suppose it is difficult for you to imagine having people here when you'll be a new mother. I'll keep everyone away—I would never let you become overtaxed." She meant that. Nettie's health was a priority. Such a faithful friend deserved all the rest and attention—or lack thereof—she wanted.

"Thank you." Nettie closed her eyes and sighed. "As long as I'm left alone, I'll be fine."

Claire squeezed her friend's arm. "Don't worry. It'll turn out all right." If only Claire could convince herself of that fact, too.

CHAPTER TWENTY-SIX

T HE ROOM WAS HUSHED, and Alice felt like tiptoeing but managed to walk normally. Nettie looked far too tired for Alice's liking. Even Ivy seemed to cower a bit.

"Gracie, Ivy, come here." Nettie held out her free arm, the other cradling the tiny bundle. "This is Malcolm."

Malcolm? But Alice had pre-approved an honorary baby sister, not a boy. She wasn't even sure she liked boys outside of their necessary uses. "He's a boy?"

Nettie laughed. "I'm afraid you can't control that, Alice. But, yes, he's a beautiful boy. Come see."

Alice walked across the room to peek at the baby. A funny little face, a mouth opening and closing like a fish, and scrunched-shut eyes. He wrinkled his nose, and Alice did think he was sweet. She liked Ned—maybe Malcolm would turn out to be another one in a million.

"Isn't he beautiful?" Nettie sighed and caressed Malcolm's cheek. "Ivy, what do you think?"

"I think he's pretty." Ivy placed a tentative hand on his cheek, then drew back. "He's soft, too."

Nettie smiled. "Yes, indeed. Alice?" Her eyes were so hopeful.

"He is sweet, Nettie." She fingered the edge of the blanket. "I think we'll be the best of friends. Will he have eyes like you? Can you tell?"

Nettie beamed. "Oh, I don't know. Tom has pretty eyes, so I hope ... but you can't tell, no, not so early on. Though, we always knew you would have black eyes, Gracie." She reached up to affectionately cup Alice's face. Her hand dropped to the counterpane after a moment. "Tom insists he doesn't see as much of himself as me in little Malcolm."

Jameson emerged from the corner of the room. "Now, Nettie, we both know he has your ears and nose. Just look at him! Stop denying it."

Alice cocked her head and examined the baby's face more closely. She couldn't see any resemblance, but parents often said those types of things. She didn't think she particularly resembled Mummy, yet people would go out of their way to compare them. Especially Nettie.

Nettie must see things a lot of people didn't.

"Oh, your guests are coming today, aren't they?" Nettie's eyes flickered to Jameson and back. "Probably on the next train. You girls will want to get ready."

Get ready? Alice was already dressed. Perhaps she could comb her hair—she'd been running out in the snow with Uncle Charlie earlier, and though she'd dried off, she hadn't cleaned up all the way.

"We'd better go." Alice kissed Nettie's cheek. "I love you, Nettie. I hope you're going to be all right."

"I love you, too. And, yes, we'll both be fine."

As Alice and Ivy left the room, she heard Nettie say something about Mr. Parker's coming today, too, but ignored it.

They found Mummy in her bedroom redoing her hair. Ivy raced forward ahead of Alice, obviously intent on a mission.

"Will Nettie be all right?" Ivy tugged at Mummy's sleeve.

Alice laughed as she shut the door behind them to preserve the heat of the flickering fire in the grate. "Of course she will, silly. It's just a baby."

"But she's sick!" Ivy scowled at Alice before redirecting her gaze upward again. "Mummy? Is she bad sick?"

"No, darling. More tired, I imagine." Mummy squeezed Ivy's shoulder. "I want to comb your hair before Mr. Knight arrives. Come along now."

In no time, they were all ready for the day.

"I don't know if we really need to get pretty." Alice glanced at herself in the mirror. She wore a simple green dress, and Mummy had drawn her hair back in a braid.

"Right." Mummy also examined her reflection. "No need to look pretty at all. It's just Miss Elton, Mr. Parker, Mr. Knight, and his son. But we can present ourselves as nicely as possible. It's common courtesy."

Common courtesy? Mummy never would keep glancing at the mirror for common courtesy. No, there must be a special reason—one Alice would definitely explore later.

She was close to making up her mind on whether or not her parents should remarry. And, well, it was good to have all the information possible on their feelings in the meanwhile.

The carriage rolled up in front of the manor, and Mr. Knight descended.

Claire took a deep breath and forced herself not to think about her appearance or what her family and the line of neatly-dressed servants must look like to him. But she couldn't resist the thought that Starboard Hall was a rich estate, she practically the mistress, and there wasn't anything amiss about her appearance.

Then she squashed the thoughts. They weren't noble, nor did they matter in the long run. She shouldn't turn her life into a competition, and she wasn't a prize to be won—nor did making a man jealous really appeal to her.

Mr. Knight had his own life now. She wasn't a part of it, really, though he kept popping back in.

Lois Elton ran forward before Claire could so much as catch his eye. "Claire, how good to see you! I was so thankful for your invitation to

Starboard. It's been so long ..." She gave Claire an overexuberant hug. "How are you?"

"I'm well, thank you." *Don't look over her shoulder at Phil. Oh, or Steven for that matter. Draw away.* "How was your journey?"

"Lovely. Steven complained the whole time, but it went smoothly. Ned hardly fussed at all." Lois glanced over her shoulder. "Steven has him, actually. He's started to take to him."

Steven shifted the boy to the crook of his arm. "I have not *taken* to him. He's clingy, is all."

Lois snorted and turned from Steven to the left—face-to-face with Charlie. And her face went pale.

Oh dear. Not this again. Claire wanted to roll her eyes, but poor Charlie didn't deserve it.

Charlie might not be entirely aware of Lois's long-time attraction to him. Claire wasn't sure. To be fair, she'd had other things on her mind.

Ivy slid her hand into Claire's, and she remembered her children existed. Jerking around, she gestured for Alice to draw near and greet their guests. Her mother was already speaking with Mr. Knight. Claire hoped she wouldn't say anything too embarrassing.

Ashamed of being so on edge yet not being able to help it, she led Lois and the girls in. Charlie trailed after her.

Really, brother. You're better than this, better than keeping a woman waiting. And Lois should have married when she had prospects.

Everyone in this world couldn't seem to move on. That was what she wanted—to move on. But no one else seemed to share the sentiment.

In the house, Claire and her mother saw the guests settled in their rooms. Mrs. Chattoway drew Claire aside for a moment afterward.

"Are you all right?" Her mother's eyes were concerned. "You're white as a sheet, Claire."

She pressed her hands to her own cheeks—cold to the touch. "I suppose I might be. It's strange to have him here."

Mrs. Chattoway placed a gentle hand on her arm. "I can understand that. I wouldn't want to be in this situation, but since you are, know that you have your mother here to talk to, if you like." She leaned forward and kissed her cheek. "Be brave. You're home; he has no right to intimidate you."

"Thank you." Claire glanced down the hallway, her eyes flickering about, looking for a servant who might overhear—or more importantly her own child. Alice would love this, but she couldn't know. Not yet. "I don't believe he's interested in me, but, I admit, it's difficult not to feel something."

Mrs. Chattoway's eyes grew distant. "We'll have to wait and pray. Remember, God has a plan for all this. He's not passive in your life. Don't be afraid; trust Him."

A constant struggle Claire doubted she'd ever perfect. Still, she could try. "Thank you for the reminder. I'm trying."

Her mother pulled her into her arms and held her tight. "Don't you worry about it. God can help you deepen a relationship with Him, too. For now, wait. Who knows what He has planned for you?"

Hopefully, something calm. Claire was ready for the drama to be over. But whatever God had planned, she would indeed wait.

Alice ran down the stairs, Ivy close on her heels. Mr. Knight stood close to the bottom of the stairs, chatting with Uncle Charlie.

"Mr. Knight?" She wasn't sure if she'd ever be able to call him something other than that, though she did hope eventually things would change. Until then, it was formalities.

"Hello, Alice." He held out a hand to her, and she slid her fingers into his. "And Ivy, too! How are you young ladies?"

"I'm very well, thank you." Alice shifted from foot to foot, unsure if she should curtsey, withdraw her hand, something. "Ivy is, too."

Ivy dropped her eyes and shuffled behind Uncle Charlie.

Her father smiled. "Good. Your uncle was telling me about a pony you have—Truffle, is it? Will you forever have horses named after sweets?"

Heat rushed to Alice's face. "I ... I don't know. Perhaps not. Perhaps not when I grow up and have a big horse ... Uncle Charlie says I'll grow out of Truffle soon." She glanced at Uncle Charlie, who nodded.

"Her legs are almost too long for the little thing."

She shot an annoyed look at her uncle. He knew very well that she didn't care for her awkwardly long limbs. "Well, anyway, I didn't name Sugarplum, did I?"

"You did not." Mr. Knight glanced toward the door. "I'd like to meet Truffle, though—and see the stables, of course. Would you mind, Mr. Chattoway?"

"Not at all."

Once they'd donned coats, they went out into the chilly air. The sky was overcast and smelled of snow, though none fell yet. Alice hoped it would, but sometimes it only looked like the clouds should release their stores but actually didn't.

In the stables, a boy led Truffle out of a stall, and Mr. Knight was introduced. Alice admitted that, much as she had loved Sugarplum, Truffle was infinitely dearer to her.

Not that she wouldn't mind seeing Sugarplum again. Especially if it meant seeing Kirk and the other servants. Pearlbelle was important to her, after all.

"It's a bit cold for a ride at the moment." Mr. Knight leaned against a stall door. "But I'm glad to have met her. We'll go riding again soon, Alice."

"All right." She looked forward to it. "I miss Pearlbelle. That's where I had the most fun." She gave him a quick glance to make sure she hadn't gone too far, but he nodded.

"Yes. I hope you'll come to Pearlbelle this summer, actually. You and your mother—and Ivy, of course." Ivy had remained back at the house. She didn't much care for horses; they frightened her.

"Yes." Alice sighed. "I'm not sure if Mummy will let us, but I'd like that very much. I have a holiday in July."

"That would be nice. Ned will be two years old, too." He absently ran his fingers through Truffle's mane. "I've been taking him up on my horse recently. He's a bit small for his own, but he's not too young to be in my arms."

Uncle Charlie chuckled. "I think if you had a wife, she'd soon put a stop to that."

Mr. Knight's eyes flickered to Alice before he met her uncle's. "I'm not sure. It depends on the woman and the amount of trust she's willing to place in you."

I wonder if he's thinking of the late Mrs. Knight or of Mummy. She wished she knew for certain. His dark eyes gave nothing away. If it were Mrs. Knight, there wasn't a great deal of grief visible—a solemn expression was all. But then, sometimes Alice felt that men didn't show as much emotion as women.

Or perhaps they simply didn't feel as much.

"Do you think Ned will ever have another mother?" Again, she spoke before she thought. Alice wanted to slap herself. "I mean ..." But there was no retracting it. She meant it, didn't she? Knowing where he stood was important to her.

"Perhaps." He stood up straight. "Actually, Alice, we should be spending time with little Ned. He knows you, I think, and I'd like you to be friends."

Alice wanted to be friends with her father, mainly, but she didn't say that. She followed him back out into the cold. Snow filled the air, and she couldn't help but smile. Christmas Eve was tomorrow, and it would be lovely. Unless one had to travel, snow was definitely an important part of Christmas.

Neither Mr. Knight nor Uncle Charlie said anything, and Alice couldn't have that. She ran up alongside her father and tugged on his arm.

"Mr. Knight?"

"Yes, Alice?"

"Did you get me a Christmas present?" It was all she could think to ask.

Uncle Charlie made a choking sound. "I'm finding your questions today very amusing, Alice, but you'd better be glad your mother isn't here."

She glared. "I want to know."

"I did," Mr. Knight said. "Ivy, as well." A grin appeared on his face. "I can't say what, of course. I did consult Lois, though, and she seems to think it's a good selection."

Alice nodded. Men really should get a woman's approval before buying a gift. At least, she was always glad when Uncle Charlie consulted one. The things he thought to buy Mummy or Grandmother were sometimes silly. "I bought Ned a gift, but Mummy wasn't sure I ought to buy one for you." She glanced up at him. "Would you have minded?"

"Not at all, but I don't need presents. It's hard to find things for grown-ups, anyway. I remember that."

They stepped through the front door and stamped snow off their feet. After their coats were peeled off, Uncle Charlie excused himself.

"Shall we collect Ned? His nanny has him, I believe, upstairs in an old nursery. We wouldn't have travelled with him, honestly, but your letter was insistent." Mr. Knight cocked his head. "Do you really care about the boy that much? You scarcely know him."

Alice narrowed her eyes. "I didn't think you'd leave him for Christmas." Only a villain would leave his child alone during a time of the year when family ought to be together. Alice believed that firmly.

"True. Not that he knows what Christmas is." They started up the stairs together. "He's very small, you know."

"But it's the first Christmas he's ever had when he's been big enough to unwrap presents," Alice protested. "And I did get him one."

"Thank you. That was kind."

Alice shrugged. "It wasn't my money."

Mr. Knight put a hand over his mouth for a bit. Alice suspected he was hiding a smile or a laugh, but she ignored the gesture.

"Would you really not mind if we came and visited next summer?" Alice paused at the top of the stairs and looked directly into his eyes. "You'll ask Mummy?"

"I will. I don't know how she'll like it, but I will." He rubbed the back of his neck. "I don't think she likes me very much."

"Oh, I think she does." *She must.* "After all, you're not that bad."

He made a little chuckling sound. "That's good to hear. I'm glad of that distinction—I suppose it's better than being very bad."

In truth, Alice wasn't sure at all what her mother thought. However, she hoped that it was favorable. If it was, that might mean she could have a family again. She wanted nothing more.

CHAPTER TWENTY-SEVEN

Seven Months Later
July 1873
Pearlbelle Park

"THERE." MR. KNIGHT MOUNTED his gelding and glanced back at Alice. "Race you to the top of the hill?"

Alice twitched the reins about in her hands. She was making the mare she rode nervous, she knew, but her own nerves were hard to control. This was her first time riding a full-size horse outside of a safe paddock. Her father said she was ready, but was she?

"It's all right. You can trust Athena." He backed Roanoke up a few steps. "Follow me. I've seen you ride much faster than we will today."

In a contained area. They'd been training for the last week, but Alice still wasn't confident in her abilities. "Are you sure?"

"I am. I wouldn't risk your safety, Alice. Trust me." He met her gaze without flinching. "Take a deep breath. It'll all work out."

A slight breeze stirred stray tendrils of hair that had escaped her braid. She brushed them aside and directed her gaze up the green hill. "All right. Let's go."

Her mother had lately decided that she should be more ladylike when riding, but even a sidesaddle couldn't curb her joy. The wind hit her face as they flew side by side up the hill. Riding Athena wasn't anything like riding Truffle or Sugarplum. It was infinitely better.

At the top of the hill, she turned to him. "You're right. But Mummy's going to be furious either way, you know."

Mr. Knight laughed. "She doesn't need to know. As far as she's concerned, we're still in the paddock practicing."

Alice wasn't about to lie to her mother, but if she didn't ask, there wasn't probably a great need to worry her. "If you say so." She only had another week or so with Mr. Knight, after all, and she wanted to maximize every moment with him.

Mr. Knight gestured down the opposite way. "There's a path through the forest, and I don't think we've followed it all the way to the border. Would you like to explore? It used to be a favorite ride of mine."

Alice nodded, and they turned toward the north. In no time, they were riding down a shaded forest path, cool and peaceful. Birds fluttered from tree to tree, and a few rustles here and there indicated some wildlife, but otherwise, it was completely silent.

"I actually have a few questions while we're here alone." He glanced sideways at her. "Would you mind?"

Questions? Alice was much more used to asking than answering them, but she certainly didn't mind. "Not at all."

"Thank you." His chest rose and fell slowly. "My first question is simple ... or at least it could be. I'm not sure of your feelings, but it's an honest question. Do you want me in your life? On a permanent basis?"

She blinked. Well, that was a ridiculous question. "Yes. Of course. You're my father."

His posture relaxed slightly. "But you don't feel as if I've ruined things? I've hurt your mother. I married another woman. Even now ... well, we had a few good moments this Christmas, but she's still wary of me. I thought you might be, too."

Alice could understand why her mother was hesitant. She'd been badly hurt. However, that just didn't apply to Alice herself. "No, Mr. Knight, I'm not wary of you, and I don't understand everything, but that was a long time ago."

"It was." He cocked his head. "But you still call me Mr. Knight. I would think Father would be better—or Papa, perhaps, if you can bear that. Why must I still be Mr. Knight?"

Alice blinked. "Well, you never asked me to call you anything different. I could call you Papa, I suppose."

"Then do!" He leaned back in his saddle slightly, and Roanoke responded instantly. When he stopped, so did Athena. "And what of your mother? Has she said anything to you?"

Alice shook her head. Though she'd asked not long ago, her mother was still secretive about her feelings toward Mr. Knight. She praised him as a man, as a father even, but made no reference to her own heart.

He sighed. "I wish she'd let me in. My mourning is completed, and I see it as ... No, that's wrong." Mr. Knight ran a hand over his face. "I was going to say that I see it as my duty to make things right, but it's more than that. I cared for her once, deeply. Now that I'm free, that we're both free, I would like to ... Oh, dash it all, I'm not sure."

Athena shifted from foot to foot and made a *brrr* sound, obviously displeased with their sudden stop. Alice let the mare have her head, and they continued on, though at a slower pace than before.

"Do you love her?" Alice kept her voice soft, as if speaking to a startled beast. "Would you like to marry her?"

He didn't respond for so long that she almost felt he hadn't heard her. At last, he spoke. "I love her. I admire her. I believe that I understand her, but her feelings at present are a mystery. She is kind—but love? I doubt she could ever care for me enough to marry me."

Well. Alice had expected to wheedle a great deal for such an honest answer. Adults almost never told her such things. "I'm not sure, either. Did you ..." Could she ask an adult such a question? "Did you ask God?"

"I did. Or I've tried to." Once again, he seemed inclined to stop, a light hand on the reins causing Roanoke to hesitate, but Alice wanted to continue on. The movement helped her think.

She urged Athena to a trot, and he kept pace until they reached a stream, which trickled across their path, already half-dry in the summer.

As they carefully crossed the partially dry, rocky bed, he turned slightly on his saddle. "I've prayed often, and I believe God is guiding me toward her. Which is what makes this so confusing. Wouldn't God make the path easier?" Mr. Knight faced forward, and she heard a soft chuckle. "I suppose I shouldn't be telling you all this. I don't want to worry you."

"You're not." Alice bit her bottom lip. How far could she go? "Can I tell you something Nettie has told me?"

"Of course. You need never be afraid to tell me anything." He turned Roanoke and made him back up so Alice could safely arrive on the grassy bank.

Alice relaxed on the saddle for a moment, organizing her thoughts. "Nettie always told me that sometimes God requires us to take leaps of faith. To trust in Him even if it means stepping where we can't see."

"That's wise."

"I thought so, too." Alice turned Athena back on the trail. "So why not take a leap? Ask her. That's what you're supposed to do, isn't it?" If she didn't need her arms, she would have crossed them over her chest. As it was, she was mildly afraid Athena would spook in this unfamiliar place.

"You're right, of course." His voice trembled a bit, but at least he said the words. "Does this mean I have your blessing?"

Alice laughed. "More than that! You really must ask her. You can't leave us again. At least try. I'd rather her disappoint me once than you disappoint me again."

She sensed he wasn't behind her after a moment of silence and turned to find him stopped in the path.

"What is it?"

"I'm sorry. I was only thinking about all that's at stake." He rode forward, squinting slightly. "I don't want you to get hurt, Alice."

"I'll be fine. Don't worry about me." Still, her heart sank at the idea of her mother turning her father down. *God, let her heart have changed. Let us be a family. Please.*

Why must she keep coming here? It was ridiculous, really. Claire shouldn't allow some ridiculous feelings of nostalgia send her back to this fountain in one of the gardens, especially not at night.

The moonlight reflected off the rippling water, and she lowered herself onto a marble bench. Her eyes half-closed. Was it wrong to pray here? Where she'd promised her heart to a man who now couldn't care whether she lived or died save to spend time with their children?

More specifically, Alice. A bitter little part of Claire's heart felt strongly that Ivy was unprioritized by her father. But then, Philip never did seem to know how to talk to her. Ivy was a reserved child and a difficult one to talk to. She couldn't blame him, truly.

But it's all for the children, isn't it, God? There's nothing about me *that compels him to become involved. So what do I do? Should I simply bear it for the girls' sake? What is my place? Would you allow us to remarry? I believe I could forgive him, but can You?*

"Miss Chattoway?"

Claire managed to control the impulse to jump up. "Mr. Knight?"

"Yes." He shuffled forward. "I'm sorry. I hope I didn't startle you. The gardens are usually empty this time of night."

Midnight? Yes, she supposed that was an unusual time to come sit in a garden. "I can leave, if you'd like."

"No, please don't. Could I sit with you?"

Claire moved slightly to the side, and he lowered himself onto the bench beside her.

"It's a lovely night. A bit chilly—are you quite warm enough?"

"Yes, I'm fine." She liked the cool air, honestly. It was wonderful at clearing her head. "I really can leave, if you came out here for quiet."

"I did, but I'd much rather talk to you." He kept his voice soft, so she felt compelled to lean in. "How have you been? Are you enjoying your stay here?"

"I'm well, and yes, I am. Pearlbelle is a lovely place."

"Oh, good. I'm glad you're here." He cleared his throat. "I believe Alice and Ivy are happy here, too."

"They are." Alice especially, but even Ivy seemed to enjoy the peaceful house and gardens. Not that it would be too different from Starboard for her, but at least she wasn't suffering any panic attacks.

"Excellent." He clasped his hands together on his knees and leaned forward. "Do you think they would like to stay here more permanently? And ... and you, too, of course?"

She forgot to breathe for a moment and had to force her lungs to inhale and exhale regularly. What did he mean? Was this a proposal? Inspired by what? He couldn't be serious, could he?

"I suppose I should clarify." She felt him shift beside her. "I'm asking you to marry me. Be Pearlbelle Park's mistress. I think it's ... it's the most sensible option."

The most sensible option. A great many marriages were founded on far less. Claire wasn't afraid of that. She opened her mouth to reply, but something kept her from responding. The silence stretched on, and Mr. Knight rose and paced to the fountain and back.

"Dash it all, Claire. That wasn't at all what I meant to say. I-I think I love you. No, I do. It's not the same mindless passion as before, no, but it's based on who you are as a person—the care you give to our children, the diligence you put into your every effort." He stood facing her, hands outstretched. "I don't know if that's enough. I don't know if anything I can ever offer will ever be enough again. But I want to try, and I pray that you can forgive me."

Claire's chin jerked. "Philip, it's not about your being enough. You ... you're a good man."

"Am I?" He offered the barest glimmer of a smile. "I abandoned you. Unwillingly, but there was a great deal I could've done to keep us together. You've gone through so much—and though my life hasn't been easy, it at least appeared honorable. I didn't suffer the consequences."

"And I haven't lived a blameless life. Nor has anyone." After all, there were still things she kept from him. But how could she share them? Claire placed a hand on his arm, lightly, not wanting to seem too forward but needing to comfort him. "God has blessed me despite it all. I don't pretend to be aware of all His plans, but He has certainly done work in my life. I can see that He's done the same in yours." *He has dealt generously with us.*

"Then would you consider ...?" Philip paused. "I suppose it's not fair to ask that much of you. But I believe I could make you happy. You would never want for anything, and I would be devoted. We could still live all the dreams of a dozen years ago." He turned to her. "God has given me the ability to make them a reality. The children, the home, everything."

Claire placed a hand on his shoulder and let herself be drawn closer. "We already have half of the children we wanted, too," she whispered. *Alice—you must tell him about Alice.*

"Yes." His gaze flicked down for a moment before returning to her eyes. "And the home—we didn't think we'd live at Pearlbelle, didn't know it would be my inheritance, but this is better than what we imagined."

"It is." Her fingers found the nape of his neck. "We'd have to work so hard to build a marriage from this rubble. There is so much I must tell you first, and I'm afraid. I won't ask you if you still love Hazel as I could never compete with a dead woman. But, even so, there is a great deal for us to contend with—the past, the present, the future."

"I concede that." Philip cupped her face, and his thumb stroked her cheek. "But I believe God can get us through it. Alice calls it a leap of faith—that's why I'm proposing."

"You feel this is a God-honoring decision?" She wasn't sure. There was reason to hesitate, certainly, after all this time and all they'd gone through, all they'd done, and she must share the whole story before committing. Still, he was free now.

"I do. And you?" His eyes searched her face. "What do you feel, Claire?"

Attraction, a bit of doubt, some regrets, and a handful of worries. But affection remained, and she believed that God had changed Philip as much as He'd changed her. "I feel a great many things, but I believe you are right."

He was silent for a long moment. "Then you will marry me?"

Claire's fingers tightened in his hair, and she kissed him. But before she could let herself go, she remembered and drew back. "Philip, there is something I must tell you—and you will be angry. You have every right to be." She bit her bottom lip. "You may change your mind about us."

Of course he protested. "Never! Darling, nothing you can say would change this."

She stroked his cheek then stepped back. She would give up if she kept touching him. "Philip, eleven years ago, I conceived and carried your daughters, twins. They were born on the first of January, 1862—but the first, who I had called Flora, only lived half an hour."

He stepped back, and she saw the wariness growing in his eyes. She wanted to about-face, to make believe she'd been joking, to tell him everything would be all right.

But that wasn't fair to either of them. Especially to him.

"I ... I lost her, and Ivy was weak. The babe was buried in an unmarked grave in Yorkshire, an illegitimate waif no one wanted. I told them the stillbirth was not mine, but my maid's."

Philip didn't speak. His eyes were vacant.

"Philip, Nettie was ... attacked. She has chosen not to share all the details with me, but Alice is the product. Nettie couldn't offer her what I thought I could. An identity. A life. So I gave her the name you chose—Alice Christina—and took her as my own. I had to—Nettie had to."

He turned away and walked toward the fountain, his shoulders slumped.

"Philip, Alice is like you—do you see it? Perhaps it was meant to be." Claire followed him, trembling, and placed a hand on his shoulder. "Please say something. Tell me to leave. I don't mind—I know what I've done, and I don't regret it."

Well, that wasn't quite true. Perhaps she could explain a little better than that. "I never thought ... I thought you would come for me, and I would tell you as soon as I saw you. If we had been in contact, it wouldn't have gone so far." She dropped her arm and stepped back. "I'm sorry, darling.

I'm so sorry."

"You did what you thought was right." Philip's voice was a dry rasp. "I can't punish you for that. Perhaps this is what I deserve."

"Oh, Philip, no." She circled around him and reached up to cup his cheek once more. "Darling, no. This isn't a punishment. I'm the one who lied—we both know what God says about that."

"But you wanted to protect Alice." Philip's face twisted. "I can understand that. I wanted to protect her, too."

Claire closed her eyes. "I know. I love her as my own. Which is why I can't give her up, even if it means giving you up."

Philip's chest rose and fell heavily, and he placed a hand on her arm. "No. You won't have to do that. I love Alice—and not being her father won't change that."

Claire blinked up at him, her eyes taking a moment to readjust to the moonlight. "Philip, I'm not asking you—"

"You don't have to ask; I'm offering. I'll raise Alice as my own, gladly." His face melted into a smile, and he squeezed her arm slightly. "Be my wife."

His wife? After all these years, even given Alice, even given all the changes to both of their lives, he still wanted to marry her? It seemed nothing short of miraculous that his heart hadn't changed toward her.

Claire blinked back tears as she whispered the word: "Yes!"

Epilogue

August 1873

N ETTIE SLID HER FINGERS into her husband's hand. "It's a lovely day for a wedding, isn't it?"

Tom smiled and shifted Malcolm against his shoulder. The boy wriggled, wanting down to try crawling once again. "Yes, it is."

Her eyes took in the lawn at Pearlbelle, dotted with the few guests there to celebrate the nuptials of her dearest friend. "I've had my happily ever after, so I'm glad she's having hers. And it's made my Gracie so happy." Even now, the child was dashing from friend to friend, parent to parent, all smiles, ready to throw herself into this new life with gusto. *My little Grace. Look at the beautiful family God has given you.*

"Are you sure ...?" Tom put his free arm around her waist and brought her close to whisper into her ear. "Are you sure this is best? For Alice?"

"The truth would hurt her too much." Nettie took Malcolm from her husband and placed him against her shoulder, enjoying the warm solidness of him. Already, he was growing so fast—she couldn't believe how quickly his eight months on earth had flown by.

"Perhaps for a bit. But, in the end, it could be healing. Especially for you." Tom drew her onto a bench next to him, and she snuggled against his shoulder. "I would love her as my own, Nettie. I wouldn't be ashamed—not for a moment."

"I know that." Tom was a good man, and in every way, he matched her. Strong where she was weak, tender when she needed a friendly shoulder to cry on, and accepting of her—all of her. Even the parts she couldn't tell anyone else but Claire.

Now Mr. Knight knew—Claire had told him shortly after the engagement—but even with his protection, Nettie had chosen to remain silent on a few points. In truth, Tom was the only one who knew the full story.

The desire to reveal everything came strong upon Nettie at times, but her loyalty to Claire, her love of Alice, and her desire for peace had always silenced her in time.

Now Alice, her very own Gracie, had the life she deserved, the life she must have. Nettie thanked God every day for His providence—for allowing even the demons of her past to be lost in a charade that had seemed impossible at the time.

How could she rip Alice out of the safe haven she'd created for her? No. She'd made the right decision. Even if her heart ached every time she looked at her child—even if Alice lived out her life never knowing.

"You'll not tell her, then? Never?" His protective arm about her gave Nettie the courage to speak of it, but her insides felt weak.

"'Never' is a long time." She sighed. "But I think not. Not unless it becomes obvious that God is directing me that way." *Please, God. Let the past remain where it is. Let my Gracie have the moon and the stars. And let me bear it from a distance, quietly and bravely.*

Her son fussed, tugging at her bodice. "I should feed him."

Tom glanced toward the garden party, his eyes flicking from man to man, seeking out a tall one with dark hair, a beard, and a charming face that hid the evil within. "I'll come with you. I don't know where *he* is."

"Thank you." Tom understood, as always. He had from the beginning, when she'd confessed it to him, afraid to tell Claire more yet needing a confidant. And she'd loved him the moment he'd pulled her closer instead of pushing her away.

As they walked back toward the big house, Alice's laughter echoed in the distance. Nettie smiled into her son's hair, pressed little kisses to his forehead and cheeks.

No child deserved the life of little Grace Atwater, the natural child of a maid and a man who'd taken his pleasure and left without a second thought to a life ruined and another begun. And, in Nettie's eyes at least, Alice's place was at Pearlbelle Park, loved and prized, the petted eldest of a country gentleman and his wife.

Too much was at risk, and Gracie came first. Always.

Yes, Nettie would keep her secrets.

A NOTE TO THE READER

WRITING A NOVEL IS not easy—and I can honestly say this is the hardest novel I've ever written.

It's gone through over twenty-five drafts, many of which had completely different endings, characters with widely variating stories, and even first to third person shifts (which, though not familiar to some, will immediately strike fear into the heart of any writer!).

I didn't think the editing was ever going to be well and truly over sometimes. When I published a draft in January 2016, I made the mistake of calling it "finished" (published books usually are), but was I ever wrong!

God had very different plans for this story. This draft, originally released in January 2020, is my boldest, my brightest, my best-edited, and my personal favorite (as well as the only one that's actually canon to the series).

I hope you enjoyed it! Perhaps you will consider posting a quick review on Amazon or Goodreads to let me know your thoughts.

Or, if you want to absolutely make my day, shoot me an email! You can find me at **contact@kellynrothauthor.com**.

As I'm writing this, book 2, *Ivy Introspective*, will be published the following summer. If you liked this one, well, you're going to love reading from Ivy's point of view. She's a fan favorite.

If you liked this book, enough to want to keep in touch with me, consider signing up for my newsletter! It's pretty easy to do. You just click on this link:

kellynrothauthor.com/newsletter

"May the Lord bless you and keep you; the Lord make His face shine upon you, and be gracious to you; the Lord lift up His countenance upon you, and give you peace."
Numbers 6:24-26, NKJV

May God's great and undeserved blessings fill your life!
TTFN!
Kellyn Roth

ACKNOWLEDGEMENTS

T HERE ARE ALWAYS SO many people to thank for these projects that it's almost impossible to include them all in a few paragraphs at the back of a novel.

This acknowledgements section is particularly difficult as I have gone through so many rewrites of this novel, so many beta readers, and even multiple editors, and I've had dozens of friends encourage and inspire me over the years.

The main people who come to mind to thank, however, are the people of YWP NaNoWriMo. If you ever stumble on this book, though we've fallen out of touch, I hope you know what a big help to me you were. I wouldn't be an author without the community.

Of course my friends, Sonja, Eva, Sofie, Bailey, and Aimee, need a big round of applause. They were, after all, my first cheerleaders for this project.

I'd also like to thank Angela R. Watts and Andrea Cox for helping me make this novel the best it could be. Your edits were so helpful!

And thank you to Makenna Pithey, Hannah Mae Linder, and Carpe Librum Book Design. All three of these artists worked hard on an edition of *The Dressmaker's Secret*'s cover.

But the biggest acknowledgement goes to my Lord and Savior, Jesus Christ. Thank You for letting me work on this project and nudging me to go back to it just one more time.

A Free Novella for You

Interested in a free novella, available only for subscribers to my mailing list?

January 1944

June Halsted moved her son to Hearthstone Cottage to escape the memories of her failed marriage and estranged family. A struggling artist in the midst of one of the coldest winters in Yorkshire, she finds herself seeking solace at church ... only to meet Mark Hayes, a kindly farmer with a limp and a knack for cheering up her son.

Inspired by The Tenant of Wildfell Hall, *this novella is a sweet romance with Christian themes.*

Go to *kellynrothauthor.com/newsletter* and subscribe to my email list to receive your free story!

ALSO BY THE AUTHOR

The Chronicles of Alice & Ivy

The Dressmaker's Secret
Ivy Introspective
The Knights of Pearlbelle Park (novella)
Becoming Miss Knight (novella)
At Her Fingertips
Beyond Her Calling
A Prayer Unanswered
After Our Castle

The Hilton Legacy

Like a Ship on the Sea
Like the Air After Rain
Like a Storm Against the Cliffs

Kees & Colliers

Souls Astray
Goldfish Secrets (short story)

The Lady of the Vineyard
Flowers in Her Heart

Standalone Short Stories

Esther Ashton's New Dress
Kind: a Christmas short story of post-WWII Munich
Eddy & the Tidepools

Anthologies

Springtime in Surrey
Novelists in November
Fingerprints in Frost
Voices of the Future: Stories of Courage & Compassion

www.ingramcontent.com/pod-product-compliance
Lightning Source LLC
Chambersburg PA
CBHW021006260626
47169CB00006B/1972